Dark Deceit

Cathie Dunn

"I love Cathie Dunn's book for its captivating characters
and vivid descriptions
of these harsh and tumultuous times."
5*, Booked Up Reviews

"Dark Deceit is a captivating read that draws you in the
plot of civil war, murder, confusion, intrigue and a
sprinkling of romance, just for good measure."
5*, The Accidental Poet

"Layered with authentic detail that will delight any
historian, Dark Deceit is a well-written tale of romance,
intrigue and dastardly machinations."
5* review, Suzanne Rogers, author

Ocelot Press

Copyright © 2012 by Cathie Dunn
Third Edition, 2020

Photography: Goonwrite.com
All rights reserved.

No part of this book may be used or reproduced in any manner whatsoever without written permission of the author or Crooked Cat Publishing except for brief quotations used for promotion or in reviews. This is a work of fiction. Names, characters, places, and incidents are used fictitiously. Any resemblance to actual persons living or dead, business establishments, events, or locales, is entirely coincidental.

To Angelika
for nurturing my love
of reading.

Acknowledgements

Dark Deceit was conceived in 2003, at a small train station in Glamorgan, South Wales.

Months of being part of a historical re-enactment group provided me with plenty of inspiration for a medieval story set in the turbulent times chroniclers called The Anarchy. I was already fascinated by the years following Henry I's death, and staying overnight within castle grounds in southern England and Wales inspired a plot I could not resist.

My gratitude goes to all the good friends I made in those fun days in South Wales, and to my wonderful critique partners for their continuing support.

Finally, a big Thank You goes to Laurence, my patient husband, who has had to share me with Geoffrey de Mortagne for such a long time, and will do so for many more years, whilst I'll be working on the other two parts of The Anarchy Trilogy.

About the Author

Cathie Dunn writes historical mystery and romance.

She loves historical research, often getting lost in the depths of the many history books on her shelves. She also enjoys exploring historic sites and beautiful countryside. Over the last three decades, she has travelled widely across Scotland, England, Wales, France and Germany.

After having spent many years in Scotland, Cathie now lives in the south-west of France with her husband, a rescue dog and two cats. She is a member of The Alliance of Independent Authors and the Historical Novel Society.

Find her at www.cathiedunn.com, and on *Facebook*, *Twitter* and *Instagram*.

Dark Deceit

Books by Cathie Dunn:

The Highland Chronicles series:
Highland Arms
A Highland Captive

The Anarchy Trilogy:
Dark Deceit
(A sequel is due out in 2020)

Standalone titles:
Silent Deception (a novella)
Love Lost in Time (a dual-timeline mystery)

Prologue

Gloucestershire, February 1141

The sound that cut through the silence was unmistakable, metal scraping against metal.

"Halt!" Geoffrey de Mortagne jerked the reins, bringing his stallion to a standstill. His two companions followed his lead. "Listen!"

A man's cry reached their ears, his voice muffled and strained.

"Outlaws." Reginald snorted. "Found a new victim. They must be behind that corner." He pointed at the bend in the path ahead. The untamed undergrowth obscured the view through the trees. "Shall we spoil their fun?"

"Aye, let's." Geoffrey unsheathed his sword and spurred Feu forward with a kick in the flanks. In an instant, his men caught up with him, swords drawn.

The view that met them as they rounded the corner was one of carnage. Three men on horseback were taunting a solitary knight, aiming their weapons where his shield could not reach. One wielded a battle axe, trying to find a clear aim while another swung a mace, looking for his chance. The third attacker prodded the knight's unprotected legs with a sword.

Geoffrey drew in his breath and signalled to his men to keep going at speed. They might already be too late. The knight was still clinging to the saddle but his surcote and hose were covered in blood. He was struggling not to be thrown, nudging his stallion with slippery knees to meet his challengers face on. There was a cleft wound on his left shoulder – in Geoffrey's full view before the knight swerved again – forcing him to hold his shield at an awkward angle.

Approaching the melee, Geoffrey steered Feu around two men lying sprawled on their backs, their bodies riddled with arrows. The knight's retainers. The set-up smelled of a trap.

Seeing Geoffrey approach, one attacker, a large man with a bushy beard, shouted a warning to his fellows who retreated towards the top of an incline. The outlaw continued to rain blows at the knight, his axe cutting chunks from his victim's shield. The sharp blade of the weapon sent splinters of wood flying, and the force of the assault weakened the knight's shield arm even further. His uncovered face drawn, he was close to dropping it.

Geoffrey swore.

He was barely a hundred feet away when the knight spotted him and turned his stallion towards him. A mixture of hope and relief crossed the knight's features as he spurred his warhorse forward. His last attacker watched him, a wide grin forming on thin lips. He took aim and threw the axe, then he took flight.

Geoffrey flinched as he watched the sharp blade fly through the air, only to bury itself into the knight's back. Eyes widened, he dropped sword and shield to the ground. His body slumped forward, only the reins remained wound tightly around his fingers, the horse broke into a canter.

Geoffrey swore as he was forced to swerve around the wandering animal.

"Guy, catch his horse. Reg, with me."

He followed the attackers retreating up the path. Reginald caught up with him and they were halfway up the hill when an arrow whizzed past them. Geoffrey reined in his stallion just as another arrow came down and embedded itself into a tree stump only a yard from him. Reginald fought to bring his horse to a halt. They stared towards the summit of the path. An archer, perched on horseback, had already nocked another arrow.

"Damn!" Geoffrey watched as the remainder of the gang

rode past their archer who waited, maintaining his aim, until the last of them escaped before he turned and disappeared.

Geoffrey bent down to pull the arrow from the stump and slid it into his saddlebag.

"This was no ordinary outlaw attack." He turned Feu.

"True, the horses were fine, and the archer gave it away," Reginald growled.

They rushed back to Guy who had pulled the wounded knight from the saddle. Kneeling on the ground, Guy placed the injured man on his right hand side and supported his sweat-soaked head in his lap. The knight's features were contorted with pain, his breathing shallow.

"I'll check the retainers," Reginald shouted, riding past them.

Geoffrey dismounted. Guy's glance met his. "I didn't dare remove the axe, Geoffrey."

"You've done right, Guy. Hold him still." Geoffrey crouched down and touched the deep cut on the knight's left shoulder. The bleeding had stopped; a light crust of dry blood was forming.

"Reg?"

"The others are dead, Geoffrey. Nothing we can do for them."

"As I thought. Go to my saddle bag and bring me the clean linen, sewing pouch and the wineskin." He had not taken his eyes off the knight. Stepping over him, Geoffrey ripped the caked fabric of the surcote apart. The chain mail underneath was slippery with blood.

He bent over the wound for a closer look. Blood was still oozing from the cleft where the blade had sliced neatly through the small metal rivets of the chain mail. The suction of the lungs kept it from falling out. Geoffrey sighed. He had seen this type of wound too many times, on too many battlefields. It never boded well.

Reginald put the wineskin, needle and thread pouch next to him on the ground and placed clean linen squares on top.

"Now watch the road," Geoffrey ordered, before he turned to Guy. "We need to roll him onto his front, then I can remove the axe."

"Argh," the knight groaned, his face contorted with pain, as they turned him slowly on his front. Guy moved back and gently laid the man's head down on his own coat, face to the side. He dabbed the face with a linen square, wiping off the sweat. The knight closed his eyes, his breathing ragged.

"I'm sorry, my lord." Geoffrey straddled the lower back of the knight to pin him down. "Guy, hold the shoulders, but avoid the cut."

Guy pressed his hands on the knight's shoulder blades. The wounded man tensed under the pressure. Geoffrey eased the axe out and dropped it to the ground. The knight screamed; his body stiffened, then collapsed. He had lost consciousness.

Blood gushed from the wound. Geoffrey pressed the linen against it while Guy held the chain mail apart. Blood ran over Geoffrey's hands and sleeves. He threw away the soaked piece and replaced it with another. And another. Eventually he had stemmed the flood sufficiently and dowsed the wound with wine, the strongest drink they had taken with them.

He mopped his brow with his elbow. "Oblivion is bliss. He won't feel the needle now. Watch his breathing." Taking needle and thread from the pouch, Geoffrey gritted his teeth and set to the task.

Chapter One

Alleyne de Bellac leapt from the chair, sending it crashing onto the stone floor of the solar. With a flick of her wrist, she dropped her needlework into the basket at her side.

"And you are certain it is Father's horse, Roger?" She adjusted her woollen gown as she addressed the grizzled steward of Bellac Manor. With her father, Lord Raymond, attending King Stephen, the inhabitants of the manor had a lax time, but that was about to change. Their lord was returning. Her heartbeat rose. How she had missed him!

She smiled, tucking a few strands of hair back inside her thick braid. She must look presentable so he would be proud of her. Where was Elvire when she needed her? Alleyne shook her head. Most likely, her maid was still in the village, taking food to the poorest families. She prayed she appeared as a knight's only daughter should.

A glance at the steward's face extinguished her smile. Roger nodded, his expression grave. "It is indeed, my lady. Ancel recognised your lord father's stallion." He shifted from one leg to another, his eyes studying the floor rushes.

Alleyne sighed and pulled the chair upright. She had known the old steward all her life and instinct told her that all was not well if he did not dare meet her gaze. She went to his side and placed a hand on his bony arm.

"So what is the matter?"

"Forgive me, my lady. But there is no sign of your lord father. Only his stallion, led by a stranger." He kept his gaze lowered.

She swallowed hard. "Whose banner do they carry?"

"None, my lady. That raised my concern."

"Let's go and see for ourselves, shall we?" She grabbed

his arm tightly and pulled him through the door.

Roger followed her down the stairs and through the deserted great hall. He reached past her and opened the solid doors to allow her through. Outside, Alleyne stopped on the bottom step, scanning the bailey. In a nearby corner, pigs and cows were tethered in a peg, ready for slaughter. Chickens roamed free, their wings flapping as they chased each other across the yard.

On the far side, women were beating clothes laid out over large boulders, trying to get the washed fabrics to dry in the chilly afternoon breeze. Alfred, the stable boy, gave her mare a brush outside the stable doors. The horse's coat gleamed in the sunlight. Plumes of thick smoke escaped through the smithy's open doors near the gatehouse. The shouting of men and laughter of the laundresses mingled with the banging of hammers on metal. Everything was as it should be.

Yet a sense of unease gripped her gut.

Turning her attention towards the gate, Alleyne stood as several men-at-arms raced up the stairs to the allure, the walkway that spanned the expanse of the wooden fence encircling the manor. The soldiers lined up against the wall, crossbows in hand.

The captain of the guard, hovering above the gatehouse, turned to meet her gaze. "My lady," he called in greeting.

"Ancel, what is happening?" She raised her voice above the clamour.

"We don't recognise the men, my lady. Strangers, all of them. We're on guard, just in case."

"But they have Father's horse?"

"Aye, it seems so. Bear with me. They're here." He leaned over the fence and demanded the men outside the gate state their business.

Alleyne waited for a sign, hardly daring to breathe. She rubbed her arms, uncertain of whether it was the biting February winds that seeped through her thin linen sleeves or premonition. In her haste, she had forgotten to bring her cloak. 'Twas too late now.

Her heart plummeted at Ancel's body language. His wariness changed to… surprise? Shock? At an abrupt signal from the captain, two guards threw open the gates. Three riders appeared through the gatehouse, one holding the reins of a warhorse.

Alleyne drew in a sharp breath. It was indeed Father's. The distinctive white mark on the long, grey forehead and the saddle were proof enough. The noise subsided, a hushed silence settling over the manor.

As the strangers crossed the bailey, she studied them with a mixture of anxiety and suspicion. The first man, clad in black, had the bearings of a knight, but there was no coat of arms stitched on his surcote. The other two had the appearance of mercenaries, the expression on their weather-beaten faces grim. She exchanged an apprehensive glance with Roger.

"You see why I'm concerned, my lady."

"Yes," she agreed, cold fear gripping her heart. "It does not bode well."

From the corner of her eye she noticed Ancel and his men on the allure had turned and now stood watching the horsemen, crossbows at the ready. Two of her guards came to stand nearby, hands on sword hilts.

Alleyne watched as the company rode towards her. The two men following the knight looked well prepared for any danger on the roads in their rough chain mail and padded gambesons, with sturdy swords at their side. Her gaze moved to the knight. He wore a pair of leather boots and a dark, thick woollen mantle, which had fallen open, revealing his unadorned surcote. Apart from his bearing, the one-and-a-half hander sword at his hip clearly marked him as nobility.

Seemingly oblivious to her scrutiny, the knight came to a halt in front of her and eased himself from the saddle. He handed his stallion's reins to Alfred who had crept forward, his head held low. The knight then turned to take the reins of Lord Raymond's warhorse and, speaking quietly to the boy, pressed them into his hands. The youth stared at the animal and nodded firmly before he turned towards the stable, gently pulling both horses behind him. The knight's men dismounted and followed Alfred.

Alleyne took a deep breath and pushed her shoulders back, her heart racing. Something had happened to Father.

"Who are you, my lord?" she called out, trying to keep her voice steady. "And why have you my lord father's stallion in your possession?"

The knight ruffled his thick black hair. She sensed his unease. He approached in tentative steps, as if preparing the right words to say. She took in the narrow, aquiline nose and thin, wide mouth. Light blue eyes met hers with a touch of arrogance. She stared back, not giving in to the sudden urge to lower her gaze. Blood pounded in her ears. Although he stopped at the bottom of the steps, he still towered above her.

"Geoffrey de Mortagne, under-sheriff of Gloucestershire." He briefly inclined his head. "I assume you are the Lady Alleyne?"

She nodded, unable to speak.

"I bring sad news, my lady, about your lord father." The seriousness of his task showed in his features.

Alleyne shook her head in refusal, wishing he would spare her any sorrow. "What..? Is he..?" Her voice failed her.

"I am sorry, my lady, but I'm afraid he's gravely wounded." When she swayed, his hand caught her elbow.

Alleyne's vision spun and she closed her eyes for an instant. Her free hand reached for the wall for support. De Mortagne held firmly onto her, his warmth strangely comforting.

Sweet Mary!

After several deep breaths, she grew calmer. Her eyes met his again.

"What happened?" Straightening up, she pulled her arm free.

"Lord Raymond was caught in an ambush on the Worcester road. His retainers are dead. We left him in the care of the Benedictines at Worcester. Their infirmarian looks after him." When she remained silent, he added: "He wouldn't have survived the journey here. At least in Worcester, he might have a chance to recover."

She nodded, her mind numb. "Thank you for your help." She hesitated but she had to know. "How did you come across him? Did you see the attackers?"

He nodded. "Yes, we saw them. They appeared to be mercenaries."

Did he hesitate? Was he telling her the truth? Her heartbeat pounded in her ears.

"But I would recognise them again, I'm certain." His words were scant consolation. If he indeed withheld information, could she believe him?

Roger stepped forward and took her arm. "Best go inside, my lady. You don't want to catch a chill at a time when Lord Raymond needs you most." He turned to de Mortagne. "We are very grateful, my lord. Would you care for refreshments while you tell us what happened in detail? Your men can make their way to the kitchens for some ale." He pointed to where a stone hut was built against the side of the manor house, smoke swirling skyward through a hole in the roof.

De Mortagne smiled at the steward. "Thank you. I gladly accept. We have been on the road for days without rest."

He nodded to his men who hovered at the stable door, and gestured in the direction of the kitchen.

Roger held open the door into the hall. Alleyne shook off his hand and went inside. Her moment of weakness had passed. She did not want to be cosseted.

De Mortagne followed her inside.

"Please be seated. It won't be long for the fire to burn." She pointed towards a chair by the side of the fire pit, where a kitchen boy struck a flint to light the small bundle of branches. A flame shot up as the dry wood crackled. The boy piled up logs, prodding them into place with a sturdy poker.

She lowered herself into her father's large wooden chair

and watched the under-sheriff who sat down, hands stretched to the flames. His timing was curious. Of course, she knew exactly who was behind the ambush, but was not as certain about de Mortagne's allegiance. After all, they were in the midst of a civil war. Loyalties changed every day.

"I know who ordered the attack." The calmness in her voice belied her fears.

De Mortagne looked up from the flickering flames. "You do, my lady? Whom do you suspect?"

"Our neighbour, of course. Philip de Guines. He has made our lives difficult these past three years."

De Mortagne straightened. "What has he done to you? Was he not called to Lincoln, like your lord father?"

"I believe he must have been. I haven't actually seen him in many months. And I know not if he has returned yet, but I'm sure he arranged it. Most probably he paid someone to make it look like an accident." Hatred slipped into her voice as bile rose within her.

Roger returned from the kitchen. A maidservant followed with a tray bearing bread, cheese, and a clay jug. She set it on a small table between Alleyne and de Mortagne, and poured wine from the jug into three cups.

"Thank you, Annet." Alleyne took the offered cup. She steadied her shaking hand with the other, unwilling to show the under-sheriff the level of her agitation. His gaze roamed the great hall and he did not appear to have noticed. A sigh of relief escaped her.

De Mortagne took a few sips, then put his goblet down and broke off a chunk of the soft white bread. He gazed at Roger seated on the bench by the fire, his own cup held between both hands.

"You wish to hear how we found Lord Raymond?" de Mortagne asked between bites.

"Yes," Alleyne said, before the steward had a chance. She straightened her back. "We would."

Roger nodded, his lined face pale. She prayed the old man was able to cope with the news, and the responsibilities that now rested on him. His health had failed him lately. Father should have replaced him months ago.

De Mortagne cleared his throat. "We were returning from Lincoln when we came across the attack. Your lord father must have left the city right after the battle, as he was ahead of us." He paused and took a draught of wine.

"We heard rumours of a battle, but no official announcement has reached us yet," Roger said. "What happened at Lincoln? Could this be the reason why–?"

"Nonsense, Roger," Alleyne interrupted him. "We know who is behind this. De Guines."

"You can't say that for certain, my lady." The steward kept his eyes averted.

Alleyne seethed. Why did he not see? It was all so obvious. She turned her attention to her guest. "You won't find any other culprit, believe me." She crossed her arms and sat back, challenging him.

"If it is him, we'll find out, my lady." De Mortagne clearly tried to assure her, then continued. "We came across Lord Raymond just outside Worcester. He fought three attackers who fled after they noticed us." He hesitated. "But before we came close enough, one of the men threw his axe. It hit Lord Raymond in the back."

She recoiled and covered her face with her hands, the vision clear in her mind. Father was not going to come back alive. Her shoulders shook as realisation hit her.

"I'm so sorry, my lady. I shouldn't have been so blunt." In a swift move, de Mortagne knelt by her side, taking her hand. She blinked at him, shocked, yet unwilling to pull her hand from his soothing grasp. She needed comfort. He held her gaze, his eyes full of concern.

"Your lord father is in good hands now. We took him to the monastery as it was the nearest place with a physician."

And a priest.

He didn't need to say the words. They hung unspoken in the air. Tears welled up in her eyes. De Mortagne pressed her hand. She swallowed, aware she should pull it free. Yet his touch was reassuring.

"I have a messenger waiting, should Lord Raymond's condition change. There was nothing more for us to do. At least now we can begin our search for the attackers."

She nodded. "I'm grateful for your help, my lord. Please be our guest at Bellac as long as you wish."

He released her hand and stood, as if suddenly aware of his improper action. "I made a promise to Lord Raymond to catch the perpetrators. Pray for our success, my lady. And for Lord Raymond's health." His voice was solemn. He sat back in his chair, giving her time to compose herself. "When you are ready, please tell me about your neighbour."

Alleyne dried her eyes with her kerchief. "That man has been harassing us for nigh on three years. Our villagers live in fear of his foreign mercenaries attacking them in the fields. These men turn up in the taverns and start fights with any man whose face they don't like." Her voice shook with anger. "But... things came to a head when they snatched two village girls whose banns had just been read."

"What happened then?" de Mortagne asked quietly.

Despite his obvious concern, she could not meet his gaze; instead, she stared at her hands.

"The mercenaries brought them back two nights later, abused like common harlots. Their families tried their best to help them cope. Even the men they were betrothed to reassured them of their love, but still the girls blamed themselves."

Nails dug into her flesh as she clenched her hands into fists. "Two days later, a group of fishermen found their bodies floating further upstream the Severn. The girls couldn't live with the shame they felt they'd brought upon their families..." Her voice faltered.

"I'm sorry."

After a long moment, she raised her head and stared at him. "Can you now see why I believe de Guines is guilty? He has hit us hard, time and time again. Father managed to fend him off but in the last year the acts have become too savage to ignore. And what does our noble king do about it when begged for help? Nothing." She spat the words, wilfully ignoring Roger's panicked expression. "I've had enough!"

Grabbing the cup, she emptied it in one large draught and banged it down on the tray. "The king has no choice but to help now."

De Mortagne cleared his throat, shifting in his seat. "Unfortunately, King Stephen won't be able to do much about anything for a long time." His expression was dark. "He was captured at Lincoln and is now in chains on his way to the Earl of Gloucester's keep in Bristol."

Chapter Two

Geoffrey's words hung in the air. Lady Alleyne stared at him, her eyes widening as the news sank in.

The steward flinched as if Geoffrey had hit him. "The king captured?" His voice shook. "Sweet Jesus! What is to happen to us with the empress ruling the country? She won't be of any help." The old man shook his head.

Geoffrey shrugged. With King Stephen captured, the Empress Matilda, the rightful heir to Old King Henry, gained control over England and Normandy. Or so she expected to. "I doubt much will change anytime soon. Matilda is going to rely on her half-brother, the Earl of Gloucester, as always. They have many plans to make now."

Roger stood and replenished the cups. "Do you really believe so? I'm certain you know her reputation, my lord. The woman's a shrew."

"A shrew who will soon be queen." Geoffrey's voice rose. He had had enough of seditious talk. It followed him everywhere. No-one was content with Stephen's kingship and his indecisive policies, but even fewer people accepted a woman as queen in her own right. In fact, many nobles regarded her husband, the Count of Anjou, as a serious threat to England's independence. King Henry, God rest his soul, should have foreseen the mess.

Geoffrey pulled himself out of his thoughts. He was not the only one who had fallen silent. The steward might have qualms about divulging his political affiliations to a stranger, but Lady Alleyne? She did not appear to be old-fashioned. When his gaze met hers, her eyes shone, ablaze with hope.

She smiled. "The empress will take up our case, won't she? She will listen, woman to woman. Roger is wrong. Surely she is bound to help?"

Roger snorted. "The woman has better things to do than listen to complaints from subjects who haven't even supported her cause."

Geoffrey nodded. "I'm afraid your steward is right, my lady. Matilda's mind is focused on her coronation. While she might present herself to her subjects across the country soon, I don't think she'll have much time to spare for neighbourly disputes. Even if they involve murder. And Sheriff Miles won't leave her side either."

Lady Alleyne's face fell.

Geoffrey sighed. "I will see what I can do when the time comes, my lady." Picking up his cup, he drained it. Lady Alleyne's obvious distress nagged him, suffocated him. Most certainly he did not wish to get entangled in her case. Solve the murder, yes. But stay away from the girl. He must get out of doors to clear his head.

This was the part of his position he hated – bringing bad news to people who had endured too much already. His mood, morose since he set off from Worcester that morning, grew gloomier. His head pounded, the extent of his responsibility weighing heavily on his mind. If only he had not given his oath to her father…

But perhaps it was just the wine, a potent red. It had been a long time since he tasted such quality, such strength. Not since Normandy. He shook off the unwanted memory, and rose.

"With your permission, my lady, I would like to start the investigation right away. We have already lost nearly two days since we took Lord Raymond to the monastery. I will take my men out into the countryside to see what those mercenaries you spoke of are doing. Then we'll speak to the villagers."

"Of course you have my permission." Her emerald eyes clouded with sadness, her voice quiet. "But I hope you will grace our company for the evening meal?"

"I certainly will, my lady." He inclined his head, grateful for a chance to discover more about the manor, and the lady who held it on her father's behalf. "Thank you."

Geoffrey strode away from the fire and left the hall, letting the door fall shut behind him. As he hurried down the steps, he took a couple of deep breaths. This was not going to be an easy task, at the worst possible time. His place should be with the court, attending the empress's progress, not here. He turned towards the kitchen in search of his men.

***

Geoffrey stood surrounded by villeins, their worries etched in their faces.

An old woman grabbed his wrist firmly, her voice hoarse with wailing. She fell to her knees, pulling two young girls with her. "But Lord Raymond will return home safely, my lord, won't he?"

"I don't know, good wife." Geoffrey had lost count of the times he had had to say those words in the last few hours. First on the fields, now in the village. He gently prised her fingers off his wrist, blood pumping through tingling limbs again. "I wish I could say yes."

Two men, dressed in shabby woollen hose and shirt, their bodies thin but not starved, glared at him. "What about us, then?" The older man took a step closer.

"You have a capable lady in charge of the manor and its men-at-arms. They will defend–"

"Have you seen them? How few we have left after Lincoln?"

Geoffrey saw Reginald approach and subtly shook his head, barely noticeable to the people around him. He must go through this alone, not intimidate these villeins any further by involving his sergeants. They were not mercenaries. "I don't know how many men you had before the battle, but I'm certain your manor isn't the only estate to lose vital fighters. The steward and the captain of the guard will prepare the manor for any eventualities. They will not forget about you."

Truth was, he had no idea what would happen. These were perilous times, and simple folk often bore the brunt. But their lord was still alive. "Lord Raymond may yet survive – you can't rule that out. He looks like a hardy fighter, reluctant to give up."

The old man smiled, gaps showing between his teeth. "Aye, that he is, Lord Raymond. Has seen many battles in his lifetime and always showed off his scars proudly."

Geoffrey took the man's arm. Here was a leader, someone to pull the other villagers with him if he only managed to persuade him. "See? You will need to keep up your spirit and pray for Lord Raymond's recovery."

The man nodded, fervour glowing in his eyes. "We will do so, my lord."

"Good. Then I can also ask you to ensure everyone is on guard here. Do not let your children or women roam outside. Never go out to the fields alone. Report any sightings to us at the manor right away. Will you do that for me? For your lady?"

The man straightened and squared his shoulders. "You can rely on me, my lord."

"Thank you." Geoffrey released the breath he had been holding. He turned to the women kneeling next to him, their whimpering in his ears. "Keep praying for your lord's health!"

Eyes filled with tears stared at him, full of sorrow. Then they lowered their heads. "Hail Mary…"

Geoffrey turned away. The villagers opened a gap wide enough to let him pass. A glimmer of hope shone on several faces but others showed only fear. He could not do any more for them. Folk had to help themselves – and each other.

He joined his companions and took Feu's reins. "Let's head back." With a flick of his head, he gestured towards the manor, the palisade barely visible in the distance. A shiver of foreboding crept down his spine.

The earlier sunset left an orange glow above the black silhouette of the forest. A thin layer of ice settled on the grass. Geoffrey and his sergeants rode towards Bellac Manor, careful to avoid the frozen puddles on the road. The cold had seeped into his body, his hands holding the reins icy. Gloves and cloaks only provided scant protection against the chilly winter air. They had not found any trace of de Guines's mercenaries; in fact, no-one had spotted them for weeks.

His mood was still sombre, his jaw set firmly, teeth grinding in frustration, when his small group finally approached the gate.

Geoffrey waved to the guard looking over the palisade. "It's de Mortagne. We're back from our search. Open up!"

"Aye, my lord." The guard nodded and turned away. A moment later, the gate opened. "Welcome back, my lord. Any luck?"

"No, Hubert," Geoffrey addressed the gatekeeper. "Still no damn trace." His voice low, he winced at the disappointment in the guard's face. Torches in the deserted bailey cast eerie shadows across the walls, the gloom matching his thoughts.

Geoffrey dismounted and handed the reins to the waiting stable boy. "Here you are, lad. Feu's tired and hungry."

Alfred nodded. "No worries, my lord. He'll love his warm home. Here you go, my boy." He spoke to Feu, patting his neck, before turning to take the other horses.

Reginald shook his head. "I'll look after mine, lad."

"So will I," Guy said. "Lead the way."

Geoffrey climbed the wooden steps onto the allure alone, grateful for a moment's solitude. He stopped between two merlons and leaned on the parapet, his gaze drifting over the forests. In between the dark outlines of two hills, barely visible in the hidden moonlight, a glimmer showed him where the village lay. The source of light no doubt came from the tavern, the meagre huts of the villeins lying in darkness. Most people settled to sleep as soon as darkness fell, to conserve their stack of rush lights. He sighed and ruffled his windblown hair.

Lord Raymond could live one day, ten days, a fortnight. Or he might die tonight.

"Christ's blood!" Geoffrey swore at the inconvenience. Sheriff Miles had ordered him to follow the court. This delay must irk his superior. It should have been an easy decision but now Geoffrey felt torn. He was keen to join Matilda's coronary procession, an event he had secretly been working for over the past three years. But he could not leave this vulnerable heiress to the wolves; this slip of a girl with green eyes too large for her own good. He shook his head to rid himself of the turmoil in his mind.

Heavy footsteps behind him alerted his senses. He turned swiftly.

"You're brooding again?" Reginald came to stand next to him, pointing in the direction of the village. "They're scared, and rightly so."

"Lord Raymond's attackers were too quick even for us; too well organised to be mere mercenaries. If they are the same men, they have an easy prey in the villagers." He nodded and brushed his fringe from his eyes.

"What are your plans, Geoffrey?" Reginald would never dare call him by his given name in company, but in the privacy of the allure they spoke like the old friends they were.

"I have to join Matilda, Reg. And we also need to find out what Queen Maude is doing. She won't rest until Stephen is freed." He glanced at his companion. "We're wasting our time here but–"

"But what? You have sworn an oath, Geoffrey. An oath to a dying man. You can't break it, Matilda be crowned or not."

"I've also sworn fealty to Matilda. But it's not just that." He stared at the manor house, shafts of light shining through gaps in the shutters. Unlike the villagers, the lady of the manor was rich enough to afford candles. "I have a bad feeling in my stomach about leaving here. Someone will take advantage and I'd rather it wasn't Philip de Guines."

"He's probably in hiding now, like the rest of Stephen's followers. We haven't heard from him in years. Could he be with the queen?"

"Well, of course! Why didn't I think of that?"

Reginald grinned. "Because your mind isn't on politics, that's why. You're thinking of the sweet Lady Alleyne, soon to be heiress of all this." He made a sweeping motion with his hands and winked.

"Don't jest, Reg. As far as we know, Lord Raymond is recovering. But it might be the right time for you to go on a journey, my friend." He slapped his sergeant on the back, the corners of his mouth twitching at Reginald's suspicious stare. "A journey to our beloved queen. To Maude in Kent."

***

The hall was warm and inviting. Torchlight flickered on the walls, throwing the tapestries on the wall into a play of shadow and light. The fire roared in the central pit, wood crackled and flames danced merrily.

The heat reached Alleyne even where she stood at the top of the wooden staircase, watching the servants prepare the hall for supper. They had moved the trestle tables stacked against the walls to either side of the fire pit and placed benches to either side of them. White linen covered the high table, with gem-encrusted goblets shimmering against its crisp colour.

De Mortagne was to join them tonight. She had arranged for Cook to bring out the best the larder could provide. Roger had voiced his concerns at such display, with Lent only days away, but Alleyne overruled him. Father enjoyed entertaining. He would approve of her showing her gratitude by providing a fine meal. The memory of her father dampened her spirit. Her smile faltered. She sent a quick prayer to the Virgin for his recovery, then shook off her thoughts and descended the stairs.

She was correcting a few minor misplacements in the setting of the high table, when the door opened and de Mortagne and his men entered. Groups of chatting manor folk, their faces flushed from the chilly air outside, followed them into the warmth of the hall, rushing forward to claim their space at the tables. De Mortagne spoke to his men, and she caught his eye as he glanced her way. He crossed the hall while his men took their seats with her off-duty men-at-arms.

As he approached the dais, she smiled. He halted close to her and took her hand. The corners of his mouth twitched before he bent to kiss it. Her skin tingled at the mere brush of his lips. She snatched her hand back and felt the sudden urge to wipe it on her gown to rid herself of the strange sensation. But she refrained, taking a silent, deep breath, her fingers entwined behind her back.

"My lady." He raised himself to his full height. "Am I right in thinking that this is what your great hall looks like on feast days?" He inclined his head and met her gaze, a glint in his eyes.

"Quite right, my lord de Mortagne. This is how we honour our guests." She waived towards the decorated high table. "Would you care for some wine?" Not waiting for his answer, grateful for a reason to look away, she turned. With unsteady hands, she picked up a clay jug brimming with rich, red wine and poured a generous measure into a goblet. When a drop splashed onto the snow-white sheet she jumped backwards, nearly losing her balance. A stain spread out over the white linen like blood. A vision of Father, lying in a pool of blood, came to her unbidden. Her shaking grew.

Swiftly, de Mortagne took the jug from her and set it down, hovering just close enough for her to feel his warmth.

What was going on? It was embarrassing to react like a foolish girl. The man must meet dozens like her throughout the year, daughters and wives of men robbed and slain. Did he pay this much attention to them all? She turned to face him and passed him the goblet, meeting his gaze. His eyes were blank, as if he had not noticed her shakiness.

"Thank you, my lady." He took a sip. "I wish your lord father was here. I'm certain we'll hear of his recovery soon."

He was still hovering close, near enough for comfort but almost too close for propriety. She took a step back but the table left her no room to escape. "I hope so. I keep praying for his health." The intensity in de Mortagne's eyes made her heart pound in her ears. His concern was genuine. Did he deal with all such cases in this manner?

In the corner of her eye, she spotted her steward. "Ah, Roger!" She beckoned him over.

De Mortagne took a step back as Roger approached, the glint in his eyes disappearing. "I just said to Lady Alleyne how inviting the hall looks."

Roger inclined his head. "Thank you, my lord. We try our best."

Alleyne ignored de Mortagne's raised eyebrow. She was relieved the spell, which appeared to turn her into a little girl, was broken. She must avoid being alone in the man's company.

She pointed towards the jug. "Have some wine, Roger. You have done very well today."

The steward helped himself to a small measure, then stared at the stained tablecloth and raised an eyebrow.

She lifted her goblet, smiling. "To Father's health!" She took a sip.

"Indeed, my lady. To Lord Raymond's swift recovery." Roger returned the gesture.

De Mortagne raised his own cup in silence, his gaze now drifting across the room.

The hall filled up quickly, men-at-arms and villeins taking their seat. The servants went about the lower tables, refilling the ale jugs that had been emptied with speedy resolve, and the atmosphere was hopeful, uplifting. For now.

Alleyne swallowed her apprehension and moved to her chair. She smiled at de Mortagne and gestured to the seat on her left. "Won't you take a seat, my lord?"

De Mortagne placed his goblet on the table and sat. "I see you keep your lord father's chair vacant, my lady."

Alleyne's heart skipped a beat. "Father is still alive, is he not? He may not be with us tonight in body but I'm certain he is in mind. He will return very soon."

Turning away, she waited for Roger to take his seat on the far side of her father's chair. Then she stood and clapped her hands. Silence descended and all faces turned towards her. She read anticipation in them, hope and concern.

"As you all know, Lord Raymond, my father, lies wounded in the Benedictine abbey at Worcester." A few murmured voices rose but were hushed immediately by their neighbours. "We are gathered here as we wish to show our gratitude to the nobleman who came to Father's rescue – Sir Geoffrey de Mortagne, under-sheriff of Gloucestershire." She raised her goblet.

"I ask you all to pray for Lord Raymond's recovery, pray that he will survive this cowardly attack..." Her voice faltered. De Mortagne leaned forward, concern in his eyes. Strangely, it gave her strength, her heartbeat slowing from its frantic pounding.

Her gaze travelled the room. "And I ask you to join me in thanking Sir Geoffrey for his intervention. Without him, Lord Raymond's fate would have been sealed." She raised her goblet to her lips and took a draught.

The room exploded in shouts of "to Sir Geoffrey" and "to Lord Raymond" as Alleyne sank into her seat, grateful for the comfort of the plump cushions at her back.

De Mortagne stood and glanced at her before he faced the crowd. People nudged each other into silence.

"I am honoured by my treatment here at Bellac." He looked around, as if studying their faces. Alleyne watched him, curious to discover how his mind worked.

"I thank the Lady Alleyne for her kind hospitality. I only wish it was a happier occasion." He paused again, eyes focused on a group of men at the end of the hall. She tried to see who he looked at but could not identify any strangers in their midst.

"Please join us in the church tonight for prayers for Lord Raymond." He nodded as he sat and picked up his goblet.

De Mortagne took a deep draught before he glanced her

way. His eyes, transformed into the shade of a stormy winter sea in the flickering torchlight, bore into hers. A deep flush crept into her cheeks as Alleyne realised she was staring. Quickly, she averted her gaze. Her fingers fidgeted, playing with the polished gems on her goblet. Sweet Mary, what was the matter with her? Not even Will d'Arques had such an effect on her senses – and Will was the one man she had expected to offer for her. She must send him a message. Guilt flooded her. It must be her mind, tired with concern for Father, that made her head spin. Nothing at all to do with the under-sheriff.

She breathed a deep sigh of relief when Roger finally gave the signal for the food to be brought. Servants entered, carrying trays loaded with roast duck and pigeon, baked eels, bowls of stewed vegetables, and the day-old bread that served as trenchers.

"How are you faring, my lady?" De Mortagne bent over the arm of his chair. His voice, deep and comforting, was barely audible above the noise of people piling up their trenchers with food and drink-induced merriment.

"I am well, thank you." She smiled, taking a cut of pigeon breast from the bowl in front of them and nibbling at the savoury meat. She normally devoured such delicacies in an instant, but tonight she lacked the taste for it.

A commotion at the door pulled her out of her thoughts. A man rushed past the tables towards hers. She leapt from her chair at the same time as de Mortagne, who raised his dagger in a firm grip. Her hands grabbed the edge of the table and her stomach contracted.

Friend or enemy?

The man's cloak was splattered with mud and dripping, his boots caked with wet soil and his beard flecked with dirt. A messenger. His expression grim, he fell to one knee in front of the dais, and bowed his head.

"I'm afraid I bring bad tidings, my lady." He did not meet her eyes. Instead, he glanced at de Mortagne who regarded him with an inscrutable expression.

Alleyne's heart pounded. "Speak!"

"I've come straight from the Benedictines at Worcester." His voice cut through the silence that had descended. "I'm sorry for being the bearer of such grave news, my lady. The Brother Infirmarian tried everything but it was God"s will. Lord Raymond de Bellac died this day."

Chapter Three

Geoffrey took Lady Alleyne's elbow, releasing it only when she sank into her chair. Her face turned ashen, her earlier glow gone. She stared, unseeing, past the messenger. Bereft.

He thanked him. At Roger's signal, the messenger rose and followed him to a side table to quench his thirst and hunger. No doubt, Geoffrey would hear the details later. For the moment, however, his mind was on the girl at his side.

He refilled her goblet and held it out to her. She gazed at him, eyes wide but dry, and cradled the goblet with shaky hands. She took a few sips, then shook her head. He put it down, scanning the room for Lady Alleyne's maid but she was nowhere in sight.

Returning his gaze to her, his mind was made up. He must take care of the lady. She still had not uttered a word. His gut clenched, and anger rose within him at the thought of this girl left alone. The vultures would soon flock to claim her. Her life was bound to become dangerous. In his line of work, he often heard of rich heiresses being snatched and forced into wedlock. Here lay an additional duty for him that he had not foreseen when he made his promise to Lord Raymond. The look of utter desolation on her face suffused him with guilt. How selfish was he to think about the inconvenience to himself when here was a lady needing his help? Guilt burned into him and Geoffrey pulled back his shoulders.

"You should retire to your room and rest, my lady. Roger can see to this." He waved his arm towards the tables. The noise level had risen considerably as villagers mourned their loss, and questioned their future. Many eyed him suspiciously as he drew Lady Alleyne from her seat. He ignored them.

Geoffrey steered her up the stairs, afraid if he let go she

might collapse in a heap. She shivered, her expression blank. Not knowing which of the three doors on the landing led to her rooms, he headed towards the first. He reached for the doorknob but the door swung back on its hinges. A stout, older woman came out, staring at them.

"We've had bad tidings," he explained. "Lord Raymond is dead."

"Blessed Mother!" The woman crossed herself, then her hands flew to her cheeks. "Come here, sweeting." She enveloped Lady Alleyne in a tight embrace. Hit by a sense of loss he could not explain, he let her take the girl to her room.

"Thank you, my lord." The door slammed in his face but Geoffrey knew the effects of shock too well to mind. He turned away. The unknown tug at his heart, he ignored.

Back at the high table, he refilled his goblet when Roger joined him. Geoffrey studied him over the rim. The old, wrinkled face haggard, the steward slumped into a chair with a sigh, ruffling long fingers through thin hair.

"What do we do now?" The old man's voice was weak with fatigue. It was clear that Roger had served too many years to bear the huge responsibility of looking after a young heiress and defending her inheritance.

Geoffrey took a draught of wine before he leaned back in his chair. "You have to be on alert now for de Guines's men, Roger. They will know of Lord Raymond's death within a day and emerge from their hiding place. If it helps, I'll stay here for a few more days. I have to send one of my men away but Guy and I will keep investigating. Both the village and the manor have to be prepared. The killers will return."

The steward nodded. "Thank you, my lord. We appreciate your help." He took a ragged breath and stood. "Now, I have a funeral to organise. I must speak with Father Anselm." Roger turned but stopped and looked over his shoulder, his gaze questioning. "The messenger said that Lord Raymond's mortal remains would be brought home for burial within a day or two. He told me you had men to cover this duty? Men to watch over the procession?"

Geoffrey nodded. "Yes. I didn't want to risk the body being snatched and defiled. Lord Raymond's remains will be transferred home safely."

A look of relief crossed Roger's features. "Thank you."

After the steward's departure, Geoffrey drained his goblet and headed for the door, signalling Guy and Reginald as he passed their table.

His men were at his heels by the time he stepped into the bailey. The light from the torches on the walls chased shadows across the yard. Groups of manor folk and men-at-arms stood huddled in the semi-darkness, their voices hushed.

Geoffrey headed up the stairs to the walkway. He felt his way rather than saw the steps in the gloomy torchlight, used to prowling in the dark. He walked to a corner, well out of earshot of any sentries, leaned against the palisade and faced his men.

"Truth be told, I expected his death, but not so quickly. We need to move fast." He glanced at Reginald. "It would be useful to have you here, Reg, but our most urgent business is to safeguard the empress. We must know what Queen Maude is plotting. She hasn't fled the country as expected, but remains in Kent. You will head out tomorrow morning and find her camp. Send word as soon as you can but stay with her retinue. We can't risk not knowing her movements. I wouldn't put it past her to attempt to rescue Stephen."

Reginald nodded. "Aye, Geoffrey. I'll leave before dawn. The fewer folk see me the better, else they think we're deserting them."

"I agree. Also, make enquiries about de Guines. Last time I heard of him he was a staunch supporter of Stephen's, so he might be at Maude's court. Unless he's changed his mind."

"Aye, it will be done."

A duty guard approached and they hushed until he passed.

Guy scratched his stubble. "What do you want me to

do?"

"You stay here with me. Speak to the manor folk. We'll go to the village again tomorrow and remain visible. If those mercenaries are lurking in the vicinity, they'll know we're still around. We wait until after the funeral before we decide what to do next."

"The villagers are worried. They don't think the old steward or the lady can protect them, though that captain of the guard, Ancel, seems a reliable man."

"Yes, he certainly appears capable, but he doesn't have enough men. This is a small manor and it's now left without a strong hand. He can expect trouble." His gaze roamed the bailey, where people headed out of the gates towards their homes. He spotted the captain at the open gate, his hand firmly clasping the hilt of his sword. Even though he must know everyone, he was still prepared to defend the manor at any given moment.

Definitely the man to have on your side.

"Guy, accompany the villagers on their walk home. Listen to their chats. I want to know everything that's worrying them."

Guy nodded and rushed down the stairs. He hailed a group of men and women, joined in their conversation, and disappeared with them through the gate.

Geoffrey dropped his hand on Reginald's shoulder. "Go back to the hall and prepare for your journey. By all means, sit down with those staying for the night and share a drink."

"Very well. What are you doing?"

"I'll have a word with our captain. See what he thinks. We have to prepare the manor together for a possible attack."

They descended the stairs in silence, their thoughts focused on the tasks ahead, and parted without another word. Six years of fighting and spying together had taught them to understand each other without speaking.

Geoffrey stopped and watched his sergeant enter the hall. Reginald was just over two score and ten years. An old soldier, but still as quick of arm as a young knight. Geoffrey could rely on him to keep him informed of any developments in Queen Maude's camp.

He wished he were able to join the Empress Matilda on her journey to London. Despite the optimism in her camp following victory at Lincoln, he doubted the path would be as smooth as she expected. She must still convince many people – nobles and commoners alike – that she, Old King Henry's daughter, was the right person to rule England. A woman.

He sighed and turned to see Ancel approaching him, rubbing his hands against the cold. The man must have read his mind.

"You heard the tidings, Captain?"

Ancel nodded, grave eyes meeting his.

"Yes, my lord. The messenger told us. We're preparing for the worst." He pointed towards his men stationed on the allure, passing each other as they patrolled the perimeter.

Geoffrey's gaze followed the captain's. He looked to the still open gate where a number of men-at-arms hid in the shadows, loaded crossbows in hand. It would have been foolish to loosen a nock in this semi-darkness, but it was prudent to be prepared. Soon they would close and bar the gate.

"Have all the villagers left?" He scanned the bailey. The yard was deserted but he still heard muffled voices coming from the hall.

"Most of them. Hubert," Ancel bellowed towards the gatekeeper. "Chase the last few from the hall and take them home. We'll lock the gate behind you. Take Harold with you."

"Yes, Captain." The soldier nodded and rushed into the hall. He emerged shortly after, shoving three men, their steps unsteady – from drink no doubt – through the door and steered them towards the gate. Ancel shot a dark glance at them. The men lowered their heads and walked briskly past, followed by Hubert and Harold.

Geoffrey smiled and regarded the captain, who supervised the gate being shut and bolted, with growing respect. Lady Alleyne was fortunate to have such a capable man.

"What are your plans in case of an attack?" He followed Ancel up the steps to the walkway. They came to a halt above the gate. 'Twould seem Ancel wanted to watch for his men's return. Well, so would he. Perfect opportunity to gauge the captain's opinion.

Ancel stared into the darkness. "Lord Raymond and I planned for all eventualities. Attack, siege, fire. Fortunately, Bellac Manor has never suffered a direct assault; unlike many other castles. The mercenaries always picked our people on the road and in the fields. The palisade wouldn't withstand fire, but the manor house is defendable to an extent." He hesitated and turned to Geoffrey. "But we couldn't withstand a serious attack."

"My thoughts precisely." Geoffrey glanced around the manor grounds. Men-at-arms spread out at regular intervals across the allure, in the bailey below him, and near the main door to the hall. A pitifully small number of men, not enough to defend the manor should some of them be wounded or killed.

"You have no reserves?"

"No, my lord. We have some villeins trained in combat but they'd be easy prey for fighting men. I'd call on them if we have no choice, but not before. We need them to work the fields. Whilst we have a well to maintain our water supply in case of a siege, the manor can't afford to starve."

"I'll leave you the rest of my men who are conveying Lord Raymond's body. That should add to your list, even if it's but a few. And I'll be staying for a while. We need to keep our eyes open for de Guines's mercenaries. They'll strike again, as I'm certain they know by now that Lord Raymond's dead."

"Oh yes, I've been expecting them." Ancel's voice was searing and he turned his back to the bailey.

Geoffrey admired Ancel's certainty. Doubts of de Guines's involvement nagged him. But without proof, he had to follow all the leads.

***

It took another three days for the plain coffin bearing Lord Raymond's remains to arrive at Bellac Manor. The constant rain had prevented the men from covering as many miles as they had planned.

A guard called out, announcing the company's approach.

In the stables, Geoffrey heard the shout and dropped the brush with which he had groomed Feu, after another day of failure. Despite searching the forests and fields within a ten-mile radius, he and Guy, with a small contingent of Bellac men-at-arms, had found no sign of any strangers, spotted no mercenaries on Bellac lands. All was calm. As if de Guines was content with the result and had re-called them. That was, if the killers had been under his command in the first place. Something in Lady Alleyne's tale had struck Geoffrey as not quite right but try as he might, he could still not identify it.

Soaked to the bone, he had turned his frustration into physical labour. Vigorously grooming his stallion allowed him time to think, to plan strategy.

Relief coursed through him that Lord Raymond's body had finally arrived home. It meant Lady Alleyne would be able to say farewell to her father before she faced an uncertain future.

Only once, almost painfully briefly, had he seen her since the messenger arrived. During a short dry spell the previous afternoon she had gone for a stroll on the allure, and he joined her. His heart pounding in his ears for reasons he could not fathom, he had spoken of his support, his plans. She had barely acknowledged him. In fact, she had withdrawn into a shell and he could not breach her defences. Disappointed and angry at once, he had escorted her back to her room.

Now she rushed through the door of the hall the moment he emerged from the stables. He pulled his sleeves down as he walked towards her. His gaze took in her appearance in swift assessment. The girl's skin was a pale reflection of her worries, in stark contrast to the dark blue of her cloak. Geoffrey stopped next to her, meeting her gaze. Was there a hint of relief in those emerald depths?

They waited for the small procession to enter the bailey. Around them, people dropped to their knees when the cart carrying the coffin, draped in the Bellac standard, rolled past them. The sound of wailing cut through the silence. Women rushed towards the coffin, touched it with shaky hands, and crossed themselves. Their voices rose high.

When the cart came to a halt, Geoffrey took Lady Alleyne's arm and led her forward. She paled.

"Oh, Father!" Her hand trembled as she reached out to touch the smooth wood. She withdrew it quickly, as if stung, and Geoffrey covered it in a grip meant to comfort.

"All will be well, my lady." Empty words, he knew.

Ancel gave instructions for the coffin to be transferred into the chapel and Geoffrey signalled to his retinue to follow Ancel's orders. Roger followed the cart as it continued its journey.

Geoffrey guided Lady Alleyne back into the hall. "Once the men have set up the remains of your lord father for the vigil, you will be able to pray by his side." He reassured her as he took her to a bench near the fire. He ordered a boy hovering by the stairs to bring hot, spiced wine, and sat beside her. The urge to reach out, to hold her hand, was overwhelming yet he held back.

"I haven't thanked you yet." Her voice quivered.

"There's no need to thank me, my lady."

Her large eyes stared into the fire and he knew she floated miles away, perhaps even as far back as her childhood. Memories were prone to attack you in moments of grief, rendering you helpless. Swiftly, he shrugged off unwanted memories of his own. This was not the place to remember Mortagne, his home village in Perche.

But Lady Alleyne was strong. He sensed it in her demeanour, saw it in her eyes. Suppressed now, no doubt her strength returned soon. She would take control when required to defend her inheritance. She must.

The boy emerged from the corridor linking the hall to the kitchen. Geoffrey took the cup. "Thank you."

Tenderly, he held it to her and she closed her hands around it. The steam rising from the hot spices brought colour to her cheeks. Her back straightened and he moved a little away from her, giving her space.

She took a draught, then stared at him as if struck. "Sweet Mary, the funeral! I haven't prepared a thing."

"Roger has organised it all, my lady. Lord Raymond left orders in place. No need to fret." Her eyes loomed large in her pale face. Too large. He wanted to brush away her fears but dared not touch her. She had to get through her pain. By herself, but not alone. He was there.

Hell, what spell has she cast? He pushed aside the fluttering sensation in his heart. He would not get close to any woman again.

"You know, it's strange," she muttered. "For the first time in days, I feel relieved." Her eyes filled with tears. "But how can I be relieved when I'm about to bury my father?"

His fingers itched to brush a drop from her cheek but he refrained. "You feel relieved because he is home. Finally, you can say goodbye and resume your life."

Geoffrey swallowed as he watched more tears spill down her face. What was so different this time? He regularly brought sad tidings to wives and daughters but none had moved him like this one. Lady Alleyne was unlike any mourning daughters he had met before. Had her dying father sent Geoffrey ambling into such a sweet yet dangerous trap with intent when he promised Lord Raymond to protect her?

She wiped the tears away with the back of her hand. "But what is there to resume? We can't hold off de Guines's attack when it comes. You've seen our poor defences."

"Ancel is a good captain. He'll defend Bellac to his dying breath. And I'll be staying as well, for the time being, should you so wish."

She met his gaze. "I would like you to stay, Sir Geoffrey.

I know you haven't found any trace of the mercenaries yet. Don't despair over this. Those men are clever. If you left now, they'd return within days, I'm certain."

He was right. The shock of seeing her father's coffin had indeed brought Lady Alleyne back to reality. She made plans. Yet something made him refrain from voicing his doubts about de Guines's involvement in the murder. She was not ready for his suspicions.

"I'm going to visit de Guines's manor after the funeral. It's worth a try. In the meantime, my men will bolster Ancel's defences."

"It sounds like you've taken care of everything already." She smiled through the tears. "I'm grateful."

The door opened and Roger entered. He stopped by their side, his face solemn. "My lady, your lord father is now prepared for vigil."

Chapter Four

The morning of the funeral dawned bright and clear. A distinct chill hung in the air. The thatched roofs of the huts and stables in the bailey were covered by a thin layer of ice that sparkled in the winter sun. Churned-up frost turned the mud into slush. Alleyne put a tentative foot down to the next step outside the hall entrance, clutching her cloak, grateful for the coney fur trim that kept her neck warm. She had dressed appropriately, wearing gloves and deer hide boots. The chapel would be cold.

De Mortagne already stood waiting. He offered his arm, which she gratefully accepted, and kept her steady as they walked over to the litter. She had never travelled in a litter before, considering it was only for damsels who did not love to ride – and she was no quivering damsel! – but the occasion demanded dignity. Jumping from her mare covered in mud, frozen and bedraggled, would simply not do. Father would thoroughly disapprove. The thought of his stern face, indignant and disbelieving, made her giggle before sadness clouded the vision again.

The under-sheriff helped her inside the litter, her gloved hand snug in his for an instant, and she leaned back against the soft cushions, hoping they would soon warm her back. Once she settled, he handed her the sheepskins to spread over her legs before he closed the curtain. Surprisingly, she enjoyed the attention he had given her in the last few days. It felt good to be looked after, cared for. Today, he made the effort to see her comfortable and protected. She pulled the curtain an inch apart and watched him mount his horse. The ease with which he had taken charge of the manor following Father's death, and the support he received from her people, puzzled her. Nobody questioned his orders. The man was a born leader.

Her opinion of him had changed. Where she had been wary at first, not knowing how seriously he took his task, she was now convinced he was on her side and doing all he could to find the murderers. His men scoured the countryside each day, and the previous nights he had kept vigil with her by her father's body in the chapel, ignoring the draughts and discomfort just as she did. He had kept himself at a discreet distance yet his presence was reassuring. Knowing he was nearby infused her with warmth.

But de Mortagne was still a stranger.

Keeping that simple fact in mind, she had followed the only route viable. She did not like going behind the undersheriff's back, after everything he had done for her, but Bellac Manor was her home. 'Twould be her shoulders that bore the brunt once he left. And leave he would, sooner or later. Besides, when she sent her urgent message to Will d'Arques, she had not been certain of de Mortagne's loyalties. Best be safe and ask Father's friend of many years to help her defend the manor until she found a way forward. Once Will arrived, de Mortagne was free to focus on his other duties, no longer bound to carry the burden of looking after her.

No longer bound by his vow to Father.

The thought should fill her with relief. Shaking her head, she brushed aside a sudden sense of sadness. Yes, she was better off with the support of a family friend who knew the manor.

Who knew her.

The movement of the litter stopped and she opened the curtain the moment it was lowered to the ground. Again, de Mortagne was at her side to assist her. The carriers had stopped outside the steps to the chapel, and she gave a sigh of relief that she was not forced to walk through more mud. She slipped through the open door and glanced around, surprised. A large gathering of villagers, men-at-arms and official mourners filled the small space. She blinked away tears. Never had she expected so many people to come and show their respects. She shivered and her breathing grew ragged. She swallowed hard.

De Mortagne nodded and, with her hand on his arm, led her through the crowd to the front. People opened a path for them, their heads bowed. Coming to a halt before the altar, he released her and took a step back. He seemed to be reading her mind. At this very instant, she needed his strength. She raised her gaze to Father Anselm, standing behind the altar.

***

Halfway through the funeral mass, Alleyne's blood reached boiling point.

What a disgrace!

Father Anselm struggled to hold himself steady. He hurried through the Latin at a speed of which, she was certain, half of what he mumbled was incorrect. She expected the priest to at least abstain from his cups on the day of his lord's funeral, but his slurred speech and swaying stance proved any such hopes misguided. Bile rose in her throat. She dug her nails into her hands. Still, the pain could not hide the anger. She glowered at the priest. He clearly noticed, and shifted his gaze.

Behind her, she heard shuffling feet and whispered protests. She could rely on her people to show their displeasure. They despised the drunkard in charge of their souls as much as she did. As soon as the funeral feast was over, she would complain to the Bishop. Again.

De Mortagne leaned forward and whispered, "Do you want me to stop him, my lady? We could find another to take his place."

She met his gaze and saw revulsion. Of course! He had not yet had the dubious pleasure of listening to the shoddy sermons delivered by Father Anselm, whose nasal voice was rising with fervour.

"No, thank you." She shook her head. "Best let him continue. The sooner he's finished the better." She turned to glare at the priest, her eyes narrowed and jaw clenched, her hands balled into fists. Grief warred with fury, draining her like a wrung cloth. The emptiness she had felt since Father's death was fast turning into rage; rage at the attackers, at de Guines, at the inebriated man of the cloth who turned this solemn gathering into a mockery; even at God for taking Father from her. She quickly crossed herself. It was not the Lord's fault that some of His priests took His teachings so indifferently.

De Mortagne edged closer. He must have felt her discomfort and she was grateful, again, for his presence. Her thoughts wandered from her anger to his likely reaction when she told him she no longer needed his help. The notion seemed callous but he would understand. Most likely, he would be relieved another man took over. She must tell him after the feast.

Her stomach knotted at the thought of him leaving. Following Will's arrival, de Mortagne could focus on finding the killers while she and Bellac were in Will's safe hands. With King Stephen captured, she wouldn't become a ward of the king's until his release. Or she became the Empress Matilda's following her coronation. In the meantime, she needed protection and Will was the right man to ensure her safety.

Alleyne pushed any traces of regret firmly to the back of her mind. Her feelings and physical reactions to de Mortagne only occurred because she was vulnerable, alone. She needed a shoulder to lean on and he had offered his. Nothing more, nothing less.

As the congregation kneeled again for the final prayers, she sank onto her knees, her hand leaning on de Mortagne's strong arm as she lowered herself to the stone floor. Soon they were going to place Father's body into the ground. Closing her mind firmly against thoughts of de Mortagne or Will d'Arques, she clasped her hands in prayer and focused on the Latin words. Her eyes rested on her Father's coffin. It had lain open during the vigil but the lid was now shut. She had taken her farewell in private, and would always remember her last glimpse at his beloved face, devoid of any suffering or pain.

***

Geoffrey frowned at Father Anselm whose voice echoed along the narrow nave. Accompanied by prayers for the dead, four men – one of them Ancel – came forward and lowered the coffin bearing the remains of Raymond de Bellac into its final resting place. The congregation bowed their heads and crossed themselves. Geoffrey glanced behind him. Several older women fell to their knees, wailing, their high-pitched voices echoing around the chapel.

Throughout the service, Geoffrey worried about Lady Alleyne. As the coffin sank into the depth, tears welled in her eyes. She pulled a linen square from her sleeve and dabbed them. He admired her composure, felt her anger at the priest's lack of respect, and another notion he could not identify. Lady Alleyne seemed torn between leaning into him and pulling away. She glanced at him when she assumed he did not notice. He noticed. And became suspicious.

Instinct told him she kept something from him.

With a thump, the coffin reached the ground. The bearers withdrew, their heads bowed. Alleyne moved forward and stopped at the end of the gap. Geoffrey did not follow. She needed her privacy for a moment, even if the chapel was filled with wails of mourning. Her head hung low, she stood still. Geoffrey sensed her tension, wanting to comfort her; to take her in his arms. To take away the pain.

He shrugged at the notion. He must not get close to her. Hunting for murderers was his job. Not seducing fatherless heiresses, as much as he wanted to.

He blinked.

Finally, Lady Alleyne crossed herself and turned away.

Roger approached her and, side by side, they walked to the door. Geoffrey pushed away the sudden pang in his heart. No longer was she looking for him. Of course, she had only taken what she needed – the support of an officer of the Crown; a man's strength to bolster her own. Now that Lord Raymond was buried, he did not have to stay. She had a chance to move on, leaving the running of the manor to Ancel and Roger while he could easily search for the attackers from his base in Gloucester.

The thought of leaving her filled him with dread. Despite his doubts, he wanted to look after her, keep her safe. That was not possible from twenty miles away.

Christ, what was wrong with him? He had never before wanted to take care of a woman. Not since Solange. Played with them, yes, but without commitment. His duties left little time for relationships, and no time at all for a family.

Family? Where had that thought sprung from? He shrugged it off and followed the congregation from the chapel. Searching for her, he saw the litter already halfway to the gate of the manor. He wound his cloak tighter around him and fastened it on his shoulder with the silver brooch.

"What a service!" Guy appeared at his side, a smirk on his face. "If he were our village priest, my mother would have kicked him out midway through."

"So would I," Geoffrey grumbled, "but Lady Alleyne wouldn't have it."

Leading their mounts behind them, they walked to the manor in silence, surrounded by chattering villagers. A funeral feast would give the people a final chance to stuff themselves with a fare seldom enjoyed by common folk. Geoffrey did not begrudge them their bit of comfort, knowing hard times lay ahead.

Again, the hall was in full splendour. Geoffrey gazed around, astonished. Much had been achieved here whilst they attended the service. The tables were set for a large gathering, with the high table elevated on the dais, facing three rows of trestles for the guests around the fire pit. People – many more than on previous nights – took their places, excited in their expectation of a great feast. Their duty to their lord done, ale already flowed freely. Cups were raised, drained and refilled. The room was buzzing. He wanted to blend in with the crowd, but Alleyne beckoned him to her table with a wave reminiscent of the Empress Matilda.

She eased herself into her chair at the centre of the table. Father Anselm already slouched on the bench on her left, drinking greedily. How the Devil had the fat priest overtaken him? The call of the wine must have made him grow wings.

The flagon from which a squire had filled their goblets with a deep red liquid was already half-empty. Surely, Alleyne must be disgusted by the priest's behaviour. It had not taken the priest long to take his fill, all propriety forgotten. Geoffrey stopped short of recoiling and reluctantly returned the priest's nod. When Alleyne picked up her goblet to do the same, he briefly covered her free hand in reassurance.

"Today you've done your lord father proud, my lady. Not many a knight receives such a splendid burial."

"Thank you, Sir Geoffrey." Her voice shook and she hesitated. "You may not believe me…but I'm grateful for your support. I find it comforting to know that your presence might deter any further cowardly attacks."

Geoffrey smiled, inclining his head. "I wouldn't go quite that far, but at least they know we're here for the time being." He patted her hand, then removed it to grab his goblet. What was wrong with him? He must focus on the task in hand.

"We're going out again at first light on the morrow. I'm sure we'll find a trace of them at some point."

The arrival of the food saved Geoffrey from further ramblings. The servants carried trays bearing roast goose, pork and pheasant and the inviting scent of rosemary and sage filled the hall. Other trays were laden with bowls of steaming carrots and turnips. Baskets of freshly baked bread were placed on the tables at regular intervals, interspersed with the meat and vegetables. As quickly as they arrived, the servants slipped away again.

Alleyne stood, clapped her hands until a hush descended on the hall. She smiled. "Lord Raymond would have wanted you to enjoy yourselves today. This is our humble way of thanking you for your obedience and hard work, for your support to my lord father. Lent is soon upon us, so please enjoy this humble offering." She raised her goblet. Shouts of acclaim filled the hall, wishes of good health and prosperity.

As she sat, Geoffrey moved the trencher they shared closer to her. He smiled as she picked a chunk of goose and put it onto her side. She returned his smile as he helped himself to a slice of pheasant and broke off some bread.

By the Rood, that smile can melt stone.

Leaning back, his goblet raised to his lips, he watched her from the corner of his eye. She nibbled at the greasy meat, her eyes gazing across the room. The bird's fatty juices dribbled down her hands and she dabbed them away with a linen square. An absent look on her face, she seemed far away.

When the priest turned towards her and grabbed her arm with a fleshy hand, she flinched.

"A fine table you got here, m'lady," he mumbled through a large mouthful of meat, the fibres stuck between crooked teeth. "A pity we don't have more such occasions."

She dropped the linen and stared at him. Ignoring her, he drained his goblet in a large gulp.

Geoffrey swore under his breath. The man repulsed him. When the priest reached for the wine jug, Geoffrey quickly took it and set it down on his other side, well out of reach. "I believe you've had enough, Father. I'm sure you don't mean to insult your lady at Lord Raymond's funeral feast." He glowered at the drunkard.

"But I—"

The words had barely left Father Anselm's mouth when Geoffrey leapt from his seat and pulled the churchman from his bench. Holding him by the scruff, he dragged him past the tables and pushed him outside. At the door, he signalled two guards. "Take this man home, and make sure he stays there until he's slept off his stupor."

He went to the horse trough, and rubbed his hands in the cold spring water. The priest's tunic had been soaked with grease and wine. Looking up, he saw Alfred the stable boy stare at him, mouth open. Geoffrey waved. The lad might be useful. But before he could call out, the boy disappeared into the stables.

As he entered the hall, Lady Alleyne was walking up the stairs, leaning on the arm of her maid, her steps heavy and slow. Damn! The drunkard had pushed her over the edge. He moved between chatting groups of guests towards the steps and hurried to reach her. A sense of duty pushed him on. Just as she opened the door to her chamber, he caught up with her.

"My lady, don't take the priest's words to heart. He's drunk and out of order."

She turned to him, her eyes wide. "Father Anselm is always drunk and out of order." Her tone was dismissive, cool.

Chapter Five

Alleyne's whole body shook. How dare the drunk! First he ruined the funeral mass, and then he had the temerity to insult her. Truly, he was no man of God. She kicked the bedpost.

"Ouch!" Crying out, she hobbled to the window, careful not to put pressure on her sore toe. But the pain in her foot did nothing to smother the pain inside her heart. On the contrary, it fanned the flames of her fury.

Elvire rushed to her side. "My lady, I'll fetch you some scented water from the kitchen to calm your spirit and then we'll put you to bed. It's been a long, tiring day."

"I don't want any of that, Elvire. Just a cup of wine." She took the cup from the maid and dismissed her. Plumping up a cushion with her free hand, Alleyne sat on the stone bench in the niche by the narrow, uncovered window, the breeze cooling her flushed face. She pushed another cushion behind her back and stretched her leg, putting the foot with the throbbing toe onto the opposite seat. She leaned back and stared out into the darkness. The cold air would help clear her mind.

The priest's words had upset her but it was not just that incident that rattled her composure. She had known the man long enough, aware of what he was like. Father should have insisted on a replacement years ago.

The night before the funeral she had kept vigil by her father's coffin in the chapel. Reflecting on her life in the long silence and flickering candlelight helped her come to terms with her grief. It was a time for memories, for loneliness and despair. And then had come the time to say goodbye.

De Mortagne's presence throughout that night had kept her calm. Sharing the silence, he had only once attended to her, wrapping his cloak around her when she shivered from the convulsions of tears, misery and tiredness. Enveloped by his scent of sandalwood, her shaking subsided. A sense of homecoming had washed over her. When she had finally risen, accepting de Mortagne's helping hand, her mind focused not on the past, but on the future. The intensity in his eyes startled her, the blue depths pulling at her heart.

Her skin tingled at the memory of the under-sheriff's touch. It thrilled and unnerved her at the same time.

Alleyne vigorously shook her head. What was going on? De Mortagne affected her in a way unbeknown to her. But it was wrong. She was in mourning, vulnerable, clinging to a stranger for support. He was the wrong man anyway. She should be thinking of Will, just as she had always done since she reached womanhood.

The sooner Will arrived – and de Mortagne left – the better.

Like her mind, her body could not relax. The breeze tugged at her hair. Defying the cold, she gazed down into the bailey. Several men stood near the torches outside the hall below.

De Mortagne stood talking to the guards, hands pointing to different directions. Eventually, the men walked towards the gate but he strode in the opposite direction, to the stables. He stopped in the doorway. An instant later Alfred appeared from within, arms crossed in front of his chest. During their brief conversation, the boy's body relaxed, then he nodded in approval.

What was that man doing now? She hoped he did not plan to use Alfred for his investigations. The boy was too young to be involved in any reckless actions.

"I will speak with him," she said aloud and drained her cup. Grabbing her cloak from the hook behind the door, Alleyne left her chamber.

She rushed down the stairs, wrapping her cloak closer around her, and threaded her way through the crowd in the hall. With ale flowing freely, the noise had risen. All earlier restraints were forgotten. As she pulled the door to the bailey open, she bumped into the under-sheriff. For a moment they stood close, her hands on his chest, his on her arms. She stumbled as his eyes bore into hers.

"Apologies, my lady." De Mortagne stepped back. He released her as she regained her balance.

"No, it was my fault. But thank you." She lifted her head to meet his gaze. What fortunate timing. "I should like to go for a walk, Sir Geoffrey. Would you care to accompany me?"

"Certainly, Lady Alleyne." He held his arm out and she put her hand on his. Dusk had fallen, but it was still light enough for them to stroll across the deserted bailey without a lantern.

She pointed to the allure. "Let's head for the walkway. I'd like to discuss some matters in private."

"No problem at all. I see you've calmed." Geoffrey fell into step alongside her.

"I've had time to think and clear my head. So, yes. I'm calm now."

When they reached the steps, she removed her hand and lifted the front of her skirt just enough to ensure she wouldn't trip over. She sought the rough stone wall with her other hand to steady herself. De Mortagne followed her careful ascent. Once they reached the top, she ordered the sentry there to join his companions above the gate and turned the other way. She leaned against the parapet near the spot where the parapet met the back of the manor house, allowing the breeze to ruffle her hair. De Mortagne joined her as she gazed over the rolling hills melting into the encroaching darkness.

"Tell me, how far would someone go to gain this?" she asked with a wide sweep of her hand. "Kill? Possibly kill again?"

"Anything for property and power for some men." He shook his head. "Those who don't live by the rules."

"I suppose many don't. By the way, I saw you earlier in

the yard, talking to Alfred." Feeling him straighten, she faced him. "What exactly are your plans to catch my father's killers, my lord?"

"Do not fret for the boy, Lady Alleyne. He'll come to no harm." He lowered his head and smiled at her. "I asked him to listen out for any rumours. Nothing sinister at all."

"I would like to believe you." Her voice shook.

He turned towards her, his expression solemn. "I'll stay until I'm certain de Guines has no other tricks up his sleeve." His voice was soft but strong at the same time, determined. Reassuring.

"Thank you. You don't know how grateful I am." She sighed, a shiver of relief rushing through her. "But you must have other duties to attend to? Especially since Matilda isn't crowned queen yet. Things could still go wrong." She dropped her head so he could not see her confusion. How could she tell him about Will without insulting him?

De Mortagne placed his forefinger under her chin and tilted her face up before he dropped his hand to his side again. When their eyes met, she saw encouragement. And something else she could not identify. Something deeper. Blushing, she smiled and opened her mouth to thank him again. His kiss came as a surprise, warm and soft. It lasted barely an instant, and at first she thought she imagined it. Then a wave of guilt engulfed her.

Alleyne took a step back and aimed at his cheek but he was quicker, catching her wrist just inches from her hand's aim. Damn the reflexes of a trained knight! She steadied herself against the manor wall with her other hand.

"Forgive me, Lady Alleyne. That was most inappropriate." He turned away.

"I could have you thrown out right now."

"That wouldn't help you much in catching your killer." He stated the obvious, her empty threat exposed for what it was. His voice gave her a chill. Gone was the warm, soothing tone. She had almost believed him. But he was an under-sheriff, a lowly knight with unknown loyalties. One not to be trusted. She straightened her back.

Will must arrive soon. She trusted him.

"It won't happen again," de Mortagne said. "At first light we'll be out of your way and focus our search on the forest again." He walked towards the steps, but turned his head. "I shall report to you on our return, or to your steward should you so prefer." Without a further glance her way, he took the stairs in swift steps.

She watched as he strode to the stables, his broad back straight and fists clenched. He kicked open the stable door. The door banged against something solid, the sound echoing through the silent bailey.

Alleyne closed her eyes. Her heartbeat pounded in her ears. If she aimed her anger at him, perhaps she could banish the memory of the eager anticipation she felt when he had turned to her. She shook her head to rid herself of the demons. No, she had not wanted for him to kiss her. All she needed was reassurance. Damn the man! Perhaps women threw themselves at him in Gloucester, but not here.

Not her.

She descended the stairs, careful not to slip. By now, the bailey lay shrouded in darkness. Inside the hall, the throngs of guests had dived deeper into their cups, their shouting and laughter loud in her ears. Alleyne brushed past them, up the stairs to her chamber, and bolted the door.

She had begun to trust him. How could she now? After this?

Will, on the other hand, would never have let her down in such a manner. After all the years she had adored him, he was still her chivalrous knight. The type minstrels sing about. Tears brimmed in her eyes.

"Oh, Will," she whispered, her hands covering her mouth as she came to a halt by the narrow window. "Come quick!"

***

A horse whinnied as the walls of the stables shook from the impact of the door. Darkness had settled fully. It was dangerous to go out alone, but Geoffrey needed to escape the confines of the manor. It crushed him like a large rock, squeezing the air from his lungs. There was no escape from her within its walls.

"Who's there?" A voice came from a pen at the far end.

"Only de Mortagne. I'm taking Feu out." He took a lit torch from the sconce by the door. Empty sconces were affixed to the wall along the corridor. Reaching Feu's pen, he dropped the torch into a sconce opposite. Only one other torch was lit further back, where the boy was.

"Do you need a hand, my lord?" Alfred called out.

"No, thank you, lad."

"As you wish." The sound of a brush on fur told Geoffrey the lad had returned to his work.

Geoffrey let his stallion sniff his empty hand. He rubbed the long nose, whispering words of endearment, before he grabbed the bridle off its hook on the wooden post. Preparing Feu, he banished Alleyne from his thoughts. Not an easy feat. He gritted his teeth. Throwing the saddle onto the stallion's back, he sighed. He must forget about nearly drowning in the emerald pools of her eyes, the sweet taste of her mouth; a mouth that seemed to respond in kind just before she realised what she was doing.

Before he realised what he was doing.

"A bad move," he muttered as he pulled the saddle straps tight. The lass had no idea about her effect on men. That could leave her vulnerable to heiress hunters.

Leaving the torch where it was, he guided Feu into the bailey and jumped into the saddle, heading for the gate. By now, torches lit the bailey, casting an eerie light across the yard. The stink of burning tallow hung heavy in the air.

"Who goes..? Oh, my lord de Mortagne. You're heading out all by yourself?" Hubert reluctantly pulled away from his stool inside the doorway of the gatehouse and shuffled towards the bolted gate.

Geoffrey nodded. "Yes, I am."

"It's not safe."

"I'll be fine. Open the gate!"

"As you wish." The gatekeeper lowered his head and muttered something under his breath about outlaws and murderers.

Geoffrey ignored the rant. As soon as the gate was open, he spurred Feu into a run, keen to gain distance from the manor. He wanted nothing more but to outrun his memories with the help of the stallion's powerful strides. But the barely visible path ahead forced him to slow down. The moon was half-hidden behind clouds, and the cold air of the open countryside hit him like the slap he had nearly received from Alleyne's hand.

As he followed the path, he marvelled at her – and himself. No woman had succeeded where she had. And there had been plenty in his life, but he had no time for the courting game. It was too dangerous. His work came first. But this girl had somehow inveigled herself into his heart. He shook his head, knew he had to leave her behind and throw himself into his work. In due course, he would forget her. She did not want him anyway, that much was certain.

He rode on under a dark cloud, accompanied only by the sounds of the night. The cold seeped through the layers of his clothes. The chill did nothing to lift his temper. Instead, it fuelled his anger.

A wall of trees loomed tall in front of him. The edge of the woods. He brought Feu to a halt as his eyes followed the path delving into the thick of the forest. The faint light of the moon barely reached beyond the first few feet. It was not safe to venture any further. Even though any potential robbers would have been scared away by the presence of armed men scouring the countryside in the preceding days, he was wary of forests. And the temperature plummeted further. Best return to the manor.

As he turned Feu around, a flock of birds rose up to the sky from farther inside the forest, their wings fluttering in frantic haste. Their screeching cut through the stillness. Something must have stirred the flock into flight. Geoffrey stopped still and listened, damning his curiosity.

A faint sound from the depth of the woods confirmed his

suspicions. Slowly, Geoffrey nudged Feu back towards the trees.

"Surely that was a shout," he murmured, reasoning with himself against better judgment. He strained to see, as he guided Feu deeper into the forest at a slow walk. The muddy ground, strewn with dead leaves, muffled the sound of the stallion's hooves. Darkness swallowed him up almost completely. After several hundred yards at snail's pace, the echoes of voices reached him. He was closing in on a camp. Trees surrounded him in the re-emerging moonlight, their gnarled branches raised skyward, playing tricks on his mind. Not too far ahead, he made out the flicker of a camp fire. He stopped Feu. The chatter of voices grew louder. Whoever they were, they did not appear worried about being overheard here, sheltered by trees and nightfall.

"Nearly there," he whispered, and nudged Feu forward again. The horse took a step and the loud crack of a dry branch disturbed the night. The voices hushed. Geoffrey pulled the reins and sat still, considering his next move.

He cocked his head and listened, scarcely daring to breathe. Feu stood still. After what seemed like an eternity, the voices rose again.

Geoffrey slid from the saddle. Winding the reins loosely around a low branch, he moved forward. The moon slid behind the clouds again and he sent up a quick prayer of thanks. As he drew nearer to the fire he crouched, mud muffling his steps. The voices became clearer. They spoke with heavy accents.

Flemish accents?

Another voice stood out – speaking with the clear intonation of a Norman lord. It sounded vaguely familiar but he could not put a name to the speaker. Cursing his luck, he crept forward. He must get closer.

Sweat trickled down his temples. His veins pumped with the thrill. Although he was used to risking his life on and off the battlefield, the rush always felt the same – exhilarating and dangerous. The pounding of his heart echoed in his ears. This was what his life was all about.

He took cover behind a large oak tree. By now, he was too close to the camp for any mistakes. Chancing a glance around the thick trunk, he saw the fire and four figures huddled around it. He made out the faces of three men, their rough, dirty mail proving him right. Mercenaries. They appeared deep into their drink, swaying and grunting. One fellow threw an ale skin to another and began imitating a stabbing motion, grinning wildly. His comrades guffawed and fell over with laughter.

Geoffrey went cold. Were they talking about Lord Raymond's murder? He held his breath. The shouting grew louder. His skin crawled but it gave him confirmation of their origin. They were indeed Flemish mercenaries.

He turned his attention to the man sitting with his back to him, head hidden in the depth of a hood. He spoke in Norman French and held himself differently, more upright, sober. While he did not join in the hilarity, neither did he stop it.

Geoffrey was sure this Norman lord was the leader. He must catch a glimpse of the man's face. The distinct voice still echoed through his head, vaguely familiar yet unknown. He had to take a wide circle around the camp to identify him. He crept back into the undergrowth and wound his way around another large oak trunk.

Geoffrey sensed the movement rather than saw it. His hand grabbed for his sword belt. Only it was missing. Damn! He had removed it for the funeral. His mind whirling, he dodged the blade of the axe aimed at his skull. The edge grazed his left arm. Pain seared through him.

Why had he not thought of a sentry? He rolled away from his assailant who lifted the axe again. The cruel mouth was contorted into the toothless grin of a living gargoyle.

"Ware!" The man shouted a warning in Flemish. That much Geoffrey understood of the tongue. The sound of scraping metal reached him. Three shapes appeared in the faint light of the fire. He pulled a knife from his boot as he jumped onto his feet and held it hidden beneath his right wrist. His opponent came towards him with the axe held high. Geoffrey sprang forward and pushed the dagger into the man's unprotected neck. When he pulled the blade out with a final twist, blood spurted from the gap. The man's arms went limp. The falling axe dug into the mercenary's shoulder. He collapsed. Death came too quickly to scream.

Accepting his poor chances against three fully armed men, Geoffrey plunged into the darkness of the undergrowth. Shouts and curses behind him proved they had found the body. He dodged branches and shrubs and hurried back towards the path, taking care not to stumble over gnarled roots cropping up on the uneven floor. The distance seemed endless although it could barely have been a hundred yards. He gained ground quickly, but dared not look around. The voices grew distant but he still rushed across the uneven earth, running into branches, cutting his face and bruising his arms – praying he had not lost his way.

Eventually, the sounds of pursuit subsided. His heart pounded in his ears and he slowed, catching his breath. He had outrun them. Blood seeped from the scrape on his arm. He clenched his teeth, scolding himself for his foolishness as he stumbled onto the path. Whispering Feu's name, he was grateful to hear his stallion snort nearby. The re-appearing moonlight bathed the forest in a mystical light.

As he had almost reached his horse, he saw a movement from the shrubs.

He turned but the blow to his head was too swift. Barely conscious, he collapsed to the ground. An instant later, someone turned him on his back, then his attacker pulled Geoffrey's head up by the hair. Pain shot through his scalp. He could not open his eyes, the lids too heavy, dancing lights making his head spin.

"Damn," the Norman voice swore. "Geoffrey de Mortagne."

Chapter Six

Geoffrey lay sprawled in the mud. A light flashed behind his closed eyes when he lifted his head, and his pulse throbbed. He groaned and propped himself on his elbows. He dropped his head in his hands and waited for the nausea to ease.

A breeze swept through leaves and birds were singing. He blinked. A forest. Hazy light filtered through gaps in the foliage.

"Argh." The ambush.

The sound of approaching hoofbeats reached him. He pulled himself up and reached for his knife, relieved to find it still in his boot. Looking around, Geoffrey took in the dense undergrowth. He was lucky the mercenaries had not dunked his face into the mud, else his would have been another corpse to be buried. But just why did they let him live?

Alleyne! He groaned. The kiss. Her reaction. His flight. He shook his head, instantly regretting the motion when pain seared through him. The hoofbeats grew closer. Where was Feu? He glanced around as he rose, brushing the dirt off his clothes. No sign of the stallion. Had the men taken him? No point in wondering; he must return to Bellac and send out a search party. The thought of walking for miles did not appeal but he had no choice.

Voices rose in the distance. Riders near the edge of the forest. But who were they? Not intending to give the mercenaries another chance – in his condition a lost cause already – he dived into the undergrowth, then darted between broad trees, keeping the path in his sight. He clasped his knife. When horses and riders came near, he crouched behind an oak trunk.

"Where can he be?"

"We scoured the whole bleedin' woods. Time to head back."

"No! We keep on searching, spread out. Feu returned to lead us to him." The voice made Geoffrey smile.

He skirted the trunk. "Guy!"

"Geoffrey?" He heard the relief in his sergeant's voice and grinned at the familiarity they normally never maintained in public. It did not matter at this moment. He pushed away the branches blocking his way and emerged from the undergrowth just in front of the group. Feu snorted and stepped forward. Only Guy's hand on his reins kept the horse from running Geoffrey over.

Geoffrey went to the stallion, took the reins and patted his neck. "Good boy!"

Grateful to see his sergeant, he grinned at Guy who stared at him. The others in the group, men-at-arms from the manor, gave him the same look.

"What's wrong?" he asked, eyebrows drawn together. "Have I grown two heads?"

Guy dismounted and threw the reins to the nearest soldier. "Are you all right, Sir Geoffrey?" Reverting back to formality, the sergeant leaned his head to the side, like a crow, blinking at him. "You're covered in blood."

Geoffrey touched his head and flinched. Crusted blood clung to his fingers.

"It's on your face, too. What happened?"

Geoffrey leaned against Feu, wiping his hand on his hose. Blood. It must have come from the blow to his head. Had the mercenaries intended to leave him for dead after all?

With a glance at the waiting soldiers, he said, "I'll tell you on the way back." He pulled himself into the saddle, ignoring stiff muscles. "I'm all right." Feu remained calm despite his uneven touch. The stallion's return to the manor had saved him from a tiring walk.

Guy grabbed his own horse and mounted in one swift move. "Hubert, go find your captain! He's scouring the fields to the south. We'll reconvene at the manor."

"Aye." Hubert nodded and spurred his mount forward while the remaining men-at-arms headed away at a trot.

Geoffrey deliberately fell behind. Guy joined him. Keeping his voice low, Geoffrey told his sergeant the events of the previous night. Guy swore, eyes wide. It was only when he saw his friend's concern that Geoffrey realised how close he had come to harm.

"They left you for dead, Geoffrey."

"I know."

He could have suffocated; bled to death. Wolves and wild boar roamed the forests. The mercenaries could have killed him without anyone ever knowing. "It was thoughtless of me to head out without my sword."

"'Twas unwise to head out alone at all."

Geoffrey winced at Guy's bluntness but the sergeant was right. They lapsed into silence.

Ancel had already returned and paced back and forth outside the gate until they came close. His furrowed brow cleared and he came forward to greet them.

"I'm sorely glad to see you, Sir Geoffrey." His smile turned into a frown. "You're hurt. Allow me to dress your wound. Then you can tell me what happened."

Geoffrey nodded, allowing the captain to take Feu's reins and walk him to the gatehouse.

"Eadgar, bring water!" A guard scurried towards the well.

Geoffrey followed Ancel into the small guardroom. The captain went to a shelf near the back and returned with jars and cloths which he set out on a small table. An instant later, Eadgar set down a bowl of water next to the jars.

Guy entered as the guard left and leaned against the doorframe, his face drawn.

Geoffrey sank onto a stool, grateful to sit. He flinched when Ancel touched his head and pulled strands of hair from the gash. Closing his eyes, Geoffrey propped his elbows propped on his knees, he locked his hands in anticipation of the sting. When it came, he winced. He felt like jerking his head away, in the same way he wanted to chase away memories of the last night, but held fast. Pain was not something Geoffrey allowed to get in his way, physical or emotional. He took a deep breath.

Ancel cleaned the wound with light hands. Bits of mud fell to the floor or dissolved in the bowl, changing the water from clear to murky.

While he sat still, Geoffrey relayed the events. Ancel and Guy listened without interrupting his flow.

"Have you any idea who their leader might be?" Guy asked, shifting his weight from one leg to another.

"I wish I had." Geoffrey met his gaze. "I'm certain I've heard the voice before but my memory deserts me. 'Twas too long ago."

"It's disconcerting to know such men are close to the manor." Ancel covered the wound in a layer of herbal ointment which burned Geoffrey's sore skin.

Geoffrey agreed. "Yes, the timing is suspicious. They were definitely celebrating some event."

"Done." Ancel stowed away the jars, leaving the cloths beside the bowl.

Geoffrey sniffed. Anything that smelled as foul as the gooey salve that stuck to his head couldn't possibly be good. His hand moved to the gash but Ancel stopped him in a swift move.

"No touching! Let it heal." His face matched the patronising tone of his voice.

Geoffrey laughed and rose. Much to his relief, he found his feet solid on the ground, all queasiness gone. Now some wine and food would not come amiss.

"Thank you. I appreciate your skills." He grinned. "How long until I can wash that muck out of my hair?"

Ancel smiled back. "You should leave it for a day or two."

"There goes my attraction. No woman will even look at me."

"Women should be the last thing on your mind," Ancel retorted. "I'll take a unit out now to search the forest. We'll speak later. Now you need rest."

Geoffrey thanked him and went outside. Guy fell into step.

"I wonder if we can get some food in the kitchen." Geoffrey's stomach growled. "I'm starving, but I want to avoid the hall for a while." He was reluctant to cross Alleyne's path.

As they walked past the hall, he noticed from the corner of his eye that the door opened. Keen to get away from the entrance, he increased his step.

"Trust me," Guy said with a grin. "Annie put some bread and meat aside for us. I arranged it before we rode out."

"Annie?" Geoffrey smirked. "Oh dear! What have you promised the poor girl?"

"I didn't–"

"Geoffrey de Mortagne, what a surprise!"

Geoffrey stopped, recognising the voice. The hairs at the base of his neck rose. He turned slowly and stared at the tall, fair-haired man who leaned against the open door of the hall.

"Will d'Arques."

Gritting his teeth, Geoffrey strolled towards his old adversary, cursing the curious timing. A long time ago, they had been friends, in the early days when they trained together as squires for the Count of Perche. But Will's ruthless ambition had torn them apart. Backstabbing. False accusations. Betrayal. Always out for his own advantage. They parted company after a sword fight Geoffrey lost. All for the virtue of a lady who had not been worthy of his efforts. Solange. Geoffrey still smarted at the memory.

He reached the foot of the steps, crossed his arms and glowered. Will coolly returned his gaze. Their appearances could not have been more different. His own worn hose, tunic and boots smudged with dirt; the other knight's pristine appearance, brightly-coloured hose complemented his short linen tunic, elaborately stitched around the hems with blue thread. The costume of a courtier. He must do well for himself.

"What are you doing here, Will?"

At that moment, Alleyne came through the door and linked her arm through Will's. "Oh, there you are."

She gazed at Will, her eyes beaming with a pleasure Geoffrey had not seen in her before. Will indulged her with a wink and a smile before he faced Geoffrey again.

A smirk touched Will's mouth briefly, but Geoffrey was certain she did not see it.

Alleyne turned to Geoffrey, her eyes widening as she spotted his hair covered in grease. "What happened to you, Sir Geoffrey?"

Her expression showed concern until her gaze met his. Let her notice the fury in him. Why should he conceal his disappointment?

Alleyne raised her head and squared her shoulders, moving even closer to Will's side. "You know each other?" She glanced from Geoffrey to the man beside her, who nodded in acknowledgement.

"Yes, we do, Alleyne." Will's voice was smooth.

The adoring look in her eyes twisted Geoffrey's guts. He clenched his hands into fists, keeping them tight to his chest. Will always got what he wanted. Money. Power. Women. Nothing had changed. She looked back at him, eyes cool now.

"I asked Sir William for help. He's an old friend of my father's. I'm sure you don't object, my lord."

"Ah," was all Geoffrey managed. His head pounded, his heart felt mangled as if crushed by heavy weights. He took a deep breath to get his emotions in check. "I'm glad to hear it, my lady. Now if you'll excuse me, I intend to have some food and drink before I make myself presentable again after my overnight sojourn in the forest." Was there a flicker in Will's eyes? "I assume the two of you have plenty to talk about."

Geoffrey bowed sharply, turned and strode towards the kitchen, hunger and thirst forgotten. His anger ran deep but he would not give her or Will the satisfaction of allowing it to show.

Guy waited a few yards away, his eyes questioning. "D'Arques wasn't here last night. I would have heard about it. He must have arrived first thing this morning when we were out searching for you."

Geoffrey saw the suspicion in his sergeant's eyes. "Very convenient, I know. I'm not certain if he was the Norman in the forest but his accent... the timbre of his voice... the timing. It all fits. But she trusts him," he added, bitterness choking him.

Geoffrey shook his head. He must get a grip. He would eat. And drink. Regain his strength. And then decide what to do next.

Later that day, his mind made up, he went to the hall. He had washed, rinsed the sticky ointment from his hair and changed his clothes. Clearly, he was no longer wanted here. Alleyne had made that fairly obvious that morning; and the previous night when she recoiled from his kiss. He must have imagined her flirtation, mistaken her sympathy for signs of affection, of trust. He had been the first man to offer her a shoulder to cry on. She had used him while she called Will for help behind his back. Geoffrey snorted. They deserved each other.

He found Alleyne and Will seated near the fire pit. Will had made himself comfortable in Lord Raymond's chair, while she sat in her seat, pulled alongside his so closely that their knees were almost touching, her hands firmly in his grasp.

All quite innocent and caring. As if!

Geoffrey stifled a grunt and crossed the hall. He sat on the vacant chair opposite her and silently regarded her through the hissing flames between them. Her eyes shone in the flickering light. Emerald pools he had dreamed of drowning in. Then he had drowned; a painful death.

Will had aged well; only a few lines around the grey eyes, his features handsome with his short, straight nose and wide mouth; his blond hair still as thick as in his youth, tumbling down over his shoulders. Yet his appearance belied the fact that underneath all that shine was the body and soul of a mercenary, hungry and ruthless. The coolness of his eyes proved his arrogance had also not diminished.

"So, the Lady Alleyne has enlightened you on the latest happenings here?" Geoffrey leaned back, slung one leg over the other and rested his elbows on the arms of the chair. He smiled, knowing well no warmth reached his eyes.

"Yes, she has." Will gave her hand a quick squeeze. "The poor girl. Of course, I'll be staying here to protect her."

Alleyne gazed at him, eyes wide with adoration and relief. Youthful stupidity, Geoffrey mused. "I'm sorely relieved to hear. Will you be searching for the killers?"

"Well, old friend, I don't want to take away your job," Will hesitated. "but then it appears you haven't been very successful so far." He tilted his head to the side. "Apart from last night, so I've heard."

Alleyne leaned forward, her eyes clouded with worry. "That was dreadful. Ancel told me all. How are you feeling?"

"Fine. Thank you for your concern."

"Oh, I'm so relieved. I was worried sick last night." She nodded vigorously.

Will raised his eyebrows.

Geoffrey should warn her about Will. But in all likelihood she would refuse to listen. Women never listened where Will was concerned. They learnt the hard way.

"I'm certain the thought didn't rob you of your sleep, my lady." He kept the tone of his voice formal, with a sting attached he knew hit home when her face fell.

He turned to the man who had made himself at home much too swiftly. "Though the Norman bastard who knocked me out did not do the best job."

"Indeed," Will said, his face unreadable, a mask that hid all sorts of secrets. Was Lord Raymond's murder one of them?

"He could have killed me, but he didn't." Geoffrey held Will's gaze. "I wonder why."

"Oh. You don't think Will..?"

The wounded tone of Alleyne's voice, and the way she

clenched Will's hand, did not alleviate his suspicions. Had she done that to spite him? At this moment, he did not care. The only thing he wanted was to escape; the sooner the better.

"No, my lady. That would be too coincidental, wouldn't it?"

Will's mouth twitched but he remained silent.

"And if Will is prepared to stay and protect you and Bellac, then my duty here has come to an end."

Her eyes widened. In the flash of an instant, he saw pain and sadness, confusion and relief in them. Poor lass. She needed a safe home with a reliable protector, not a notorious womaniser, to look after her. But if that was what she wanted, who was he to try and convince her otherwise?

"I will continue to have my men search for the killers and will send word should there be any developments. In the meantime, I'll pack my belongings and will be gone by sunrise on the morrow." He rose. "I'll leave you to catch up on the remainder of the gossip." He bowed to Alleyne, then aimed a cool look at Will.

"Won't you join us tonight, Sir Geoffrey?" Was she pleading with him or did he imagine disappointment in her voice?

He studied her. She stood, her fingers entwined until her knuckles showed, luminous eyes imploring him.

It was too late. "I'm afraid not. I want to retire at a reasonable hour. As I said, I'll have an early start." Her face fell. "But I won't forget my promise to your lord father. His killers will be brought to justice. Farewell, my lady."

Chapter Seven

Alleyne rubbed her temples. Her pulse throbbed. The headache had hit her as she sat in the hall chatting to Will, wondering about the change in Geoffrey's demeanour. Soon after the under-sheriff left, she retired to her room. Will knew the manor well. He would settle quickly.

Lying on her bed, she pulled the fur covers to her chin and closed her eyes. She wanted to calm her mind in the silence of her bedchamber. To rid herself of the headache, and of the turmoil that engulfed her. Memories flashed through her head, of Father, of Geoffrey, of Will. Her heart ached to mourn without distraction. But her brain would not let her.

An heiress without a protector was an opportunity for any man to grab hold of a profitable estate – and a young, malleable wife to boot. With King Stephen captured and the Empress Matilda not yet crowned, Alleyne was alone. With the country held in the grip of a civil war, nobody would wonder about her fate.

Had she really expected Geoffrey to stay after Will's arrival? Geoffrey's attentions had comforted, even flattered her. His audacity the previous night had both thrilled and shocked her. Her cheeks burned as she remembered his kiss, strong, demanding. Her heart fluttered. Had she encouraged him, only to push him away? She shook her head, wincing at the sudden stab in her heart.

Alleyne covered her eyes with her hands to banish the picture. For an instant, she had responded to his kiss, felt a bond between them, a fire inside. Felt his heat, his passion. It excited her.

It scared her.

With a sigh, Alleyne turned to her side and curled her knees up to her chest, wrapping her arms around them. She stared at the tapestry hanging on the wall, the vivid colours blurred. There was no denying she enjoyed the way he kissed her. She shivered. It had been her first real kiss, not just a chaste peck on the cheek. Naturally, that first experience was bound to leave its mark. But it was just a kiss.

Then Will had arrived. She sighed again, absently stroking the fur coverlets, letting her hand glide through the soft hairs. Will had always remained close to her heart. Ever since she first set eyes on him, he was the one she wanted to share her life with. She often imagined him kissing her, leading her to his bedchamber as his wife. But Father never encouraged such a union, even though Will was a friend of his for many years. Of course it was only because Father had simply not wanted to let her – his little girl – go. Much unlike other fathers who sought a speedy, profitable marriage. Dear Father!

She blinked away the tears.

She could never trust Geoffrey the way she trusted Will. Geoffrey was dangerous where Will was safe. After all, Will had fought alongside Father. Drank with him, became part of the family. She knew him well.

Yes, she was doing the right thing. She would let Will woo her, and her future happiness would be secured. After a suitable time of mourning, of course. Surely, her need for a protector was reason enough not to wait for a year?

A knock on the door stirred Alleyne from her musings. Elvire entered without waiting for a reply.

"Are you not well, my lady?" The maid came over and placed a soothing hand on her forehead.

"I'm well. I just needed to rest a while." She rose from the bed, ignoring the sting in her temples.

"You rested for half the day. Maybe you should stay abed for the remainder?" Elvire fussed.

Alleyne shook her head. "We have a visitor and I should be there to entertain him. Is dinner being prepared?"

"Yes, my lady. The tables are set."

"Then fetch the green velvet gown." She watched the maid pick the dress from the clothes-pole behind the door and began to undress. "And bring me some cold water."

A little later, refreshed and changed, Alleyne descended the stairs. Will slouched in Father's chair. Her heart skipped a beat as a sense of unease prickled down her spine. The speed with which Will took over shook her a little.

I'm doing the right thing.

She smiled and joined Will. He stood as she neared the dais and pulled her chair back. Her gaze lowered, she sat down demurely and folded her hands in her lap. Will gestured to a hovering servant to fill her goblet. He behaved as if he were already lord of the manor. She swallowed. Was that not what she wanted? For him to make himself at home because it would soon be just that? She glanced at his handsome profile as he watched the manor folk – back to only a handful now after the funeral feast the night before – settling at the trestle tables. Will's brows were drawn into a frown and his mouth set in a firm line. Clearly he disapproved of something.

She followed his gaze. The people behaved as always, as they had done in Father's day. It was what she wanted. Life continued. Gone but not forgotten. She touched Will's arm and he jerked. A moment later, he sent her a dazzling smile and lifted his goblet. Their eyes locked as they drank. Yet there was something in the depths of his gaze she found unnerving, almost calculating.

'Twas probably only her tiredness. She set down her goblet.

The servants entered the hall carrying plates of sizzling pork and bowls of steaming carrots and turnips, the spiced aroma teasing Alleyne's nostrils. They distributed loaves of warm bread at each table.

Will filled her trencher with succulent meat. She inhaled the tantalising scent of rosemary. She noticed several of her people nudged each other at Will's gesture. They must become accustomed to it.

"Thank you." She waited until he had taken his fill. Only then did she take a bite.

"You are the perfect host, Alleyne." Will's eyes showed approval. "We will speak of your future later."

"My future?" Her hand stopped halfway to her mouth. She quickly swallowed the morsel and dabbed her fingers with a linen square. Warmth spread through her at his smile.

"Aye. The reason you called me here, remember?"

Her cheeks burned. Had he always known her feelings, only to wait for his chance?

She finally pushed away the trencher, having filled her belly. Will, long finished after taking his share, took her hand and kissed her knuckles, his lips hovering just a little too long for propriety. She withdrew her hand as heat shot into her face and swiftly scanned the room but folk continued to chat to each other, paying no heed. With an inward sigh of relief, she briefly closed her eyes.

"Shall we retire to the solar?" The twinkle in Will's eyes sent shivers down her spine. It was like in the olden days. This was the man she had always adored. She nodded, not trusting her voice to come out steadily. As she rose, the crowd stood and people lowered their heads. Dark glances darted Will's way. How suspicious her tenants were! Will would soon look after their welfare. Folk should be grateful. She smiled into the room, trying to reassure her people, but none would meet her eye.

Tears stung at the rejection. She blinked them back. Will led her up the stairs to the solar.

After he closed the door, Alleyne walked to the window and gazed outside where dusk was settling.

"Care for a cup of wine?" Will poured two cups from a jug on a small table and held one out to her.

She took it gratefully. As she sipped the rich red liquid, she spotted Geoffrey standing on the allure, his now uncannily familiar broad figure outlined by the orange glow of the sunset. It surrounded him like a halo. She snapped the shutter closed with her free hand, cutting out the cold breeze together with any thoughts of the under-sheriff.

Smiling at Will, she sat down on the window seat. He lowered himself next to her, his body shielding her from the draughts whistling through gaps in the shutter. She sighed.

"How are you faring, Alleyne?"

Wine ripples swirled as she spun the cup gently in her hands. "I'm well." She turned to him. "Thank you for coming here so quickly. I wasn't sure if and when my message would reach you. I didn't know if you were at your manor after what happened in Lincoln." Will was on King Stephen's side. It was fortunate he had not been caught during battle.

He nodded. "Of course I had to come. I was preparing to join Queen Maude in Kent when your message arrived. The queen is most angered. We have to regroup and find a way to gain Stephen's freedom."

"Do you think that's going to happen? I thought Matilda has won now."

"Ah, little one." He took her free hand in his, entwining their fingers. "Don't fret about politics. Leave that to those who live for it. Matilda won't get anywhere." His thumb circled the inside of her hand, pressing and caressing. Then he took her cup from her, setting it onto the floor. He tucked away a strand of hair that had escaped her braid. His thumb brushed her cheek, fleetingly touching her lips. At his open smile, her heart skipped a beat.

"But first I have to look after you." He cradled her hands in both of his and planted kisses into her palms, on her fingertips.

Alleyne gasped, her unsteady breath betraying her inner turmoil. He had never been so openly affectionate, never dared to come so close while Father lived. But this was what she had dreamed of during countless nights spent awake. Now it was real. Yet her mind could not completely banish the memory of the night before. She squeezed her eyes shut.

Will's lips closed on hers, soft but cold. Shocked, she drew her head back. Her eyes met the grey depths of his, clouded by something akin to anger.

"Forgive me. I presumed..." His body drew back but he held onto her hands. "You looked so lost when you closed your eyes." He smiled again, the anger in his gaze replaced by warmth.

"There's nothing to forgive," she whispered. "It's a little rushed but it's not unwelcome." She blushed and stared at the tips of her slippers. With his forefinger, Will tilted up her face.

"You don't know how glad I am to hear you say those words." He bent his head to plant a soft kiss on her nose. "You make me a very happy man."

His mouth came down on hers again, hard at first, then softened. His hand moved from her cheek to her nape, the other sliding up her arm. She left her hands in her lap, uncertain of what to do. His left hand roamed down her throat, trailing along the neckline of her gown.

She gasped for air. Her body responded but something was amiss. The euphoria she expected did not appear. Her heart remained distant, unattached. Unable to explain it, she gave in as he lent forward, his lips soft on her throat, her chin, and she pushed her doubts aside. Soon, she would be his wife.

When he pulled up her skirt, she jerked upright. "No!"

He sat back with a sigh, his jaw clenched. "I'm sorry, Alleyne." He grabbed his cup, drained it and slammed it onto the floor.

She stared at him. They were not wed yet. It did not matter if she enjoyed his caresses or not. She would not allow Will to go any further without a blessing. Her insides in turmoil, Alleyne picked up her own cup, cradling it in both hands until her breathing steadied. Then she drank deeply.

Will rose and bowed to her. "I shall leave you now, else I might not be able to resist temptation any longer." He strode to the door. "I bid you good night." He let it fall shut behind him.

"Oh, Will," she sighed, setting the cup down with shaky hands. What had she done? She sent away the man she wanted for the sake of her virtue, something he would take from her sooner or later anyway. Scowling, she pulled the shutter open to find the world in darkness. The cool breeze fanned her flushed face. Her eyes searched the allure for a sign of Geoffrey but he was gone. Curious, she leaned over the rim, peering down into the bailey. Only her men-at-arms patrolled the grounds. All was quiet.

She secured the shutter again, took the candelabra from the table and went to her chamber. Her hands still trembling, Alleyne set the candleholder onto the small table beside her bed and undressed. Shivering, she blew out the candles, dove underneath the covers and curled into a ball. She was awake, her heart a battlefield. Staring into the darkness, she wondered why she had not felt any sensations when Will kissed her. Yes, her body responded to his touch like the strings of a harp. But her heart remained quiet. No embers growing into a fierce fire as she had expected.

Like the fire that raged when Geoffrey kissed her.

She shook her head and closed her eyes. Well, clearly it could not be the same with every man.

***

Geoffrey stood in the shadow of the stable door and watched Alleyne gaze across the bailey. Was she alone? He snorted and quietly closed the door. In near darkness, he went to Feu's pen where he had prepared a corner for himself, the fresh hay covered by his cloak. He could not bear the thought of spending a night inside the manor house, knowing Will was there. He lay down and pushed his bag beneath his head.

Alfred snored at the far end of the stables. Geoffrey smiled. Sleeping in stables came with his job at times. Here, away from people, he found peace. Solitude. Even with the boy nearby, it felt like he had the place to himself.

Geoffrey stared into the darkness. Sleep eluded him. Of course he had seen them seated together at the high table. Alleyne and Will. He had peeked through a window into the hall, had seen the little touches and looks they shared. By pure chance, he later spotted them at the solar window, an instant before she closed the shutter. God only knew what followed.

Anger surged through him. He clenched his hands into fists and swallowed hard. Aye, the lass would give freely to Will what she had denied him. He saw it in her eyes. Ultimately, she was simply another girl Will seduced – and then dropped.

Visions returned of the youth he and Will had shared in Perche. Young lads keen to sow their oats, they had both set their aims on a comely dairy maid working in the kitchens at the Count of Perche's castle. The girl had toyed with both of them but ended up lifting her skirts for Will between bags of grain in the barn. Geoffrey had entered the barn on an errand and the triumphant gaze she sent him as she straddled Will sent him to attack the quintain with much force.

His lord's steward recognised his anger and took him to Rouen where, in the luxurious surroundings of a town house with more well-equipped bedrooms than any manor, a fourteen year-old Geoffrey had tasted the peachy delights of Madame DuBois. Geoffrey grinned. Will's fury knew no bounds when he heard that he had missed out on the entertainment. For once, he had bested his former friend.

From that moment onward, their rivalry continued until, three years later, Solange – the daughter of a lowly knight – stayed at the castle while Perche and her father discussed her fate.

His grin turned into a scowl. He had loved Solange. Her radiant smile and wide blue eyes bewitched him. In a serious attempt to woo her, he made her giggle at his jokes and presented her with costly gifts. Combs adorned with semi-precious stones and silver torques delighted her. They talked as they strolled through the gardens. He amused her with poetry and stories. Yet in the end, behind his back, she had fallen for Will's charms. Geoffrey had left for England, and swore never to fall in love again.

Until Alleyne.

He let out a slow, long breath and unclenched his hands. Alleyne was just like the others before her. Just another of Will's whores.

He swallowed hard to rid himself of the bitter taste in his mouth. He turned to his side. It was to be a long night.

***

Geoffrey woke with a start and opened his eyes. It was still dark. The scent of hay and horse was overpowering. He felt Feu's warm body near him; the horse's hot breath on his skin. He touched the stallion, gently rubbing his nose. He chuckled at the sound of Feu snorting.

Still smiling, he threw off the blanket and rose. He felt his way towards the stable door, finding the bailey cast in flickering torchlight. A faint glow rose in the eastern sky.

He brushed the hay from his clothes and strolled to the watering trough. The air chilled him. A thin layer of ice covered the water. Leaving any last memories of the warm bed of hay behind, he thrust his hands through the ice and scooped up some water, splashing his face. Shivering, he quickly rubbed the moisture off with his sleeves. 'Twas a shock to his body, but it dispelled any drowsiness.

Refreshed, he crossed the yard and slid into the hall. In the dim light of the embers in the central hearth he saw outlines of sleeping men lined up near the walls. He tiptoed past them until he spotted Guy. As quietly as possible, he crouched and touched Guy's shoulders. His sergeant jerked up, knife in hand.

Geoffrey fell backwards, cursing his stupidity. Of course Guy would be alert, even in his sleep. Already the sergeant had hidden his knife in the folds of his tunic and grinned.

"It's time." Geoffrey stood. Guy pulled on his boots and wrapped his cloak around his shoulders. He picked up the saddlebag he had used as pillow and followed Geoffrey outside. Nobody else had stirred.

"Get the horses ready. I need to speak with Ancel before

we leave." Geoffrey strode to the gatehouse, knocked on the closed door and entered without waiting for an answer. The captain was seated on a stool near the lit brazier, yawning. A guard sat nearby, legs stretched towards the warmth of the coals. He scrambled from his seat.

"Good morrow, Sir Geoffrey." Ancel nodded. He turned to his man. "Go and keep an eye on the hall, Oswald? See that d'Arques's men are still asleep. If anyone wakes, keep them indoors somehow."

"Aye, of course." With a quick bow to Geoffrey, the guard left, closing the door behind him.

"You are on your way, then?"

Geoffrey grabbed the vacated stool and lowered himself onto it, rubbing his hands near the flames. The heat warmed him instantly.

"Aye. Guy's preparing the horses. Alfred will hear us but he won't cause a stir."

"No, the lad is reliable. Can't say that for d'Arques's men, though. They caused a ruckus in the village late last night, almost ended up in a fight. I had to intervene."

"Grim days lie ahead for you, Ancel." Geoffrey stared into the fire. "If his men are anything like their lord, they're scheming troublemakers. Trust me, I know the man. You can be assured d'Arques has his own agenda. He'd never get involved here if there were naught to gain. Keep a tight rein on your men." He glanced at the captain. The deep lines under Ancel's eyes showed lack of sleep. There would not be any sleep at all for him if Will remained at Bellac. "The worst thing is you aren't likely to get your lady's support. She's blinded by him."

"Lady Alleyne has always been fooled by d'Arques. Unlike Lord Raymond. He kept d'Arques close but not too close. I think he used him for information. And in turn told him what the man wanted to hear. Truth or not."

"Lord Raymond spied on Will d'Arques?" Geoffrey grinned. "With Will on Stephen's side that must mean Lord Raymond was inclined towards Matilda?"

Ancel nodded. "I thought so, too, though he never

declared his allegiance openly. And he fought for Stephen at Lincoln."

"True." Geoffrey nodded. This lead must be followed. It could be the missing link that held the clue to Lord Raymond's murder. He rose, reluctant to leave the warmth of the room. "I have to go."

"I'll send word about what happens here. Where will my messenger find you?"

"Send your messages to Gloucester Castle. The steward will make sure I get them." He extended his arm.

Ancel nodded and took it in a firm grip. "Then I pray you'll get them in time. Godspeed, Sir Geoffrey."

Geoffrey and Guy rode through the gate in silence, keeping their horses at a quiet walk as not to wake the manor. Ancel closed the gate behind them.

They remained on the road only until they approached the forest before veering off onto the open fields that bordered the woods. Geoffrey turned his head, but to his relief the manor was already too far away for anyone to possibly spot them in the dim light. The road was deserted. Morning sun rose on the horizon. Soon the manor would be bustling. And Will's men no doubt would come searching for him. To make sure he was truly gone. Or to finish off what they had started in the forest? The notion seemed more and more likely.

Geoffrey glanced at his sergeant. "We must hurry. Ready?"

Guy grinned, adjusted his cloak over his shoulder and fastened the clasp. "Aye."

"Then let's leave this mess behind." He kicked Feu in the flanks. The stallion started, and within seconds had picked up speed with ease, clearly relishing a good run. Guy was beside him, a smile on his face. The chill in the air was just a minor inconvenience. Giving in to Feu's rhythm, Geoffrey blanked out all thoughts of Alleyne. For now, he intended to enjoy the ride.

Much later, they slowed to give their mounts a rest. "Where are we heading?" Guy pulled a flask from his pack.

Geoffrey took the flask and drank deeply. The liquid soothed his parched throat. Neither man had drunk or broken his fast. And they were not likely to fill their bellies soon.

"To Bristol. We need to see how Stephen fares. Once we know the situation, I'll stay with Matilda's retinue while you seek out Reg in Kent. Maybe someone at Queen Maude's court knows what Will has been up to after Lincoln." He handed the flask back to Guy, who took a deep draught before he put the stopper back on.

"That makes sense." Guy stashed the flask away. "Are you expecting a message from Reg when we arrive in Bristol?"

"I hope so." Geoffrey scanned the landscape. They had just skirted the forest and in the distance ahead he spotted people moving. "That's the Gloucester road ahead. We'll stop off at my house there on the way." With a sidelong glance at his sergeant, he spurred Feu into another run.

Chapter Eight

Alleyne awoke, shivering, her arms exposed to the chilly morning air. Her skin covered in goosebumps, she slid them beneath the covers and rubbed them until the skin burned. Daylight filtered through the gaps in the shutters.

Geoffrey was gone, she was certain. Perhaps it was for the best. After all, he didn't seem to like her. He must surely be relieved to be on his way.

Shouts from the bailey disrupted her thoughts. A moment later, spurs clicked on the wooden floor outside her door.

Curious, she pushed the covers aside and tiptoed to the clothes hook. Quickly, she pulled a woollen dress over her shift and tied a simple belt around her waist. What had happened? Pushing her feet into her slippers, she untangled her ruffled hair and tied it in a loose braid. Then she hurried to the door and drew the bolt. The landing was empty. Her gown hitched up with her hand, she rushed down the stairs. Only the kitchen boy was in the hall, kindling a fire. She darted past him, ignoring his greeting. On the top step to the bailey she stopped, staring. Her mouth dropped open.

Dozens of men-at-arms milled about, shouting orders at Alfred, who struggled to take care of the many horses. The gate gaped open. More men rode in. Ancel stood at the gatehouse with several of his guards, watching. Eyebrows pulled together and mouth twisted in disapproval, his arms crossed in front of his chest, he glowered at the riders. She called out to him but he couldn't hear her above the clamour. Treading carefully in the mud, she walked through the chaos, ignoring wolf whistles and shouts. Ancel finally saw her and pulled her to the side, out of the way of the next wave of incoming riders.

"What's happening, Ancel?"

"Just what I expected, my lady. Sir William's reinforcements." He spat the last word. Anger blazed in his eyes, his brows furrowed, as he viewed the scene in front of him.

"What do you mean, reinforcements? For what?"

"For holding Bellac, of course."

Alleyne released her held breath. "Ah, they've come to protect us." She gazed around, appreciating the numbers in light of Ancel's revelation. Geoffrey hadn't come anywhere near this with his two sergeants and few men-at-arms who could now go home. Will made the effort.

"If you say so, my lady." Ancel's voice dripped with sarcasm.

She sent him a sharp look. "Do you think differently?" Her voice cooled.

He met her eyes. "I believe Sir William has his own plan, my lady."

"I'm certain he has. To take care of me." She touched his arm, wanting him to understand. Why was he so full of doubts? "It's lovely of you to care so much. But there's no need."

"We are perfectly capable of defending Bellac, Lady Alleyne. Do you want us to take orders from d'Arques from now on?"

"Aye, of course." Ancel jumped at Will's voice behind him. "It's in Lady Alleyne's interest that everyone follows the same orders."

"My lord." Ancel's voice grated.

She beamed at both men. Why would Ancel not see? "Will is right. Now Bellac will be safe."

Ancel glared at Will, who held his gaze with an eyebrow raised. "Safe from whom?"

Alleyne sighed. "The mercenaries, Ancel." She was pleading with him, desperate for the captain to value Will's help.

"Mercenaries? Take a good look at these men, my lady! To my eye they look just like mercenaries, with their scars, their blood-stained gambesons and assorted axes and swords." Ancel stepped back. "If you'll excuse me, I have men to advise." He marched off towards the gatehouse, his back stiff and straight. Alleyne stared after him, her shoulders slumped.

Will touched her arm. "I think you should go inside, Alleyne. It's not the safest place for a lady, to wander amongst soldiers."

Alleyne cocked her head as she watched Will. His cheek marred with red blotches, most unbecomingly, he seemed angry. Ancel must have irritated him. How strange that a mere captain of the guard rattled the composure of this proud lord. She must soothe Will's ruffled feathers before he sent Ancel packing. Bellac could not afford to lose him.

Will kept his hand at the small of her back as he nudged her towards the hall. The noise of men shouting became overpowering. Across the bailey, she spotted the blacksmith outside his hut, arms crossed, his face dark. Two kitchen maids stood close behind him, too curious to hide away from the soldiers' eyes but not bold enough to venture out by themselves.

Alfred ran between the riders, picking up reins as he went. He kept his head down, not looking the men in the eye. One called him a dolt and whacked him on the back of the head. Alfred hurriedly took the reins from the man and rushed towards the stables, tying horses up outside and leading the first one in.

"Did you see that? How dare he!" Alleyne pointed at the offender.

"Alleyne, inside!" Will's voice was like ice as he pulled her through the door into the hall. She stumbled and would have fallen, had he not tightened his grip on her arm. Several men laughed but stopped on his brisk orders.

Once the door was shut behind them, she rounded up to him. "How dare that man hit Alfred?" She stamped her foot. "I want him punished. Nobody treats my people like that."

Will pushed her into her chair and shouted to the kitchen boy to bring some wine. The lad scurried away, leaving the fire in the hearth burning brightly.

Alleyne struggled to rise, the flames heating her face, but Will held her down by the shoulders. "Stay where you are!"

"I beg your pardon?"

He sighed and released his grip. "Will you please stay here? Outside's no place for a lady. Those men aren't used to seeing noble ladies parading in their homespun before their eyes."

Heat rose in her cheeks, but determination still ran deep. "Are you going punish that man?"

"If it makes you happy." His voice changed, the tone now soothing.

The boy returned and put a tray with two goblets and a jug of wine on the small table. Will waved him away and filled the goblets.

Alleyne took hers with shaking hands. Geoffrey had barely left, and immediately Will had taken charge. She should be relieved, delighted even. It was what she had wanted. Surely Will's intentions were honourable?

So why could she not shake off the feeling in her gut that something was amiss?

She felt his eyes boring into her and lifted her head. Will had regained his composure. He pulled a bench near to her chair. Taking her goblet from her, his hands reached for hers, grasping them tightly when she wanted to withdraw them.

"I would do anything to keep you safe. The men outside are for your protection. They will help me chase those criminals who killed your father. They're good, reliable men."

"I'm sure they are." She shivered under his touch. Her hands trembled. Surely, he felt it. "But Ancel should be in charge of our defences. I cannot afford to lose him."

"You won't, sweeting," Will said, his eyes filled with a longing she had only noticed the day before. She blushed at the memory. "But he will now be under my orders, just as he was under Lord Raymond's." His thumb traced her vein up from her wrist, gliding along her underarm. "I'm acting in your name, Alleyne, as Lady of Bellac." He smiled.

Her gaze followed his hands as they wove their way up her arm. Finally, he cupped her face and kissed her lightly on the mouth.

Blessed Mother! So many years she had dreamt of this. She must put her doubts from her mind. Will cared. Ancel was wrong. Geoffrey was wrong.

Father had been wrong about Will. None of them knew him like she did, saw the warm, loving side of him. Only she knew it existed. He kept it hidden deep inside.

Will drew back and rose. "I need to see how the men are settling in. Perhaps it is wise if you stayed in the solar for your meals for the time being."

She nodded, feeling bereft as his hands left her skin. "You're right. It will be safer. And it won't be for long, will it?"

He brushed a lock from her cheek. "No, it won't be for long. I promise."

Alleyne stood. "Best I retire upstairs, to ready myself for the day. You will dine with me later?"

"Of course I will." His smile sent waves of heat through her system. She nodded inwardly.

"Oh, and Will?"

"Yes?"

"See that man punished. I don't want my people upset." Alleyne tilted up her chin and sent him a stern glance.

"As you wish."

She nodded, walking towards the stairs, her back upright. It was a gamble. But being so close to fulfilling her aim, she must now set aside any doubts she had earlier. Will would be hers. He would take care of her. And Bellac.

Geoffrey was gone. And soon she would forget him.

At the bottom step she turned and smiled at Will. He raised his goblet. She climbed the steps and began to plan the night's dinner, pushing any thought of what went on in the bailey from her mind.

***

Several times throughout the day, Roger burst into the solar, disrupting her spinning. Alleyne glowered at him when she pricked herself because of his latest sudden entrance. "What now?" She dabbed the tiny wound with a clean linen square to stem the flow, the sight of her own blood not helping her curb her growing impatience with his constant disruptions.

"Pardon me again, my lady. I have a complaint from a kitchen maid. One of the men tried to get his hands under her skirt. This is the third such incident and the men have only been here but a few hours. The hall is in turmoil, the kitchen boy harassed and made fun of, and Alfred is at the receiving end of their boots. Literally!"

She sighed, checking her finger. The bleeding had stopped. "Have you told Sir William?"

"No, my lady, I couldn't. He's in the centre of the mayhem, making himself right at home."

"Which is what I permitted him to do, Roger," she said sharply. "These men are here for our protection and I will not have Will insulted."

"But the maids–?"

"The maids more than likely flirted with the men. And then got cold feet." She grew bored with this. Will would make sure his men did not harm anyone at Bellac. "He said the man who slapped Alfred was punished, so that's the end of it. Alfred's a big boy. He can take a few jibes." She picked up the spindle again.

"Those are no jibes, my lady. They are punches."

Her head shot up. "Punches?"

Sir William has his own plan. Alleyne shook off Ancel's words of warning as she stared at Alfred.

"Yes. They punch him. See for yourself, if you care to look outside?" The upset tone of his voice, his indignant gaze, made her give in. Resigned, she dropped the spindle in the basket by her side and went to the window, leaning out for a clear view of the bailey. Her eyes widened when she spotted six men near the stable door, pushing Alfred between them.

"Stop!" The culprits twisted their heads to stare at her. She could barely see Alfred's face but the bruises around his eyes and cheeks were easy to notice even from the height of the solar window. "Leave him be!"

To her annoyance, the men laughed. One made a rude gesture with his fingers, sending his companions roaring. They turned back to where the boy had stood but Alfred had fled into the stables. He must have bolted the door. Their fists pounded on the solid wood that did not give in. She knew they would not try to break in for fear of scaring the horses. For the time being, the lad was safe.

"It's just sport," one man with an eye patch and long straggly hair shouted. He rubbed his crotch. "Why don't you join us for some, now that the pup's run away?"

Her cheeks flamed. "You insolent dolt! I'll report you to Sir William."

"You do that, sweetheart. You do that." The men laughed, slapping each others' backs.

"He will see you punished." Their laughter grew louder. She slammed the shutter closed.

"You are right, Roger. This is out of hand." In rough moves, she pushed loose strands of hair into the thick braid. "Where is Sir William?"

"He's downstairs in the hall, playing dice." He stopped her at the door, his hand gripping her arm. "His mood is foul. It seems he lost money. I tried to reason with him, but he wouldn't hear of it." He shook his head, a resigned look on his wrinkled features. "Now if I were a few years younger–"

"You're not. But I am." Alleyne rushed down the stairs, Roger close behind her. The sight that greeted her in the hall stopped her halfway. Trestle tables lay overturned. Chairs and benches were pulled towards the central hearth. Men lounged in small groups, playing dice and drinking. Everyone had cups in their hands, with Elvire and two kitchen maids rushing around to replenish the jugs. Elvire slapped a man's hand away from her rump. Roger moved forward.

Alleyne's hand on his arm stopped him. With a flick of her head, she sent Elvire and the girls from the room. Whistles accompanied their departure. She glared at the crowd, repulsed at their behaviour. She drew her mouth into a thin line and swallowed the bile rising in her throat. Eventually, she spotted Will at a table on the dais, surrounded by several coarse men. Skirting filthy hands that reached for her, she strode over to him, Roger by her side.

"Will!" Her voice boomed over the noise. A hush fell across the hall. Now she held everyone's attention.

Will stared at her and raised his cup. "To your health, m'lady. You have some wonderful wines in your cellar."

She wrestled the cup from his grasp and threw it into a corner, the wooden vessel bouncing off the wall.

"What the–?"

"A word, Will." She stood in front of him, feet rooted on the ground, hands on hips.

He smirked and looked her up and down. How dare he! She bit back a sharp response.

This was not the same Will who had kissed her earlier, not the knight she had known so many years. Fear rose in her chest, constricting her throat.

Something was horribly wrong.

"Your men abuse my people. Tell them to leave them alone." She glared when he chuckled. His gaze scanned the hall before he threw his head back and roared. The room erupted in raucous laughter. She drew in a sharp breath.

Will recovered quickly and touched her arm. "They are just having some sport. To vent their built-up vigour. No harm done." He shot out his hand and gripped her wrist. Ah, he was not completely drunk after all.

"No harm done?" She tried to pull her hand away but was thwarted by his iron grip. Frustration sent tears pricking at her eyes. "Alfred's face is bloodied, and the girls are being molested." She stamped her foot, angered at her inability to keep a cool head.

"The girls were flirting. What did they expect?" His eyes challenged her. "You know what maids are like when they see a strapping man paying them attention?"

"Not like that." Roger interjected.

Will ignored him, his gaze not leaving Alleyne's. "And Alfred's a big boy. The men must've thought he mistreated their horses."

"Alfred has never mistreated a horse in his life."

The door to the bailey opened. The soldiers she had seen pestering Alfred marched in.

"That's them." She pointed her finger. "They are to leave Bellac forthwith."

"Oooohhh," came from the other side of the room. "Someone tame that shrew!" The crowd roared. The sound chilled her. Some brave drunks staggered towards her. Amongst them was the man with the eye patch. He rolled his eye as his hands went down to rub his crotch. Just like earlier.

She turned away in disgust and glared at Will. "If you can't get your men under control, leave!"

"Enough!" Will's shout silenced the whistles. He straightened in his seat. "Peter, apologise to the lady for the treatment of her stable boy." He looked coolly at the man with the patch.

"I what?" The soldier scratched his head.

"You apologise. Now." Will stood and placed his hand on Alleyne's back. She was too terrified to push him away, angry with him yet grateful for his presence. She had heard of soldiers out of control but never dreamt of witnessing such terrifying behaviour. She clenched her hands for strength.

With a flourish, the man bowed to her. "My apologies, my lady. Didn't mean to offend."

Will dismissed him and turned to her, a smirk playing on his lips. "Is my lady content now?"

"I hope this man won't cause any more harm or he'll have to go." Her voice shook. She was still uncertain about the apology, the lack of sincerity. Roger had not moved from her side but clearly he was overwhelmed. Still, his presence was comforting. He took her arm.

"Let me take you upstairs," he said. "You will be safer in the solar."

Will stopped him, his fingers digging into the steward's shoulder. "You should never have allowed her down here, you old fool."

Roger straightened. "You didn't listen to me. At least you have to listen to Lady Alleyne. She owns the manor." He turned and led Alleyne to the stairs.

Her mind was whirling, sending a dizziness through her head. How could she stop this mayhem?

She stopped Roger at the bottom of the stairs, and sent a swift glance around the hall. Conversations resumed; men returned to their games.

"Roger, ensure Cook adheres to the rules of Lent. Give those men only pottage, boiled eels and stale bread. And arrange for the ale to be watered down. After all, it is Ash Wednesday. I told Elvire earlier what I want for myself and Will. Make sure that lot doesn't get a glimpse when she brings it to the solar. Make haste!"

"Will you be safe alone?" His eyes were full of concern, and not just for her. She knew he worried about their tenants, their villains and servants, himself.

"Yes, perfectly," she assured him. "Nobody will dare come up." She took the steps, aware of men watching her. She must make plans.

Fast.

***

Alleyne sat and surveyed the solar, pleased with Elvire's efforts. The table was set, with a trencher to share between herself and Will. Freshly baked bread lay steaming in a basket. Small bowls were filled with vegetable stew. The aromatic scent of rosemary and thyme hid the pungent smell of the grilled eels. She hated eels, but Lent was upon them.

She sighed, tapping her fingers on the wooden table. Where was Will? She had sent Elvire some time ago to inform him all was ready. They began to serve the pottage and fish downstairs when Elvire left. She had ordered the maids to stay in the kitchen and the boys to serve, overseen by Roger. She hoped the men would not notice the watered-down ale, as they had already consumed a barrel. At their pace, Bellac's cellars would be empty within a week.

Will threw the door open, then kicked it shut with his heel.

"Have you been waiting long?" He had changed into his best clothes, bright hose complementing a crisp linen shirt. Clearly he had sobered up and was sorry for the earlier incidents.

She gestured towards the vacant chair. "Please be seated."

He bowed and took her hand to his lips. "Please accept my apologies for what happened. The men were out of control, but they aren't used to being cooped up indoors." He sat and picked up his brimming goblet of wine. "They will search the area tomorrow, so it will be more peaceful in the keep then." He smiled.

Relief washed through her, her shoulders relaxing. "Thank you. You understand why I don't want my people upset."

He nodded. "I completely understand. It won't happen again." He sipped at the wine. "Much nicer than the brew downstairs, Alleyne. Glad to see you hide your good stuff from the crowds." His tone light, he winked. This was the old Will. The man who always made her smile, chivalrous and charming. Perhaps he had to be tough when he was with his men. After all, they would not follow his orders otherwise.

He helped himself to a generous portion of stew and eel and looked very much at ease, almost as if he felt like being home.

She picked at her own fish, then broke a chunk off her bread and dunked it into the stew. She was not hungry but, despite herself, found the taste comforting. The heat and scent gave her strength. She broke off more bread and scooped up the spiced vegetables. Who said that food had to be bland during Lent? Her spirits rose. She smiled and caught Will's eye.

"Something amuses you?"

She nodded. "Yes. I'm in the company of a trusted friend, and the manor is safe." She dabbed her mouth with a linen square and picked up her goblet, glancing at him over the rim. His eyes shining, he returned her smile. He pushed himself away from the table and came to her side. Kneeling, he took her hands, then kissed each of her fingertips.

A shiver ran down her spine. This morning she had woken, fully certain he was the one. The events of the day had raised doubts, but of course Will knew what he was doing. She just had to remind him of that occasionally.

"Alleyne, sweeting," he whispered between gentle kisses pressed into her palm. His eyes grew misty, his breathing heavy. She gasped as the sensations travelled across her skin. Her breath became shorter. She wanted to close her eyes but did not dare. She must not give in so easily. Another shiver rattled at her resolve.

"Be my wife."

Her eyes widened. "What?" Her voice trembled. She did not trust herself to say more as dreams and doubts warred in her mind. She had asked for his help. Should she now take a path she had always wanted, or await the summons from Court? It was utterly unexpected, at least this early during his stay.

He laughed softly, clearly misreading her hesitation. "You heard me. I know it's early days yet but…" His eyes danced. "What say you?"

Dizziness overcame her and she closed her eyes. Safety or uncertainty? She swallowed, knowing the only answer. "Yes."

"Alleyne." Will's mouth was on hers. At first hesitant, gentle, then demanding as his kiss grew deeper. His hands slid up her arms, roaming her face, her throat. She drew in a ragged breath.

She was safe.

Chapter Nine

The icy rain had been drumming on his head in a steady rhythm since they left Bellac the day before. First Geoffrey had sought shelter at an inn by the roadside, forced to stay the night, but as the weather showed no sign of improving, he and Guy set off again at dawn, huddled deep into their cloaks. The delay was most untimely. He swore at the thought of his wet armour.

Finally, they passed St Peter's Abbey and entered Gloucester at a walking pace. A slippery mixture of mud, human waste and sleet covered the uneven cobbles. The horses' hooves slid on the mess. The city stank despite the cold breeze. After weeks in the countryside, Geoffrey shuddered at the smell. He steered Feu towards a narrow lane not far from the abbey. He halted outside a smithy and heaved himself from the saddle. A boy hurried to greet him.

"Sir Geoffrey," the lad cried. "It's been so long. We worried you had come to harm in Lincoln."

Geoffrey laughed and handed him Feu's reins. "Sorry to give you a fright, Edwin. I was delayed on my return. Has aught happened since I left?" The lad was a prime source for gossip, dealing with Gloucester's burghers daily.

Edwin held out a hand to take the reins of Guy's horse, but Guy shook his head. "I'll sort out my stallion."

The lad shrugged and stepped through the stable door adjacent to the smithy. "As you wish. You can use the pen over there." Geoffrey followed him as Guy took his mount to the pen where Edwin pointed.

Edwin removed Feu's saddle and placed it onto the partition. "Sheriff Miles is with the empress in Bristol. He left Oswald in charge here and now all hell's broken loose over a burglary at Aelfric's house." The boy grinned as he picked up a brush. Having tied Feu to a ring in the wall, he brushed the stallion's wet coat.

Geoffrey leaned back and watched. Exhausted from the journey, he craved wine and sleep. But he must stay focused. Oswald was inferior to him yet Miles had left him to look after the town. Not the best option but clearly one sprung from necessity. The sheriff had to stay with Matilda while Geoffrey was forced to detour via Bellac. "Aelfric, the wool merchant? Was anyone hurt?" Inwardly, he groaned. The merchant had to be handled with care and respect; not exactly Oswald's virtues.

"No. Aelfric's wife was visiting her sick mother and he stayed at his mistress's." Edwin smirked as he circled Feu, safe in his experience to know the stallion let him handle him. Geoffrey was still amazed at the lanky lad's skill and daring, given Feu's temperamental nature. He brushed away the memory of another capable stable lad, Alfred.

"So what's Oswald doing about it?" Geoffrey crossed his arms, the metal rivets of his mail shirt clinking. He could not wait to rid himself of his armour, his skin sore from the soaked gambeson beneath his chain mail.

"Oswald marched in like a wild boar, scaring the wits out of the wife who returned immediately, concerned for her household. He went on and on about the mistress, right in front of the lady. Aelfric's furious and wants him removed but Sheriff Miles is ignoring the matter for the time being."

Geoffrey laughed. "That sounds like Oswald. Fair enough, I'll stay well out of his path. Don't want to get caught up in that squabble."

"No, best stay out of it, my lord. As you know well, Aelfric hates being made the laughing stock of the town. And neither does the wife appreciate the attention the mistress is getting."

"I bet."

Geoffrey decided not to let Oswald know he was in town. He would go home, take a bath, eat and rest. There was no point in pushing themselves, and their horses, in the appalling conditions.

He turned to Guy. "Go home when you're finished. Report back to me at dawn."

Guy nodded. "As you wish." He threw a blanket over his horse's back and grabbed his saddle bags.

"Edwin, can you get the horses ready by daybreak? We have to get to Bristol swiftly."

The boy nodded. "Aye, my lord. Would you want Father to repair those?" He pointed at some broken rivets on Geoffrey's right arm.

"No, not this time. He can sort the whole damn thing when I'm back."

As he pushed open the door, a blast of chilly air hit him, followed by sleet stinging his skin. "Until the morrow," he said, without turning back. Pulling his cloak around his head, he clutched his bags and hurried up the street. He turned into a narrow lane and stopped outside a whitewashed cottage.

Home. Relief washed over him. Here, in his refuge, he could simply be himself. And he had a chance to think.

"Bloody freezing," Geoffrey swore as he dumped the bags on the beaten floor, scattering the fragrant rushes.

He grinned at his startled servant rushing through from the kitchen. "Hello, Arnulf."

"I, I... You could have sent word, my lord." Arnulf swallowed and straightened his back. "But it's good to have you back."

Arnulf picked up the bags and carried them up the narrow stairs at the back of the room. Geoffrey glanced around. A solitary candle stood on the large beech table by the only window, and the seats of four chairs were tucked neatly beneath the surface. Two padded armchairs faced a wide stone fireplace, their footstools lined up symmetrically in front of them. The fireplace lay cold and empty, cleared of embers and ash. Arnulf had kept the place tidy. It held none of the cosy warmth of Bellac's hall with its wall hangings and torches.

Pushing away the unwanted memory, he crossed the room and opened the oak door to the small kitchen at the back. The shutters were closed against the elements but, to his delight, a fire danced in the hearth. He threw his wet cloak over a bench and sat down on another near the warmth, stretching his legs towards the comforting flames. Arnulf entered, carrying a bundle of dry clothes which he placed on another bench.

"If I had known of your arrival, I'd have prepared your front room." He tutted as he viewed Geoffrey's bedraggled state. "Let's get you out of those first, then I shall kindle a fire in your room." He poured a cup of hot wine from a pot near the stove.

"Sorry, but there was no time to send word." Geoffrey smiled and took the cup gratefully. He took several draughts, relishing the warm, sweet taste, before he set it beside him on the bench. Then he held out his arms to let Arnulf remove the braces.

Later that evening, bathed and dressed in crisp linen hose and shirt, his feet propped up on the footstool near fire hissing in the grate, Geoffrey reclined, staring into the flames. Another cup of mulled wine warmed his insides. Home meant peace, recovery.

At Arnulf's discreet cough, he glanced up.

"My lord, these were delivered but a few days ago. I deemed it best to keep them here rather than send a messenger in search of you." Arnulf held out two neatly folded notes.

Geoffrey took them and stared. One held the intact seal of Sheriff Miles – a summons, no doubt, to join Matilda's court. The other showed his older brother's.

"And a short while before you arrived, I received this." Arnulf pulled a stained, roughly-folded letter from inside his shirt. "A message from Reginald."

***

Alleyne stared at her maid.

"Roger dead? But he only just…" Her hands sought the wall for support as she dropped onto the clothes chest. "I spoke to him but moments ago." Tears brimmed in her eyes as the news – stark on Elvire's face – sank in.

"Apparently, he fell down the stairs. So says Sir William."

"Will? But he wasn't even in the hall when Roger and I passed through a short while ago. How can he be aware of what happened?"

Elvire vigorously shook her head, as if trying to rid herself of a memory. "I just entered the hall from the kitchen when I heard a shout. I looked up and...and saw Roger stumble forward. Dear Lord, help me." She gasped, her hands covering her mouth, tears streaming down her face.

Alleyne pulled Elvire down beside her, winding her arm tightly around the old maid's shoulders. "Shhh. Calm yourself." She held her until the trembling subsided a little. Her hand brushed away a stray lock from Elvire's flushed face. "What happened then?"

"Roger fell all the way down the stairs. Everyone rushed to him but not to help...no!" Elvire hiccuped. "No, they went forward to gloat. I could see it in their faces, clear as day." She looked at her, a determined look in her eyes. "The men didn't let me anywhere near him but I had seen enough."

"I'm sure you–"

"Beg your pardon, my lady, what I mean is...I'd seen the blood on Roger's body. An axe cleaved open his chest."

Alleyne's face drained of all warmth as her ears hummed. Black spots danced before her eyes and she blinked sharply. Her father killed by an axe. Now her steward shared the same fate. A coincidence?

"I know what you think. The same notion struck me. Oh!" The maid gasped as the meaning of her words sank in.

"You've done the right thing by coming to me. But how did they let you come up here, with Roger's...body on the floor by the stairs?"

"I withdrew into the corridor to the kitchen, watched them heave Roger onto one of the tables. And then the lord d'Arques came in. He…he took one glance at Roger and said, 'Clearly a case of an accident. He fell into his own weapon. Get him out of my sight.' Yes, my lady," she hastily added when Alleyne drew back, biting her hand to cover a scream that wanted to escape. "Yes, just as I thought. So, while they were busy moving Roger's body out into the bailey, I fled up here. I know it's cowardly of me to hide but I didn't want you to be on your own, not knowing the truth. And 'tis the truth, so God help me." She crossed herself, murmuring a little prayer.

Alleyne leaned her head against the wall and closed her eyes. If this were true – and why should she doubt the word of her mother's maid, her lifelong companion? – then Will should be held responsible for Roger's death. His men had killed her steward.

Tears stung behind her lids, as realisation hit her like the spikes of a mace. Will's sweet words exposed as nothing but lies. Ancel was right. Father had been right. Both men had mistrusted Will but she had dismissed their doubts. Instead she had given in to foolish girlhood dreams. She only prayed the captain of the guard knew how to look after himself. There was naught now that she could do but–

Geoffrey.

The under-sheriff's name came to her head unbidden. He presented her only chance of survival. But where was he?

"Gloucester." She opened her eyes, her mind made up.

"My lady?" Elvire turned to her, a frown forming between her brows. "What's in Gloucester?"

She stared at her maid. "Geoffrey de Mortagne. He will help us."

Elvire's eyes filled with skepticism. "Are you certain? Because, when he departed, the lord de Mortagne was in a right foul mood."

Alleyne's mind raced back to the day Geoffrey left. True, he had been rather mulish, and insensitive. But that didn't warrant the foul mood. "Why so?"

The maid rolled her eyes. "Because you sent him away and welcomed Sir William instead."

Alleyne blushed at the bluntness of Elvire's words. They stung. But they held the truth. Shame filled her as she remembered her words, her actions. She had clung to Will like a drowning puppy to a stretched-out hand.

But Will had betrayed her.

Elvire's jaw was set in fierce determination. "I'm going to find de Mortagne."

***

The soldier at the outer gate of Oxford Castle mumbled something unintelligible to his fellow as he opened it, but Geoffrey cut him short. Darkness had fallen and his eyes were heavy with tiredness.

"Make haste, man! We've been travelling hard and I'm in no mind for delays."

It was not the gatekeeper's fault that Geoffrey and Guy had faced another day of sleet and rain on the roads, but the sheriff's letter did not allow for any delays. Why had Matilda demanded his presence at her Easter court? The feast was still three weeks away. What he knew, though, was that if he stayed until then, his brother might likely be dead by the time he eventually reached Perche. Geoffrey would not be given the chance to bury their disagreement. Anger and shame warred in his heart, his gut twisted with lost opportunity as he remembered Bertrand's scribbled words.

If Bertrand died, the family manor became Geoffrey's. The news that Bertrand suffered from consumption had nearly felled him. Once there, he would also have to visit his godfather and liege lord, Count Rotrou of Perche, in honour of whose father he had been named. It appeared that after more than ten years' absence, his life in England just as he wanted it, Geoffrey's past had caught up with him.

He swore as he urged Feu through the barely opened gate. The gatekeeper scrambled away for safety.

"Thank you," Guy shouted. "Geoffrey, slow down! If you approach the empress in your current mood, the Lord only knows what she'll do with you."

The slush on the cobbles in the outer bailey made footing treacherous, so Geoffrey brought Feu to a walk, grumbling. "Thank you, Guy. If I wanted to be reprimanded by my wetnurse, I'd have stayed at home."

"Fine, my lord." Guy's voice held a note of ice.

Geoffrey shook his head as Guy brought his horse up beside him. "I'm sorry. I shouldn't scold you simply because this journey is so untimely. We were meant to travel to Bristol, to speak to Stephen, instead we're here. And now I need to travel to Normandy as well."

Guy shrugged his shoulders. "It's just that I don't like being compared to a woman, 'tis all."

Laughing out loud, Geoffrey slapped his grinning sergeant on the arm. "I don't know what I'd do without you." The man finally managed to crack his shell. Relieved – if reluctantly so – Geoffrey guided Feu along the deserted lane towards the keep. Uncertain if there was any accommodation for them in the no doubt crowded quarters, he decided to play safe.

"You remember the inn we stayed at during our last visit?"

"Aye, of course. How could I forget the charms of the red-headed serving wench?"

They were back to their usual banter. Geoffrey chuckled. "The dame in question was the innkeeper's wife. As you well know. Do you think you can find it again?"

"I'm certain. You want us to stay there instead of the castle?"

He nodded. "Aye. I'd like to stay away from the high and mighty."

Guy pushed his horse towards a lane crossing theirs. "When I've arranged the room, do you need me there at the castle?"

Geoffrey shook his head. "No, just make sure my bed isn't completely invaded by bed bugs."

With a wave of his hand Guy turned back. "No worries. Leave it to me."

Determined not to stay long, Geoffrey approached the high wall surrounding the inner bailey. He repeated the ritual of identification before he was allowed in. So, Matilda was still careful. Not just hesitant but mistrusting her own people. Geoffrey marvelled at the time the court wasted here instead of arranging a hasty coronation. The sooner that took place the safer Matilda's position would be. But no, she had to dither.

He left Feu with a stable boy who eyed the stallion warily. Geoffrey patted the horse on the neck and turned towards the hall. His armour stained from the hard ride, he would use the hurried summons as an excuse for his shabby appearance. First he needed to know why he was called there, then he could clean himself. As he was likely stuck for several days, he might as well make the most of it, exchanging news with Miles and the earl of Gloucester.

***

Alleyne jumped to her feet. "I can't let you do that, Elvire. No!" She shook her head vigorously, pacing the room. "I won't allow it."

"But it's the only way." Elvire rose, too, holding her hands out, pleading. "De Mortagne is our only chance. Everyone else is caught up in this pointless war with no winners."

"No, Elvire. Under no circumstances are you to leave the manor on your own. I forbid it. We can send someone else. Ancel will have a man who can search for him."

"No, my lady. We need every one of our men here. We can't afford to let go even one."

Alleyne stopped, her voice hoarse. "We have already lost one. Blessed Mother, what are we to do?" She wrung her hands, her eyes tilted heavenwards.

"I'll go, my lady. I won't be missed. One of the girls can stay with you."

"It's too dangerous. You know we can't have any of the young girls near the hall any more. And Will would notice immediately you're gone."

"Well...then we'll have to devise a scheme so he can't enter your room. Keep him out and stay safe."

"Ha! You think this door would hold out against an axe? No, no, no, no." Her mind whirling, Alleyne began to pace again. "There has–"

Heavy footsteps sounded from the other side of the door. Elvire took position next to her, a strong arm around her waist, and Alleyne felt a rush of affection for her lifelong companion. Never would she allow Elvire to risk her life.

A bang on the door – expected though it was – still made her jump. Her heart pounded in her ears. She cleared her throat. "Who is it?"

"It's Will. Open the door." His voice strong, menacing, not allowing rejection.

The latch was lifted then rattled, but the lock stayed true.

"Alleyne!"

"I...I'm resting, Will. My head aches. I shall receive you later."

"Damn your head. Open!" A sigh followed the demand, then Will's tone changed to a mellow drawl. "Alleyne, sweeting. I come bearing sad news. There has been an accident."

"An accident?" Alleyne held her breath, stunned by the swift change in Will's demeanour. Had she ever known him? Really known him? "What kind of accident? Is anybody hurt?" It took all her strength to hide the tremor in her voice.

"I'm certain Elvire has informed you already. Your steward fell down the stairs. My men saw him take a tumble. Sadly," the pause was subtle, "sadly he fell into his own sword. The men tried to help him but it was too late. I'm so sorry."

Elvire shook her head, her eyes wide, blazing. "An axe," she mouthed.

Alleyne held her forefinger to her lip. "Roger?" she gasped. "Oh no! How could this happen?" Her eyes scanned the room for a hiding place for Elvire and fell on the bed.

There was space underneath but Will would see through the ruse. Glancing back at the door, the chest caught her eye.

"Help me carry it back," she whispered. "Quietly." They tiptoed to the chest and heaved it up, suppressing a moan at the sheer weight of it. With a thud Alleyne thought loud enough to wake the dead, they dropped it in its place. She opened the lid and lifted a couple of dresses. "Quick, inside!"

Elvire's face turned white in shock. "In there?"

"Alleyne? Sweeting, what are you doing? I want to see for myself that you are all right."

"Aye, quick," she whispered. "I'll have to let him in."

With a final glance, Elvire squeezed herself into the chest and Alleyne draped the gowns over her, leaving a gap for the maid to breathe. She ensured the lid was not fully closed, but held open a couple of inches by the iron catch so Elvire would have air.

"I'm just dressing again, Will. Surely you can't expect me to receive you in a state of undress?" Her tone held a light note she did not feel, as dread took hold of her insides. Her blood pumped in her ears.

How could she have been so wrong?

She shuffled to the door and lifted the latch. An instant later Will swept past her, his eyes scanning the room before they came to meet her gaze.

"I was so worried about you." He led her to the window seat and pulled her down next to him, holding her hands in a firm grasp. "You see, I heard of a misunderstanding in the corridor to the kitchen. I hope you don't bear a grudge. Marten is particularly concerned. He never meant you harm."

Alleyne suppressed a shudder at the memory, still vivid in her mind. Forcing herself to remain calm, she let Will keep hold of her hands. Struggling would only make him angry, and he might discover Elvire's presence. Yet she could not keep the chill from her voice. "That man is not sorry, Will, nor is he concerned. He attacked me as I left the kitchen." A shudder racked her body, and she swallowed back the rising bile. "He grabbed my–"

"My poor lass." Will pulled her into his arms.

Tears stung her eyes. She had to force herself to relax her stiff back, to ease herself into his embrace. Anything, as long as he left soon and didn't suspect she had company. Her hands flew up to cover her face as Will whispered soothing words in her ear. Meaningless, now she knew the man behind the mask.

Alleyne raised her eyes and met his. Raging inside at Will's duplicity, she smiled. "Perhaps...perhaps it wasn't quite as I thought it was."

"Let me assure you, Marten would never lay hands on a lady. It was a simple misunderstanding. And the dark, narrow corridor can conjure up all sorts of imagined fears. He sends his apologies if he scared you."

"But Roger?" She sniffed, forcing him back on the issue.

"Ahh, dearest." He gradually released her, and stood. "Poor Roger has lately become weak in the leg. I sometimes saw him stumble up or down the stairs, uncertain of his footing. Old age must be difficult, especially for a man bearing so much responsibility."

Will strolled towards the door, then changed his mind and sauntered towards the clothes chest. Alleyne held her breath. Had he suspected all along? She nearly screamed when he slumped down on top of it, the heavy lid falling shut with a thump, depriving Elvire of air. His eyes calculating, he watched her. She had to stay focused.

"It was unfortunate Roger fell into his own sword. The poor man must have carried it in his hand though I can't think of any reason why. There was nothing to be done but to move him to the chapel."

Alleyne stood, knowing that time was of the essence. Elvire must not suffocate. "I would like to see him."

He rose and came towards her, taking her by the arms. His fingers dug ever so slightly into her flesh, only a hint of force yet unmissable. "You have just buried your father. I won't allow you to see another dead body." His eyes glinted in the fading light.

"But–"

"I'm quite certain Roger is in no fit state to be seen by a lady. He'll be buried tomorrow."

"Tomorrow?" She blinked. "Why the haste?"

"The poor man's body is badly mutilated. The sooner he is in hallowed ground the better for his soul." Was there a hint of sarcasm in his voice?

Alleyne froze.

"I have to leave you now." A hand on the latch, he paused. His eyes, inscrutable yet cold as slate, held hers. "Never keep me waiting again." The door slammed shut.

Alleyne dashed forward and locked it before she scurried over to the chest, lifting the heavy lid.

"Elvire?"

Chapter Ten

Queenship did not suit Matilda, Geoffrey thought as he kneeled in front of her. She sat in a large, cushioned chair, her back ramrod straight, hands closing over the armrests. When he approached, he had seen her raise an eyebrow at his mud-stained armour. He berated himself for his haste.

"Rise." Her tone was abrupt, with her habitual note of arrogance.

Slowly, he raised his head to meet her gaze. Her dark glance down her nose assessed him coolly.

She was too haughty, too dismissive. He felt like a piece of untreated meat, left in the heat to rot. Perhaps he should have cleaned himself up, after all, to appear more presentable but the summons had seemed urgent.

'Twas too late now. The sniggers of several courtiers reached his ears. Whispers filled the room. He groaned inwardly.

"Welcome, Sir Geoffrey." Matilda cut short the murmurs. At the wave of her hand, he rose fully. "We are pleased to note you have not dithered for wasteful pastimes on your way to us."

His bile rose. He swallowed it back before he cleared his throat. "I apologise for my appearance, my lady. Your message seemed urgent so I did not wish to waste time."

"We understand, Sir Geoffrey. Tell me, what are the latest plans of Maude, my cousin?"

Geoffrey tilted his head. "The quee–" He cut himself short as Matilda's eyes turned into thunderclouds at his blunder. "The lady Maude seeks to free her husband, Stephen, and fight for his throne. She rejects any suggestions of giving up, of leaving the country for her home of Boulogne."

"That dreadful woman!" Matilda rose and paced the dais, her fingers fidgeting with the elaborate golden embroidery elaborately stitched on her belt. "How dare she defy me? Me? The rightful heir to the throne." Her footsteps rang loud on the wooden boards.

Geoffrey marvelled at the contrast between the two women. Stephen's wife, Maude, soft-spoken and utterly feminine, yet with the steely courage of a warrior princess; and Matilda, former empress of all Germans, now Countess of Anjou and soon to be Queen of England, a cold woman with a prideful mind. She would not win many hearts with her fits of temper. Yet, somehow, as the daughter and heir of King Henry, God rest his soul, she demanded loyalty. Loyalty from men like him.

"My lady, if I may speak freely?"

Hard eyes met his. "Continue!"

"I'm sure your advisors have already, well…you must proceed to London at your earliest convenience. The lady Maude has the city quaking in fear of an attack while she is camped south of the River Thames with a strong following. Hurry forth to London, and have yourself crowned queen immediately. That way you can–"

"We thank you for your opinion, Sir Geoffrey, but we regard it as just that. Your opinion. A frenzied ride to London is not only undignified, it is also utterly unthinkable. It reeks of desperation. We shall remain here, in Oxford, to celebrate the holy feast of Easter. Then we will plan for my journey across the country."

"My lady." Chastened, Geoffrey inclined his head, grinding his teeth.

She laughed, a sound so alien Geoffrey stared at her to believe it. A smile graced her thin, wide mouth. "Don't you worry on our behalf, Sir Geoffrey. We shall drive that woman from our realm. And then we shall deal with her hapless husband. You may now leave us to clean yourself up." She rose and turned away. Geoffrey bowed as Matilda left the hall through the curtain separating her private quarters from the rabble.

"Just put your oar in, de Mortagne." Miles, Sheriff of Gloucester, chuckled at his side. He slapped Geoffrey's shoulder. "Come with me."

Geoffrey grinned. "My lord? Surely I'm not the only one in favour of a swift move?"

Miles led him to a corner seat away from the chattering crowds and gestured to a servant to bring wine. Once they held cups filled with a potent red liquid, Geoffrey relaxed. He pulled off his braces and dropped them at his feet.

"You're not alone with your opinion, Geoffrey. But unfortunately the empress won't listen. She thinks she has all the time in the world now Stephen is incarcerated. It's dangerous."

"Agreed." Geoffrey took a sip. "Mmmhh. Rhenish?" The heady scent played havoc with his tired mind.

Miles laughed, the heavy lines for once not creased with worry. "Aye, some things are better imported to this country. Potent German wine is one of them."

Geoffrey relished the taste for a moment before he returned to the matter at hand. "Maude is gearing up for an assault. She's not the beaten woman Matilda pretends her to be."

"I know. That's what makes our situation so volatile. Maude and d'Ypres, her Flemish mercenary, are they indeed conniving to rescue Stephen from Bristol Castle?"

"Yes, but I don't have any exact details. My man is still in Maude's camp so we will no doubt hear more soon. I have instructed Reginald to send his messages to you. I must go to Perche, with your permission. My brother is close to death…if it's not too late already." He clenched his teeth. Seeing the sheriff's raised eyebrows, he added, "I received a letter from home, urging me to come soon as Bertrand my brother has contracted consumption."

"I'm sorry. I know you're estranged. You will need to make your peace whilst you can. I'll try to convince Matilda to grant you permission to leave on the morrow, but I'm unsure if she'll agree." The sheriff shook his head, his brows drawn together in thought. He drained his cup in one long draught and rose. "Go and refresh yourself. In light of your intended journey, I may have a mission for you."

***

Alleyne gnawed at her nails as she watched Elvire's shadow, garbed in a thick black cloak with the hood pulled down to cover her face, gliding through the gate, dragging a grey mare behind her. Then the maid disappeared from sight. Alleyne pushed her berating conscience to the back of her mind. They had no choice.

Ancel locked the gate, his eyes scanning the bailey before they met hers across the distance. Despite the sparse light from the torches, she saw worry in them, and encouragement. He knew, like she did, that Elvire's mission might end in tragedy. It was vital for their survival that it did not. He nodded, then slid into the gatehouse.

She closed the shutters, cutting out the wind and rain. Tears welled up. With the back of her hand, she wiped the moisture from her cheeks. A sob escaped her as she gazed across the empty chamber. Her only confidante was gone. Despite the positive tone from the maid, they both knew Geoffrey could be anywhere, even abroad. Gloucester was perhaps Elvire's first stop of many.

Alleyne threw herself onto the bed, her fists pummelling the soft fur of the coverlets. 'Twas all her fault. Had she not opened the gates and invited Will into her home? Almost allowed him into her bed?

By the Saints!

She crossed herself and whispered a short prayer of thanks, realising how close she had come to dishonour. But how close would she come to death? Clearly, Will did not intend to stop at the steward. Was he behind the attack on Father, after all? The thought was unbearable. Had she asked her Father's killer for help? Set a wolf amongst the flock? A moan escaped her, despair warring with only a tiny flicker of hope. Elvire must succeed.

She closed her eyes and let the tears flow.

A shout roused her from a dream. Relieved to escape the dark shadow of foreboding lurking in the back of her mind, Alleyne stretched, rubbing her arms to dispel the goosebumps. When had she fallen asleep? The candle by her bedside had burnt down three notches – three hours had passed since Elvire's escape.

The temperature in the chamber chilled her limbs. Another shout rang out. She sat and blew out the candle. Her icy feet sought and found her slippers and she went to the window, unfastening the latch of the shutters with trembling fingers. She pulled the shutters open just wide enough to peek outside.

The moon stood high above the manor and the rains had abated. The rain would have slowed down Elvire's journey but the moon might betray her whereabouts. Alleyne sent a quick prayer heavenward for Elvire's safety while she eyed the three soldiers on horseback who had just entered the bailey. Their laughter and boisterous slapping of each others' backs made her skin crawl. She grimaced, then froze when a distinctive voice reached her ears – Marten's. A shiver ran down her spine. Where had he come from?

"That was merry, lads." He chuckled, sending his two companion into fits. They nearly fell off their horses, their bodies shaking with mirth.

"Aye, Marten. Especially when she punched your nose."

Marten's hand shot out to grip the other soldier's throat. Alleyne fell back, not wanting to attract their attention. With one eye she watched the despised mercenary shake the other man who had gone quiet.

"That...was not funny. However, this is."

"Stop, man! He was only joking," the third mercenary interjected.

Marten turned on him, dagger in hand. His adversary backed off, hands held high. "Hold it, Marten. You got her in the end."

Alleyne closed her eyes, her body shaking in convulsions. Were they talking about Elvire? She strained to catch more of their words.

"Aye, I did get her, didn't I? Oh, and how she squirmed. Bet she'd never been serviced like that. Some fun before the final–" Marten drew his hand holding the dagger in front of his throat.

Alleyne bit her lip and slowly pushed the shutters back into place with shaky hands. Hysteria welled up from inside as she slid onto the stone bench. He must be boasting about Elvire. Sobs racked her body. Will must have watched the maid leave, and sent his men after her.

Sweet Mother, help us!

***

Geoffrey left the sparse bedchamber clean and refreshed. His shirt and braies tidy, his stubble shaved, even his hair gleamed now he had washed out all the dirt from the roads. With his neat appearance came renewed hope that he would be allowed to leave for Perche.

He whistled as he walked up the muddy path to the castle outside the north gate, careful not to get his boots covered in filth again. Not for a second time would he allow Matilda to put him down in front of her court.

When he entered the great hall, Sheriff Miles waved him over. "I'm pleased to see you made an effort to look like a human being again, de Mortagne. I trust you remember Brian FitzCount?"

The tall, handsome lord in his company, dressed in a linen shirt with embroidered cuffs and well-cut braies, grinned.

"Aye, of course. My lord." Geoffrey inclined his head.

"Welcome to Oxford, Sir Geoffrey. You must forgive the empress's earlier outspokenness." He smiled affably. "She can be a little blunt sometimes but she doesn't mean to offend those who have her best interest at heart."

"No offence taken, my lord. I know well when she speaks the truth." He returned the smile, arms outstretched in acceptance. Brian FitzCount, everybody knew, was

Matilda's favoured supporter. Evil tongues hinted at a more intimate relationship. Geoffrey did not care for such gossip, especially as he knew the man to be the most selfless knight he had ever met. Fair, level and good-natured, Brian was also a force to be reckoned with when it came to battle.

But not quite as adept in strategy as the man leading Matilda into the hall. Robert, the Earl of Gloucester, her half-brother. With regret Geoffrey noted deep lines on Gloucester's face, signs of the continued struggle that took its toll on the man who would, by rights, be king, had he not been born a bastard. Yet the glow on his face as he took his half-sister to her seat spoke of pride and affection.

Geoffrey rose, wishing again Matilda would hurry. The earl deserved the peace that was bound to descend on the country following a swift takeover. They all deserved it.

"If you will excuse me." Brian moved towards the dais. Geoffrey raised an eyebrow. Perhaps the gossipmongers were right, but it was still none of his business.

Miles leaned over, his voice low. "I have spoken with the earl and he agreed to let you handle your affairs at home as a matter of urgency. In the unfortunate event of your brother's death, you will be required to swear fealty to the count of Perche. As you know, Perche is not an easy man to please. You'll have to tread carefully."

"I know. That is just another reason I have to go." Geoffrey bit his lip before he blurted out that visiting his liege lord was bound to bring up unwelcome memories. "I'm grateful for your intervention."

"You don't have to thank me, Geoffrey. Gloucester isn't just Matilda's half-brother – he's also the driving force behind her campaign, as you well know. He never lets anyone leave without reason. So he has a message for Matilda's husband Geoffroi, the Count of Anjou, that he doesn't entrust to any messenger. He wants you to deliver it in person."

Geoffrey snorted and shook his head, amazed at his own naivety. Of course those in power would use men like him whichever way they saw fit. But as Anjou was progressing through Normandy, laying waste to one strategic city after another, the man could be anywhere. Further delays. Geoffrey cursed this dreaded squabble for the throne.

They moved away from the masses gathering at the trestle tables to one of the benches cut into the wall. "Not surprising, really. What do they want Anjou to do now? And where is he?"

Miles grinned. "I'm not certain of his whereabouts but I'd suggest you start in Falaise, so you may not have to travel too far out of your way."

"Now that's a relief."

"No sarcasm, Geoffrey." Despite the sharp tone, the smile did not leave the sheriff's face. "Anjou is invited to join Matilda's journey across the country."

Geoffrey had to stop himself from laughing out loud. "When pigs fly!"

"Aye, that's what I think. But Gloucester is convinced Anjou will listen this time. After all, he is to become consort of a queen. Like it or not."

Geoffrey's response died on his lips when he saw a man at the door, blood trickling from a gash at his temple, running down his cheek onto muddy armour. He was trying to shake off the sentries and scanned the room, wild eyes finally meeting his.

Dread settled in Geoffrey's stomach as he mumbled a quick excuse to Miles and took off after the man now being dragged from the room.

Ancel.

***

Alleyne pulled the shawl tighter around her shoulders. The spring breeze still chilled her even though sunlight burst through the window. She sat on the stone bench and let her gaze sweep over the bailey thronging with men. The mercenaries prepared for another outing, pushing her own guards out of the way.

The night of Elvire's departure, Will locked Alleyne in

her chamber. He had wrestled the key from her hand, shoved her to the floor and slammed the door before she could scramble up to stop him. She swallowed back the bile that rose in her throat each time she thought of him now. Not that he kept her company, for which she was grateful.

How had she ever considered him a friend? A suitor?

She had searched for a means of escape but found none. The window was too high, the sheer drop into the bailey fatal. A soldier with a drawn sword accompanied the servants who brought her food she barely touched. Her only distraction had been watching the bailey. For the past fortnight, large numbers of men had been leaving the manor at first light, to return only late at night. They brought no prisoners, no game. What were they doing?

She craned her neck to get a better view of the guard at the gate. She had not seen Ancel in a sennight, and her concern for his safety grew stronger. She bit her lip, ignoring the pain as she dug her teeth deeper into her flesh. Had the soldiers killed him?

Surely, if Elvire had succeeded in her escape, Geoffrey would have arrived by now. She held her breath. The thought of him refusing to help was unbearable. Tears stung her eyes.

A deceptive calm settled on the manor after the mercenaries departed. Daily life began later now, with many villeins not coming to the manor any more at all. And when they did, 'twas only the men who came. She had not seen a woman from her village in weeks. Was that what the soldiers were doing? Attacking her tenants? Raping the women?

She shuddered at the thought of her people in danger. Danger she had inflicted upon them. Her guilt was as large, no, even larger than Will's. Hot fury raged inside her, the pounding of her heart loud in her ears. She sent a prayer heavenward in the fervent hope Geoffrey remembered the bond between them which she had denied him.

The creaking of the gate pulled her from her thoughts. Resigned that just another villein arrived to barter goods, she barely glanced in that direction. Then her breath froze in her lungs.

Geoffrey.

She blinked hard. Had she conjured him up? Was this some kind of witchcraft? She closed her eyes and crossed herself, sending a quick prayer heavenward. Then she opened her eyes again, only to stare at the man seated atop his fiery stallion. It was him, accompanied by his sergeant; what was his name? Guy.

Instinctively, Alleyne ran to the door, only to remember as she lifted the latch that it remained solidly locked.

She spun on her heel and raced back to the narrow window, leaning out as far as she could.

Just as she was about to shout his name, her tongue stilled. Will stood below her, near the door to the hall, with two of his men bearing crossbows aimed at Geoffrey and Guy, arrows nocked. If she called out now, Will's men would kill them. Swiftly she withdrew, holding her breath to hear.

"What do you want?" Will's voice was like ice.

"I was passing," Geoffrey drawled, his stance relaxed. "And I thought to visit the lady Alleyne. Is she–?"

"She's unwell and doesn't receive visitors. Now I'd leave if I were you."

"Well, as I'm here now I'd like to share the famous Bellac hospitality. Or is her steward incapacitated as well?"

Alleyne winced at the mention of Roger's name. Did Geoffrey somehow know of the steward's death? Hope rose within her chest.

"I'm afraid so. The old man fell down the stairs. At his age a fall like that is fatal."

Geoffrey crossed himself, his face serious. Alleyne balled her hands into fists and bit her knuckles, else she would cry out, praying Will would disappear.

"God rest his soul, poor man. Still, you won't deny weary travellers a refreshment, would you?"

"Leave, Geoffrey! My patience is wearing thin. The sooner you're out of my sight the better."

"I still want to see—"

"Am I not making myself clear?" Will's voice turned to a snarl, his body tensed. His hand went to the pummel of his sword. "You won't see her and you won't get inside. Now I wish you godspeed." Will turned his back on Geoffrey and disappeared into the hall, leaving his two crossbowmen to watch them leave.

Alleyne kept her gaze on Geoffrey. He scanned the grounds, clearly in no haste. This was her only chance. She jumped forward, banging the shutter against the inside wall, the racket alerting him instantly. His head shot up and their eyes met.

"Geoffrey, help!" She yelled from the core of her soul. All the desperation, the pain she had suffered, drained from her as her body convulsed. She gripped the window ledge for strength to stay upright and let the tears flow. "Help me!"

"Alleyne."

Two bolts shot past his head and he pulled his shield up in front of him. Warning shots. If they had wanted to kill him, they would not have missed. She had to let him go. Fear gripped her heart. If he stayed, Will's men would kill him right here, in front of her eyes.

"Go, Geoffrey. Go!" Tears streamed down her face. All her hope shattered as he turned Feu and headed for the gate. He sent her a final glance, a promise hidden behind his burning gaze.

The sound of spurs hit the floor outside her chamber. The key grated in the lock.

In a final effort, she raised a shaky hand in farewell. "Don't forget me," she whispered.

Geoffrey spurred Feu through the gate, Guy at his heels, just as another volley of bolts flew after them. Alleyne stared at the spot where her only hope had just disappeared, until strong hands pulled her away from the window, and threw her on the bed.

As she looked up, Will's eyes were wild with fury. His hand lashed out and hit her cheek, sending her tumbling onto the stone floor. She touched her stinging cheek. Her hand came away with a smudge of blood. The ruby ring on his index finger had cut her. Her body numb with grief, but beyond care, she cast him a defiant glance.

He raised himself to his full height. "You're going to pay for this."

Chapter Eleven

Alleyne's eyes haunted Geoffrey, their shine drowned by tears. Damn Will! He should never have left her alone with the man. 'Twas his pride that had led to her being kept prisoner in her own home.

They had retreated into the forest to where Ancel and a small band of his men waited. The captain's face was contorted with rage, his usually cheerful manner abandoned. He pulled a leather flask from his saddle bag, removed the stopper and pushed it into Geoffrey's hand. Geoffrey took a deep draught and returned the flask, his mind made up. When Ancel's gaze met his, he knew they were thinking the same.

"Are you sure your man will open the side gate for us? How will he know?"

"Because he's on his way back in now." Ancel pointed at a muscular, tall man, bushy brows drawn together, who stood nearby holding the reins of a piebald gelding. The blacksmith. Clearly, he awaited his orders. When Ancel nodded to him, the blacksmith mounted and slowly cantered in the direction of the manor.

"I have instructed him to unlock the side entrance once the rabble has fallen asleep. We're certain d'Arques is unaware of this door. It's hidden neatly behind the smithy. Cook is to add a stronger dose of hops to the ale tonight, so the men should sleep soundly."

Geoffrey smirked. "Good work, Ancel. That should ensure a safe escape." Will often refrained from drink but, if needed, he would deal with the knight personally. Anticipation grew within him. They would rescue Alleyne.

Not daring to light a fire, he camped with the other men

in a clearing deep in the forest. He must take Alleyne to a safe place. His house in Gloucester was too close. Will would find her in a matter of days. Matilda's court was too fickle and she was still not established enough in her power to ensure the safety of a wealthy heiress. Even an heiress temporarily robbed of her inheritance.

Bellac remained in Will's hands for the time being. Geoffrey shook his head and banged his fist into the dry ground. He did not have enough men and it could take weeks, nay months, if Will forced him to besiege Bellac. With Will's reinforcements secure within, the manor was too well defended.

Around him, men-at-arms dozed, whispering as not to alert Will's mercenaries. Noise carried far at night and Geoffrey was grateful for the thick needle trees that ensured the duty guards on Bellac's walkway did not spot them.

He took a draught of ale from his flask and leaned back against the trunk of a beech tree. Lulled by the soft swaying of branches, he closed his eyes. Alleyne's face appeared in front of him almost immediately, her dark eyes imploring him to help her. Not only had he given his oath to her father, he realised he could not bear to leave her with Will. The man would break her. Hatred fuelled Geoffrey's blood as it pounded its way through his body. Alleyne had chosen Will, and now she paid for it with her life. Geoffrey clenched, then slowly unclenched his fist. He could not allow Will to win this time.

Yet where could he take her? Where would she be safe from Will's clutches? His eyes opened sharply.

Perche.

He would take her to his family manor. Will would never suspect he subjected Alleyne to a channel crossing and a gruelling ride both sides of the water. And by the time Geoffrey had dealt with family matters, he would find a way to regain her inheritance.

"Ancel?" He waved the captain over. "I have a plan."

***

Alleyne shivered despite the warmth of the sheepskins she had wrapped around her. Her heart pounded in her ears at a speedy rate, sending spasms through her body. She clenched her fists to stop the shaking but to no avail.

Will had finally left her lying on her floor. The memory increased her shivers and she snuggled deeper under the covers. Her arms hurt where she had defended herself against his superior strength. They would be covered in black spots on the morrow. Her cheek swollen, she lay on her other side, careful not to put pressure on the sensitive skin. Will had pushed her, hit her when she could not avoid his fists. But somehow she had escaped the worst. Something had happened that she could not comprehend.

"Damn you, whore."

Will's words rang in her ears. She was no whore. Despite his pitiful attempts he had not-

Alleyne's eyes flew open. That was it! She sent a quick prayer of thanks to the Virgin, certain that the Lady had kept her safe. Whatever it was men did when they forced themselves on women, he had not been able to do it. Tears pricked her eyes as her breathing steadied and her heart rate slowed.

She wet her dry lips and closed her eyes again. Moments later heavy steps halted outside her door. The key ground in the lock and the door banged against the wall. She pretended to sleep, hoping to delay his revenge. Spurs scraped on the floor as the footfall came closer. Surely he would go away.

"Alleyne, sweeting." Will's honeyed tone sent shivers down her spine. His deception scared her. She did not react, keeping her lids firmly shut, breathing steadily.

A strong hand dug into her shoulder, shaking her roughly. "Woman! I know you're awake." She opened her eyes to find him hovering over the edge of her bed.

"What do you want?" Her voice hesitant, she could not hide her trepidation. Had he come to continue where he left off?

Will grinned, a wolfish snarl. She held her breath.

Releasing her, he took a step back. Only then did she notice his other hand hidden behind his back. What was all that about?

"I have something for you, sweet lady. Something that might just stop you from seeking an escape." His grin widened.

She swallowed hard. "What do you mean?"

His hand shot forth and he dropped a bundle of fabric on the bed. Her eyes widened.

Elvire's travel cloak, ripped, covered in congealed blood.

She recoiled, pushing herself to the other side of the bed. Dizziness overcame her as the truth sank in. She shielded her face with her hands, fighting nausea. "No!"

Will's hysterical laughter echoed in her ears as he left the chamber and slammed the door shut.

***

Silence surrounded him as Geoffrey stood next to Ancel, barely half a mile from the manor. Their small band of men hovered behind them, nodding to unspoken orders. Alfred held the horses' reins, as Guy and two of Ancel's men followed them. The lad had joined them, keen to help, after the blacksmith returned to the manor.

Will had not bothered to send his men after them. Geoffrey shook his head. The man was so certain in his own capabilities that he did not waste time chasing enemies. Well, they would give him a surprise he would not forget anytime soon.

He glanced at the sky where thick clouds gathered. The perfect cover. He only prayed it did not rain. His gaze met Ancel's as he gave the sign to move. Like him, the other men crouched low in the muddy field as they approached the palisade. Not taking his eye off the manor, Geoffrey prayed their ruse would work. It was their only chance of saving Alleyne. They must not fail.

Not a sound came from behind the wall rising high above him. He followed Ancel's lead to a small side door hidden from view by a double wall. With little time to admire the ingenuity, he held his breath as Ancel turned the round handle. The captain swore softly but after a final twist the heavy oak door creaked open. Surely the grating sound would wake the manor? They stood still but all remained calm. The captain nodded, then pushed the door just wide enough for them to slide through one man at a time.

Once inside the bailey, they left the door ajar and halted in the shadows behind the sooty walls of the blacksmith's hut. Geoffrey unsheathed his sword and glanced around the corner. As his gaze swept the yard, he counted two sentries by the gate, and three men-at-arms pacing the allure. Ancel nudged his ribs and pointed to another two men staggering from the hall. They skidded down the steps, holding onto each other for support. Drunk and drugged. Geoffrey smiled, satisfied the ruse was working.

He waited until the two disappeared into the stables before he turned to the captain. "Where is that window you told me about?"

Ancel pointed at an opening that appeared barely wide enough to allow a child through. It was set into a wall several feet above the walkway but close enough to jump. "It's just big enough for us. It looks smaller from down here." Reading the hesitation in Geoffrey's eyes, Ancel grinned. "Trust me."

"There's no other way in apart from that, or the hall?" Geoffrey did not relish the thought of stretching high above the allure wall – easily spotted from anywhere on the walkway, and a fair way down to the ground either side of the palisade. "How do we deal with the men up there?"

Ancel's grin widened. "We don't." He nodded towards the far side of the yard. A boy emerged from the kitchen, a clay jug in one hand and several tankards in the other. He sauntered over to the gate where he was brusquely stopped. The soldiers took the jug and whacked the boy around the ear. The tankards clattered on the stone flags as the boy scurried back towards the kitchen. His glance their way was brief, but the line of bared teeth showed his mirth. Ancel gave a quick nod and the boy disappeared inside.

As Geoffrey turned his attention back to the gate, the three men-at-arms from the allure joined their mates, eager to get their hands on the steaming liquid to warm their insides from the chilly night air. Their loud jests as they clinked tankards made him sink deeper into the shadows. Such noise might raise Will's suspicion. Yet nobody came to check. Could Will be fooled so easily? Geoffrey dared hardly hope.

After what seemed a lifetime, the men slumped against the gate, their voices slurred and muted. At Geoffrey's signal, Guy slid around the front of the smithy and – as if just woken up – sauntered leisurely over to the men. Kicking the first with his toe, he paused for a reaction before he gagged the prone figure. He swiftly tied the man's hands and pulled him into the gatehouse.

"It's time." Ancel nodded, and together they hurried across the bailey, skirting the thin beams of torchlight. Swiftly they dragged the limp bodies inside, bound and gagged them, and took their weapons. Ancel removed all tankards and jugs from outside. The bailey was deserted.

Geoffrey led Guy and Ancel up the steps and, crouching to stay within the height of the palisade, rushed towards the window. The two remaining men in their party returned to the side gate, waiting.

Geoffrey eyed the narrow, open gap of the window. His heart sank. He drew in his breath. Ancel was slimmer in size, more sinewy, and should have no problem getting through, as would Guy, but he? Having left his armour with the horses, he would still struggle. He was too broad.

"After you, my friend." He gestured to Ancel to lead the way. Using Guy's hands as a lever, the captain raised himself up to where the tips of the wooden stakes of the palisade met the window, balancing for a second before his hands and feet found firm ground inside the opening. He pushed through and waved.

"You stay here, Guy." Geoffrey gritted his teeth as his sergeant nodded. Ignoring Guy's grin, he heaved himself up like Ancel had before him. Briefly he fought nausea as he glanced down the outer side of the palisade. The drop meant certain death. He closed his eyes for an instant, then followed Ancel through the gap. As he had expected, his shoulders grazed the uncut walls, tearing at the fabric of his gambeson. He swore as he hunched his shoulders and squeezed through the opening.

Ancel had his back to him as Geoffrey quietly slid off the window ledge. They found themselves in the narrow corridor leading to the private quarters of Alleyne and Lord Raymond. Ancel put his forefinger to his mouth, gesturing towards a far door wherefrom raised voices reached them. "Lord Raymond's chamber. Now d'Arques's."

Geoffrey stood still, every sinew strained. "Will," he mouthed to Ancel. The captain nodded. Anger rose in Will's voice as he screamed abuse at a man muttering apologies.

It could not be any worse. Geoffrey's gaze travelled the short length of the corridor but only three doors led from it. Two were private quarters, with Alleyne's and her father's rooms adjacent to each other. He stared at the third door.

As if reading his mind, Ancel whispered, "The solar. Nobody should be in there. We can hide in there until d'Arques calms down."

Geoffrey agreed. As they stepped forward, an object crashed into Lord Raymond's door. An instant later, it flew open.

"Get out of my sight!" A rotund man stumbled backwards, landing on his backside on the wooden floor, scrambling away from the door. His eyes, full of panic, met Geoffrey's.

***

Alleyne startled at the sound of something crashing against a wall. She sighed and sank back into the cushions, accustomed to Will's temper outbursts. The whole manor suffered when Will exploded. Which happened frequently. But that Cook shouted apologies was news to her. So far he had not quarrelled about the food, but perhaps Cook had disobeyed him and served boiled eels instead of the birds and game Will had ordered for himself lately. As if Lent meant nothing.

Heavy steps on the stairs told her Cook was making his way back to the kitchen. Then silence descended once more. She closed her eyes, certain in the suspicion that Will had murdered Elvire. She should never have allowed her to leave. Elvire's death was on Will's conscience, but it also pricked hers. Tears stung behind swollen lids. She must avenge her.

A moment later a scratching sound on the door roused her. In the faint light of the candle beside her bed, she tiptoed to the window seat and picked up the jug of wine Cook had brought her earlier that night. Not wanting to dull her senses, she had refrained from drinking. But, wondering about Will's outburst, she sniffed the content yet could not detect anything untoward. He must have been dissatisfied with the food. She opened the shutter, relieved to see nobody about, and slung the liquid into the bailey.

When she heard the key softly turn, she hurried to stop behind the door, jug firmly grasped in both hands, her breath coming out in short bursts. She would show him this time. The door eased open an inch. This was most peculiar behaviour from Will. He usually barged in, especially when he suffered from one of his moods. Impatience tore at her nerves. She raised the jug above her head, poised to strike. A head full of hair black as night appeared through the gap. One of Will's other mercenaries, wanting a piece of the pie?

Alleyne's arms came down with force just as the intruder turned and swerved. The jug slipped from her grasp and was inches from the ground when it was deftly caught by a strong hand. Her heart in her mouth, she did not believe her eyes.

Geoffrey.

Her heart pounded in her ears.

The under-sheriff pushed himself through the door, followed swiftly by Ancel. She could have sung with joy but the muted whoosh of the door closing gently brought her back to reality.

"Geoffrey," she whispered as her outstretched arm sought his.

He passed the jug to Ancel before his hands clasped hers. "Shhh."

Worry written in his eyes, she swallowed hard and blinked away tears. "You have come."

"We must hurry." Ancel's urgent voice reached her and realisation finally hit her. She would be free. Her heart raced.

Geoffrey smoothed a tear from her cheeks, then looked around. "Where is your cloak?"

She pointed towards the clothing hooks and he took the woollen mantle, wrapping her inside its warmth. "I'll also need my–"

"There's no time for anything else, my lady. We have to get out now before Will knows something's afoot."

"Why? What's going on?"

Ancel grinned, keeping an eye on the door. "Cook drugged them all."

Hysteria welled up inside her and she stifled a giggle. Was it really that easy to escape Will's clutches? She glanced around her bed chamber, the familiarity of each item hitting her. Sadness washed over her. Would she ever see this room again? With a final nod, she turned. Ancel's hand touched the latch when another door was thrown open and spurs hit the wooden floor in the corridor outside.

"Cook!" Will's slurred words made her shudder. "Where are you? You'll pay for this."

Horrified, she held her breath, not daring to look at either man. None of them moved. As Will's steps receded down the stairs, Ancel nudged the door open, checked the corridor, and slipped through.

"Make haste!" Geoffrey pushed her out, towards the window at the far end. Why would they..?

Sweet Lord!

"You don't want me to–"

***

Geoffrey's smile was strained. They had little time to lose. "Aye, my lady. You will crawl through this window, or stay with Will?"

She shook her head, eyes wide in fear.

Geoffrey kept an eye on the stairs while Ancel squeezed through the gap. A moment later the captain whispered an order from the outside.

"Go!" Geoffrey repeated, sensing Alleyne's hesitation. He cursed all headstrong women – and this one in particular. "Forgive me."

"Why?"

He wrapped one arm around her waist and the other behind her knees, lifting her high so her feet found the ledge. She gave a little yelp which he prayed did not filter down into the hall. When she had gained her balance, he let go. "Ancel awaits you on the other side. Hurry!"

He watched her shuffle forward, smiling as she shoved her gown down her legs in an attempt at propriety. When she reached the edge, she gasped.

For an instant his heart skipped a beat. What if she lost her footing and fell over the fence? He closed his eyes, but hearing Ancel asking her in a soothing tone to reach out to him reassured Geoffrey.

Will's raised voice echoed from the hall. Geoffrey winced as crashing noises followed. Will must have another of his infamous outbursts, destroying Bellac's furniture. As the sounds grew closer, he glanced at the window to find Alleyne had jumped. Ignoring the lump in his throat, he heaved himself onto the ledge and crept forward, his shoulders hunched, just as footsteps sounded on the stairs.

"I'll find the whoreson. And when I do, he won't escape punishment." Clearly, Cook was hiding from his new master. Most likely he would not return.

As Will's head appeared at the top of the stair, their eyes meeting for an instant, Geoffrey pushed himself out of the window. Landing with a heavy thud on the wooden planks of the allure, he rushed after Ancel and Alleyne who had already reached the steps.

Down in the bailey, he glanced up. Will leaned over the window edge, glaring at him. "Traitor!"

"To the side gate, quick." Geoffrey took Alleyne's hand and pulled her after him, past the sooty walls of the smithy.

"Guards!" Will's voice echoed from above across the deserted bailey. "Stop them!"

Worried they had overlooked any men-at-arms, Geoffrey scanned the yard. Nobody appeared. He nodded, satisfied. By the time Will reached the door, they would have gained a safe distance.

Outside, Alfred waited with their horses while Ancel's men secured the gate behind them. Geoffrey mounted and reached for Alleyne. Large, questioning eyes stared at him. "Give me your hand. Quick." The sound of crashing doors reached them and Alleyne swiftly took his arm and sat sideways in front of him. At Ancel's signal, the party galloped towards the forest. His arms firmly draped around her, holding the reins tightly, Geoffrey urged Feu forward.

Only near the line of trees did he dare turn to see Bellac's gate thrown open. Will stood, waving his sword in the air while three guards clumsily readied their horses. By the time they had completed their task, under much shouting from their lord, Geoffrey disappeared into the forest last.

Darkness surrounded them as they rode at slower pace, their eyes adjusting to the faint light. Dawn was breaking but the light did not reach into the shelter of the trees.

"I don't think they'll come after us." Ancel turned to look around him. "They're too unsteady."

Remembering Will's determination, Geoffrey shook his head. "He'll make them. We have to move."

"Will is going to kill you," Alleyne said, echoing his thoughts. "And me."

Geoffrey stared at the woman leaning back against his chest. She kept her head high, her gaze straight. He nodded. "Aye, if he catches us, that is."

His words were meant to cheer the sombre mood but

Alleyne remained quiet. The girl had lost everything apart from her life. And even that was not worth anything if Will caught her. Thinking of Lord Raymond, he wondered again who was behind the attack – if it was Will, or de Guines, whom Alleyne had suspected. His bet was on Will.

A faint glow showed the path in front of their small group and they rode in double file, with Ancel leading, Guy and Alfred following, and the two men-at-arms covering the back. Shouts alerted them to their followers and Geoffrey ordered Ancel to speed up, a dangerous undertaking as he could barely make out the ground. Alleyne's body shivered against him. She wrapped her cloak tighter around her.

"Damn," he muttered, nestling her closer against him. "I'll find you a blanket when we finally stop."

"I'm fine, thank you. You…you came." Her voice filled with wonder, she turned her head.

He swallowed, and sent her a quick smile. "I couldn't really leave you, could I?"

She lowered her head. "It surprised me a little after our last encounter. I didn't exactly appear…grateful."

Did he detect a scarlet tint in her cheek? Must be the faint light of dawn. "I understand. I know from the past that Will can be persuasive when he sets his mind on something, or someone. We have a long way ahead of us, my lady."

"Do we? I assume we approach Matilda?"

He gave a short laugh. "I'm afraid not, my lady. The empress is not interested in minor squabbles as she prepares for her entry into London. And Will has the advantage of holding Bellac."

"But–"

"I'm afraid we have to go into hiding for a while."

"Into hiding?" She held her breath, her body stiffening. "Where?"

"Perche."

Chapter Twelve

Alleyne huddled into thick fur coverlets. The meagre shelter provided on the ship barely held off the chilly April gusts. She shivered. When she had last dared emerge from the feeble canvas cover, sleet stung her skin. Keen to find out how much longer she was bound to endure this hell, she lost her balance as her feet slid on the treacherous slush. Tears mingling with the downpour, she could not even muster a smile when Geoffrey and Guy helped her up. Geoffrey had carried her inside again, and buried her chilled body in this bed of furs. Before she had a chance to enquire about their trip, he had vanished again, leaving her to ponder on her losses.

Perche. It might as well have been the moon. The late outburst of winter, in the middle of spring, made their journey difficult. At the same time, Geoffrey withdrew from her. His responses – when they came – were short and vague. As if she was a hindrance. Which, of course, she was. She burrowed herself further into the warmth of the coverlets.

They had left Ancel in Gloucester, where he searched for potential sightings of Elvire. Alleyne prayed he would send word of the maid's safety and, if he found her, they would follow. If Elvire was alive… The vision of the blood-smeared cloak Will had shown her made her shudder.

For the moment Alleyne's fate was sealed. Father dead, Bellac lost. Anger welled up inside her at the memory of Will. Had he always been so ambitious, so uncaring? Had Father known and kept her from Will, aware of his flaws? 'Twould seem so. She had blindly trusted Will, allowed him to take over her home without any hesitation. Perhaps it was not surprising Geoffrey treated her with distant politeness. He had done nothing wrong by assuming his duty was done and she was safe in Will's care and protection. She had sent him on his way, insulted his skills at resolving Father's murder, doubted his allegiance.

Now, deceived by Will – the man she had trusted instead – Geoffrey was her only hope. She closed her eyes as shame washed through her. Waves crashing against the hull made her sink deeper into the furs, the regular whoosh eventually sending her into restless slumber.

The canvas flap opened. Alleyne startled and peeked out from the furs. She blinked as Geoffrey crouched next to her pallet. "It's nearly time, my lady. You'll be relieved to hear we're nearing land. Barfleur harbour will soon be in sight."

She smiled. Tonight she would sleep in a proper bed. In a dry room.

"Are we going to stay there for a night or two?"

Please!

He stood, nodding. "Yes, we'll rest for a couple of days while I await news. Then we have to move on."

"News of what?" Puzzled, she stared at him as she pushed the covers away.

"Nothing to concern yourself about." As if sensing her fears, he added, "It might be weeks till we hear from Ancel. All you can do in the meantime is pray." He turned, lifted the flap and secured it again behind him.

Alleyne kicked the covers off. Why had he rescued her if he clearly thought her an inconvenience? He had taken her with him out of duty, mayhap even pity. She was but a hindrance in his work. She should have approached the empress directly after all. Now it was too late. Now she was approaching the wrong side of the channel. Normandy. A strange new world for her.

She stilled. Of course, that was it. Matilda's husband. She would seek help from the Count of Anjou. Then Geoffrey would be free of the burden of looking after her.

The ride from the harbour to the inn Geoffrey had chosen sorely stretched Alleyne's already frayed nerves. Seamen, dressed in filthy rags, whistled as she rode past, only silenced by a flash of Geoffrey's blade; crates were thrown across her path; at the entrance to a waterside inn, a buxom whore exposed her breasts to their party, the garish paint on the woman's face pronouncing, rather than hiding, her age; the stink of decaying fish hung in the air, making Alleyne retch. If only she could have closed her eyes against this onslaught but, riding between Geoffrey and Guy, she still had to watch what went on around her.

Finally the bustle of the harbour receded as they turned from High Street into a quiet lane. Whitewashed cottages lined the street, and only a clean sign – its black letters shiny against white – revealed the inn hidden at the far end. At first glance, the Mermaid's Haven seemed like an ordinary town house, only several times the size of its neighbouring buildings. Buckets bursting with crocuses in an array of colours, the petals shivering under a thin layer of sleet, sat either side of the solid oak door.

At their approach, a boy appeared through a narrow arch and took their reins. "Good day, Sir Geoffrey. Madame."

Clearly Geoffrey had stayed here before. "Hello, Jean. How fares your mistress?"

"Madame Claude is well, my lord." He grinned, exposing a row of gaps between white teeth. "She'll be delighted to see you again."

"No doubt." Geoffrey chuckled and dismounted.

Alleyne's heart skipped a beat. She startled, wondering for an instant what linked Geoffrey to the landlady. Had they been lovers..? No, she was certainly not jealous.

Guy helped Alleyne dismount, making sure she avoided to step on the dirtiest slush. He pushed the door open and immediately a comforting surge of heat embraced her. Alleyne stepped across the threshold into a small, clean serving room. Benches and tables stood in neat order, and a large fireplace dominated one wall, the flames dancing in the breeze. Geoffrey followed them inside. The fire calmed after he closed the door. The few customers sent them only a perfunctory glance.

Behind a long, wooden counter stood a woman of at least twice Alleyne's size. Unruly, curly hair escaped her kerchief as she mopped her brow. When she spotted them, a wide smile spread across the chubby features and she rushed forward with the power of a war horse. In an instant, Geoffrey was engulfed in a close hug which he returned in kind.

"My, it's been too long." The landlady took a step back, her hands clasping Geoffrey's, and looked him up and down.

He laughed. "Aye, nigh on five years since I last visited. And you haven't aged a day."

"Liar!" Claude sent him a coquettish smile, turned and sauntered back towards the bar with a swing of her ample hips. "I'm sure you're thirsty. I'll fetch a jug of my latest batch."

Alleyne watched in astonishment but Guy gestured her forward with an encouraging nod. "Take a seat by the fire, my lady."

"I bet it's still the best cider in Normandy you're making, Claude." Geoffrey shed his cloak, dropped it over a bench and held a chair out for Alleyne. "My lady, you're in for a treat."

Alleyne removed her mittens and her cloak and Guy draped it over another chair, to dry in the heat, before he straddled a nearby bench. Geoffrey sat in a large wooden chair close to hers, stretching his legs to the flames. She risked a glance at his attire. Like hers, his garments were sodden and grimy. Oh, how she craved a bath.

Claude arrived with a tray bearing a clay jug and three cups, and set it on the table next to Guy. As she poured, the sweet scent of hot cider reached Alleyne's nose. Claude handed her a cup and stood back, arms crossed.

"My best batch yet. I'm mightily proud of it." The landlady grinned as Alleyne took a tentative sip.

"Mmmhhh." The warmth spread through her while the

sweet scent of apple teased her senses. "This is wonderful, Madame, er, Claude."

The landlady's ample bosom shook as she giggled. "See, lass. I told you." Turning to Geoffrey, she said. "Will you need rooms?"

He nodded.

"Well, let me see what I can do. After all, unless you're married to the pretty lass, I need to find her a suitable room. Has she a maid?"

When Claude's gaze met hers, Alleyne shook her head. "My maid is–"

"Her maid couldn't make the crossing, Claude. Do you know of a girl who could assist?" Geoffrey's eyes roamed Alleyne's gown.

Claude clapped his shoulder. "Of course, I've just the girl to help the lady. My goddaughter Beatrice has assisted many a lady over the last year or two. I hope the lady finds this agreeable."

Alleyne nodded, grateful for Geoffrey's suggestion. "I'd be very happy to accept Beatrice's helping hand. Thank you."

"So be it. I'll send for her right away and have water heated for you." The landlady turned on her heel and disappeared through a side door.

"You'll be safe here." Geoffrey leaned back and closed his eyes, cradling his cup on his chest.

Alleyne sipped the potent cider again, watching him through narrowed lids. Lines furrowed his forehead, and signs of bags under his eyes revealed his restlessness. His hose was covered in mud, his hair unruly. He had not only pushed her, but also Guy and himself, to the limits. Now he finally relaxed but it would not be for long. Of that she was certain.

She had barely emptied her cup, her head feeling light as a feather, when Claude appeared again, a lanky girl of no more than fifteen years at her side. "My lady, this is Beatrice." The girl curtsied, a blush settling on her cheeks. "She'll help you while you stay with us. But first of all, your bath awaits in your room."

A bath! Alleyne smiled, at her happiest in weeks.

***

Geoffrey woke to the screeching of seagulls. His gaze raked the narrow chamber. A sliver of daylight streamed through the shutters. On a pallet near the door, Guy lay snoring. Geoffrey grinned. Their clothes were scattered across the floor, discarded without thought after several jugs of Claude's delicious cider.

He heaved himself from the bed and his grin froze on his lips. A shaft of lightning pierced his eyes and his temples throbbed. He moaned. He could not afford the after-effects of too much drink on a busy day like this. With a sigh, he sat, closing his eyes and cradling his pounding head in his hands.

"My, my."

Geoffrey prised his lids open to find Guy staring at him, a slow smile turned into a chuckle, then a grimace. "Oh, ouch!"

Geoffrey sniggered and pushed himself from the bed, letting his crumpled shirt fall loose. "A fine pair we are, Guy." He grinned down at his sergeant who had lain back, covering his eyes with his arm. "Time to rise. Now, which are my clothes?" He ruffled through the items on the floor and picked up his hose. Where were his boots? Ah, yes, at the bottom of the bed.

Guy sputtered as Geoffrey nudged his side with a bare toe. "Steady, Geoffrey! My head's spinning."

"Aye, that's Claude's incomparable cider. The only way to get rid of it is by starting off with the same."

"What?" Guy sat up and blinked. "I swear, I'll never touch that Devil's stuff again."

Geoffrey laughed. He secured his hose and grabbed his boots. The filth stuck to the soles reached his nostrils. No time to dither, though. Accepting that needs must, he pulled them on and tied the laces tightly. Then he stepped over

Guy's pallet to throw open the shutters. The glare of the morning sun blinded him for a moment before his eyes adjusted to the light. He dipped his hands, grimy with mud from their journey, into the bowl of water on a bench below the window. The water was freezing, sending a surge of energy through his body. He took the bar of soap from the dish next to the bowl and lathered his hands, frowning at the muddy mess he created. Had he forgotten to wash last night? He shook his head. The evening had been a blur.

They descended the stairs together. As expected, the floorboards were scrubbed to the core. The scent of lavender wafted through the corridor. Guy opened the door to the inn's main room. It was deserted at this hour. Only Alleyne sat by the fire, giggling to something Claude said. Geoffrey coughed.

"Good morrow, lads." The landlady turned, the twinkle in her eyes unmistakeable. "Have you slept well?" She clapped her hands and a maid polishing the bar dropped the cloth and disappeared into the kitchen.

"Good morrow. And yes, too well." Geoffrey returned her cheerful greeting, deliberately ignoring the sting behind his eyes. "I fear our chamber has become quite messy. And dirty."

"Men!" Claude winked at Alleyne. "They always keep the maids busy. I'll see where your food is to break your fast." She tutted as she walked past him, the laughter in her eyes not subsiding.

"Good morning." Geoffrey bowed before he dropped into the chair opposite Alleyne's. "I hope your night was quiet."

"It was most pleasant." She beamed, a relaxed happiness radiating from her Geoffrey had not seen before. She wore a clean gown of pale yellow linen, a thin, embroidered belt emphasising her narrow waist. The colour suited her well, bringing out auburn highlights in her hair falling loose over her shoulders. Claude must have arranged for the change of clothes. He must thank her suitably for looking after the lass so well.

"I'm relieved to hear. After our torturous journey, a good night's sleep can work wonders."

"And a bath," she observed, a becoming blush creeping into her cheeks. "Madame Claude is so helpful. How do you know each other?" She leaned towards the nearest table and picked an apple from a bowl.

Geoffrey swallowed when she bit into the shiny red orb. A trickle of juice slid down her chin and it took all his willpower not to bend forward and scoop it up with his thumb. Then the moment was gone.

"Oh, I'm sorry." She pulled a linen square from her sleeve and dabbed her chin. When she met his gaze, she burst into a giggle, quickly stifled by her hand.

He inclined his head and smiled. A jug of cider would just do to douse the sudden urge racing through his body. Where was Claude when he could have done with a distraction?

"I've known Claude since our childhood. She grew up in Mortagne, my home village, but married a brewster here in Barfleur. Shortly after they wed, they opened the Mermaid's Haven and discovered she had a dab hand at making cider. So, instead of weak ale available everywhere else, this inn serves the best cider in all Normandy." He paused when she took another bite, his eyes darting from hers to the apple.

He coughed, trying to regain his composure. "Sadly, a score years ago her husband died of a fever. To make ends meet, she had to keep the inn going alone and has done so ever since, with firm permission from the guilds. No man is allowed to tell this woman what not to do."

Alleyne returned his smile. "She is a formidable lady, I agree. I'm pleased to have her on my side."

At that moment the kitchen door opened and Claude returned, clutching a jug and balancing three cups. Behind her, a maid followed with a tray bearing hot porridge and a plate with slices of roast duck.

The morning had just improved. Now all he needed was news of Anjou's whereabouts, so he could pass on Matilda's message.

***

Alleyne breathed in deeply. She opened her eyes again to the glaring sunlight reflected on the water. Soft waves rushed in, their white crests collapsing as they swept across the soft, white sand.

"This is wonderful, Beatrice." She smiled at the girl sitting next to her. "You are fortunate to live in such a beautiful place."

"I believe so, my lady." The maid nodded as she furrowed her bare toes into the sand.

They rested on a blanket after a gentle stroll along the beach, away from the bustling, narrow lanes of Barfleur. A burly man stayed out of earshot but within reach, clearly keen not to let them out of his sight. No doubt, a warning from Madame Claude was enough to make even such a large man, ordered to watch over them, quiver.

"Look, another ship leaves for England." Beatrice jumped up, pointing her finger at a large vessel exiting the harbour. They watched as the cog steered safely through the rocks that dotted the harbour entrance. "This time it's a bigger one."

Alleyne nodded, shielding her eyes from the sun as she strained to see the flag. 'Twas none she recognised, though no doubt it carried a person of high standing. Matilda's reinforcements?

Her gaze fell on the sharp edges of the rocks protruding from the seabed. She shuddered despite the warm spring sun. What a cruel twist of fate had brought them here! Had it not been for the White Ship's drunken crew, King Henry's only legitimate son, William, would have ascended the English throne on his demise. Peace would reign across England and Normandy. Instead, the lives lost here that fateful night paled into insignificance over the number of people who had been killed since then.

She straightened and brushed the sand from her gown. "I think we must return. I need a few essentials for my journey onward. Do you know a good seamstress?" She stepped off the blanket and waited until the maid had shaken it out and folded it neatly. Their watch rose, too, ready to escort them back.

Later that afternoon, Alleyne threw herself into the chair by the fire, vacant as if it had been reserved for her. The guest room was bustling with patrons, good natured banter and shouting so different from the silence that morning.

Beatrice giggled, nearly losing her balance with a large basket she carried with both hands. "I'll take these to your room, my lady." She nodded and darted out the door connecting the room to the part of the house which held the bedrooms.

Alleyne shed her cloak and stretched her legs towards the fire. The sunshine had been warm but the breeze that blew through the narrow lanes of Barfleur still held a chill. Most likely 'twas the same in all seaside towns.

A beaming Claude, having spotted their entrance, came over with a jug. She poured some of the steaming, sweet liquid and handed her the cup. "Here's something to warm your blood, my lady. I see you've been busy?"

Alleyne nodded, cradling the warm cup in her hands. "Yes, I've made some purchases and visited the wonderful seamstress Beatrice suggested. I needed new gowns. After all, I can't impose on your kind generosity too much."

Claude shook her head, her eyes twinkling. "Nonsense, chérie. You're not imposing at all. The pleasure is all ours."

After a sip of the cider, its crisp scent lingering in her nose, she cast the landlady an appreciative glance. "I'm immensely grateful for everything you've done. And you don't even know me."

"You're a friend of Sir Geoffrey – which makes you a friend of mine." Colour rose in the older woman's plump cheeks. Was she blushing? It appeared the formidable goodwife had a soft spot for the under-sheriff.

"Thank you. I'm honoured." Alleyne smiled, then remembered the man himself. "By the way, where is he?"

"He's at the castle. Been gone all day."

"The castle? What is happening there?"

"I believe he's waiting for news. Something to do with the Count of Anjou's whereabouts. Sounds like he'll go after that Devil." A shadow crossed Claude's face and she quickly topped up Alleyne's cup. "I'm certain he'll be back soon." She shuffled back to the bar, muttering to herself.

Alleyne's gaze rested on the fire, sparks flying up in a merry dance. So Geoffrey was looking for the count. What a stroke of good fortune!

So was she.

Chapter Thirteen

Geoffrey shrugged his shoulders. A silent nod to Guy sent them on their way. The wooden gate of the castle closed behind them as they steered their horses back towards the town.

Frustration raged through him. He gritted his teeth and glared at the path ahead. He had wasted a full day on empty promises. The messenger was supposed to arrive with news of Anjou's location, but the man never came. The residents had eyed him, whispering, clearly wondering why a nobleman from Perche, in the guise of an English under-sheriff, hovered within their walls. His temper flared.

"By the Cross! Why does it take so long to establish where Anjou is hiding? The man is all over Normandy, taking bites out of Stephen's territory here and there. Someone must know!" He shook his head as he urged Feu into the sunset.

"I think the count's tactics make it difficult for–"

"Don't make excuses for him, Guy! The man leaves an impression wherever he goes." Geoffrey clenched his teeth else he lost hold of himself completely.

"I'm not making excuses, Geoffrey. Just stating facts. That's why you take me along all the time, remember?" His voice held a sarcastic note. "To keep you calm."

Geoffrey chuckled despite himself. Guy was right. But his patience was wearing thin. While he traipsed after the Count of Anjou, his brother lay dying. Perhaps Bertrand was already dead.

But guilt about his brother was not the only reason for Geoffrey's foul mood. He had left Alleyne alone all day. They had parted after breaking their fast. Fact was, he was grateful for the distance. It cleared his head after their last encounter. He was in no position to woo her, nor the kind of man to take advantage of her. Which was exactly what he had considered that morning.

No, Alleyne was a lady in mourning, bereft of support, cheated by a so-called friend, in search of a way to regain her inheritance. And he was only by her side to help. Nothing more.

Yet he had left her alone all day, in a foreign town, a fishing port. What if she had met with undesirables, with soldiers, or sailors? His heartbeat drummed in his ears, the thought unbearable. Then he shook it off. No, Claude would take care of her. She promised. And Claude never broke a promise. Alleyne was probably enjoying the change, the respite.

Outside the Mermaid's Haven, Jean took the reins and led the horses through to the stables. Geoffrey scanned the lane but nothing struck him as untoward. If Will had an inkling of where they were heading, his men would have found them by now. Geoffrey assumed Will did not want to leave Bellac's grounds, just in case someone came to take it from him. He was quite likely fuming over Alleyne's escape but her value clearly did not warrant a pursuit. With Stephen jailed, and Matilda occupied with her progress, no-one asked twice about Will d'Arques taking over a small manor.

"You coming in?" Guy held open the door.

Geoffrey nodded, realising he had stopped outside, staring into the distance. "Aye." He stepped over the threshold.

The calm outside changed to a crescendo indoors. The room was packed; local dialects attacked his ears. Folk were worried about the Devil's advance – as they called the Count of Anjou's attacks. But not too worried to stay at home and barricade themselves in. The Cotentin peninsula was safe.

For now.

His eyes searched for Alleyne and he found her in her usual place, by the fireside. With Guy in tow, he weaved his way through the crowd, drawing curious glances. Then the men's attention drifted away again.

"My lady." He gave her a curt bow and settled into the vacant chair opposite. "My apologies to leave you on your own all day." He took an empty cup from the small table between them and filled it. The scent of spiced apple brought back memories he did not wish to explore. His head had pounded most of the day.

He looked up. In fact, he had half expected her to sulk, to reprimand him for his omission. But the gaze that met his was all sweetness and smiles.

"My day was good, my lord. Quite successful, in fact. I took a stroll by the seaside. Claude sent a man as big as a barrel to guard us. Then Beatrice and I visited a seamstress on Draper Lane after I'd purchased linen for two new gowns." She folded the needlework in her hand – an apron or something suchlike, no doubt Claude's – and placed it into the basket by her side. Seeing him frown, she laughed. "I carried coin sewn into my travel cloak. Elvire always reminded me of the necessity to be prepared."

He nodded. "Ah." Of course she would not leave home without money. Piqued she had not confided in him, he pursed his lips.

Leaning back, she cocked her head. "And how was your day?"

"Not as good as yours, it appears," he grunted. "Still waiting for that messenger. But I left word of where he can find me, so I can spend tomorrow with you."

"That's…" she hesitated, then a smile lit up her face, "wonderful, Sir Geoffrey. What are we going to do?"

He ignored the heat pounding through his veins at her smile. "I thought we could visit St Nicholas Cathedral. Or perhaps explore the coast?"

"How exciting!" A becoming flush rose in her cheeks. Since when did she react to his suggestions like this?

He frowned, quickly hiding it by sipping his cider. "Then that's what we shall do, my lady."

The day ahead suddenly seemed promising.

***

Having enjoyed the meal, Geoffrey reclined, cup in hand, unable to eat another morsel. Claude had excelled herself, serving up roast duck with crunchy root vegetables and freshly baked bread. The waffles covered in sugar that followed the main course rounded up a pleasant meal.

Alleyne chatted animatedly, giggling when Beatrice showed off the ribbon Alleyne had given her.

Between anecdotes of her day's discoveries, the odd wistful smile broke through. Once or twice she mentioned Lord Raymond, each time a cloud descending over her. But then she shrugged it off. She was strong.

His mind wandering, he startled when she stared at him in silence.

"Apologies, my lady. My mind wandered."

She waved a hand with a cheerful smirk. "So I noticed. So let me repeat myself. Why Perche?"

The smile froze on his lips. Memories of Bertrand came to his mind. Memories of days when they were brothers. Close. Now the only vision of his brother was one of Bertrand on his death bed.

"My brother is dying. Or perhaps even dead already." His attempt to hide the bitter note in his voice failed miserably. "We haven't talked in years. I didn't want him to leave this world without an attempt at reconciliation. He's in fact my half-brother," he added, as if the exact type of their relationship explained the feud.

"Ah, I see." Her eyes showed concern. "You didn't want to part ways forever without making up."

"I've no apologising to do." He swallowed hard. "I'm merely wishing to lay our misunderstandings to rest." He winced at the poor analogy.

Alleyne leaned forward and took his free hand. "You're a good man. For certain, I can't be the only one to say that. Your brother will accept your willingness, no doubt."

"If he's still alive. I received his letter before Easter and the feast has now passed."

"Don't despair. Easter was barely a fortnight ago. Did you send word?"

"Word? To whom?"

"To your brother, of course. To let him know you were on your way."

Geoffrey shook his head. "No. I didn't want to give him…hope. Or whatever else he might think." He drained the cup and set it down with a thud. Her unmoving gaze unnerved him. "I didn't mean for you to be dragged along. Our village of Mortagne in Perche is the place I was aimed for when Ancel alerted me of the danger you found yourself in. I still believe it's the safest spot to hide. Once there, we'll start planning how to recover Bellac."

She nodded. "I'm very grateful to you." The intensity in her eyes made his pulse race. "Very grateful."

The tension broke when the door burst open, and a sudden gust of wind howled through the inn. Geoffrey glanced up to find a man heading towards him – as if he had been given his description. The messenger? He nodded in confirmation.

"My lord de Mortagne." The man knelt at his side, his words barely audible above the noise. "Greetings from his lordship, the Count of Anjou." His gaze scanned the room – the patrons' attention had reverted to their drink – before it rested on Alleyne. He raised an eyebrow.

"Speak freely! The lady is with me."

"As you wish. My lord the count is keen to meet with you. He is in Caen, awaiting your company at the castle. Will you travel on the morrow? My lord is keen to return to camp following your meeting." The man's voice faded to a whisper. Not surprisingly so, given the patrons of the Mermaid's Haven, however mellow their mood might be now, would waste no time in stringing up a man in the service of the Devil Count.

Geoffrey nodded, part of him sad that he would not be able to spend a day with Alleyne at leisure in the peaceful setting of Barfleur after all, but also relieved to move on. "Tell your lord I will see him in four days' time. I have a lady travelling with me so our pace won't be too fast."

"As you say. My lord shall await your arrival. Sir Geoffrey." A curt nod, and the man disappeared through the crowd. Only the door falling shut reminded them of his presence.

Geoffrey leaned back and found Alleyne's eyes on him. Her earlier flirtatiousness was gone, replaced by… calculation? Yes, the lady had heard everything – no problem, as she was bound to accompany him anyway – but the determination in her gaze raised the hairs on his neck.

Alleyne was plotting.

***

Alleyne paced her chamber, her mind too restless for sleep. Did Geoffrey suspect she intended to present her case to the count? Throughout the evening he had been highly attentive. Following the messenger's departure, they had only chatted about unimportant issues. Barfleur's turbulent history; the assumed healing properties of fresh sea air; the architecture of St Nicholas Cathedral. No more talk about Geoffrey's dying brother. Or Bellac. Or politics. Yet she could not deny an undercurrent so strong she was almost swept away. Shivers ran down her spine. She wanted to scream.

Now she had to tread with care, plan her approach to the detail. They would travel for four days, enough time to come up with a solution. The Devil Count's reputation preceded him and she hoped to gain his favour if she dressed appropriately. The new evening gown, ready on the morrow, should be most suited. If she played it right, the Count of Anjou might send a letter to his wife, the empress, telling her to aid Alleyne. The good lady was bound to follow her husband's counsel, was she not?

"Of course she will help," Alleyne muttered to herself. With determined steps, she reached her bed, threw back the covers and slid into their warmth. Claude had insisted on the softest of furs to be used for her. The crafty landlady appeared prepared for the highest visitors. At this moment, Alleyne was simply grateful for whomever Claude had purchased those costly covers. They kept her warm, and she needed her rest before their onward journey. Her mind had to be alert.

The sound of her latch being lifted woke her. Alleyne blinked, but relaxed when Beatrice entered, carrying a bowl of water.

"I'm sorry to wake you, my lady. 'Tis still early – barely past sunrise – but Sir Geoffrey is keen to be on his way. It's a glorious day for travelling." The maid put the bowl on a stool. She turned on her heel, a shy smile on her face. "I'll be back in an instant to help you."

Alleyne stared at the door that softly closed behind the girl. What was going on? The girl had certainly looked mischievous.

She shook off her musings and slid from beneath the covers, giving them a longing glance. How long until she would be this comfortable again?

She pulled aside the curtains and averted her gaze from the sun's early morning glare. When she dipped her hand into the cool water, a knock on the door announced Beatrice again. The girl stuck her head through a gap, beaming, before she pushed the door open. An array of gowns hung over her arms, and she kicked the door shut with her heel.

Puzzled, Alleyne watched her gently laying her load onto the bed. "What's this?" She stepped closer.

"Your gowns, my lady." The maid spread the colourful display of gowns on the unmade bed. Wools and linens, their hues of green, blue and yellow overwhelmed her. She had but ordered two gowns – one for travelling, and the luxurious evening dress which Beatrice draped on top of the others. There must be at least half a dozen.

"But I didn't order them all." Her gaze still moved over the array of embroidered girdles and laces.

Nudging a girdle into place, Beatrice kept her head low. "Sir Geoffrey enlisted the help of Madame Claude…and me. We thought, with your clothes back in England, you would have need of more than two new gowns."

Alleyne swallowed. "You assumed I couldn't afford more?"

The girl stared at her. "Oh, no, no, my lady. Not at all. 'Twas merely to help you get back on your feet." She turned back and picked up the evening gown, its shade of summer grass bold in the light of the morning sun that streamed through the narrow window. The thin thread of gold woven into the delicate girdle glinted.

Alleyne held her breath. The gown was stunning, its flowing skirt and low cut bodice perfect for her plan. She smiled as her hand roamed the soft fabric. "It's beautiful."

"Yes, it is." The maid giggled. "I wish I could see you dressed in it. Lords will be drawn to you like, well, flies?"

They burst into laughter. "I certainly hope the lords don't smell."

Giggling, Alleyne bent over to pick up the solid brown travel gown. "I shall wear this for our journey. As for the others," her gaze roamed the array, "I must thank Sir Geoffrey and Madame Claude for their consideration. At least I am now suitably attired for whatever lies ahead."

The Devil Count's assistance was assured.

***

The castle to Caen, a solid stone structure with an impressive square tower, sat high up on a rocky mound in the centre of town. They spotted its ramparts from a distance but the approach had been slow, hindered by quarrelling tradesmen, desperate families – their belongings on their backs – beggars and monks. Geoffrey sighed as he thought of all those dispossessed tenants.

This time fortune had accompanied them all the way, the weather pleasant, perfect for swift travelling.

Now Geoffrey glared at the back of a fleshy man, clearly a butcher from the blood-stained cleaver slung almost carelessly over his shoulder, making the good people of Caen swerve out of his way. The man's girth demanded a slow pace and Geoffrey had no desire to be on the receiving end of his wrath – or weapon. But he had never favoured patience, and his was wearing thin.

He glanced at Alleyne. The lass had been in good spirits throughout their journey. His mind wandered back to Claude's guest room the morning of their departure, where Alleyne had almost kissed him in gratitude for her new gowns. It had been a small sign of his responsibility, happily shared by Claude and Beatrice who advised on suitable fabrics and colours. Alleyne's exuberant way of thanking him made him smile. And a little suspicious.

Her gaze was aimed straight at the castle looming ahead of them, an expectant look reflected in her eyes. When she saw him stare, she smiled.

"Nearly there, Sir Geoffrey."

He nodded and turned back, just in time to see the butcher enter a shop displaying cut meats on rickety tables outside. Thanks be to God. Their path was clear. He urged Feu forward.

Something irked him about her reaction. She appeared almost excited. Of course Alleyne knew whom he was due to meet, but he had no plans to linger. The Count of Anjou was renowned for his womanising, though, and Geoffrey intended to keep her out of the man's sight, and clutches.

Then a thought struck him. Had Alleyne planned a meeting with Anjou, without him? He prayed she had not betrayed his trust again. He forced his hands to unclench.

Having crossed the moat, the stench of stale water in their noses, they entered the cobbled courtyard through the narrow gate where the noise from the city streets abated, only to be replaced by the clamour of a busy castle. Sounds of hammered metal came from a smithy at the far side of the bailey; pedlars shuffled past them, their carts laden with trinkets he knew were worth little; servants carrying baskets with firewood towards what must be the kitchen. The scene across the large bailey suggested Anjou was here to stay. At least for a while.

Geoffrey shrugged and headed for the stables, keeping

Alleyne between him and Guy for protection. A boy with reddish-blond hair, his face covered in freckles, rushed from the stables and reached to take their leads.

"Steady, lad." Geoffrey eased himself from the saddle. "Feu has a temper."

"I'm used to stallions like him, my lord. My lord the count has a whole stable full of 'em." He grinned as he stretched out his small hand to Feu's nose. The stallion sniffed, looked up and allowed the boy to stroke his neck.

Geoffrey laughed. The boy's arrogance was not misplaced. He knew how to handle horses.

Guy handed the lad the other two leads. "Where do we find the steward?"

The boy's index finger pointed at a man standing at the top of the steps to the hall. "See the man dressed all in black? That's him." A coin from Guy's hand made him grin, then he turned and led the horses away.

"Guy, check with some of the soldiers about the latest stages of the campaign. I want to be fully aware of Anjou's movements."

"Aye." Guy nodded and turned on his heel to join a band of soldiers practising further inside the bailey.

"Right." Geoffrey offered Alleyne his arm and, sending her an assessing glance, led her towards the keep looming before them. "Let's hope we won't have to dally too long."

The corners of her mouth twitched.

Chapter Fourteen

Geoffrey gazed at the keep of Caen Castle, the four round towers proving old King Henry's construction to be an impressive architectural feat. Every time Geoffrey saw it, he felt its immense pull, its display of power. Memories of when it was built sprung to mind. He had been a boy when Henry built this statement for the world to see who was in charge.

Geoffrey hailed the steward just as he turned towards the gatehouse.

A man of middle age, his lanky, brown hair tied at the back, black hose and tunic spotless, he displayed an air of importance as he raised his chin and glared down his long nose. "You wish..?"

Geoffrey's blood boiled. Arrogant sod. "I'm Sir Geoffrey de Mortagne, here to see the Count of Anjou on the order of the empress his wife." Geoffrey watched the colour drain from the steward's face, not completely without a hint of satisfaction. The steward instantly ushered them inside.

"My lord count awaits you, Sir Geoffrey." He gestured him towards a stairwell to the side. "He is in the great hall upstairs, keen on your report." With an apologetic shrug, he added, "We have had an influx of turncoats – not entirely unexpectedly I must say – throwing themselves at my lord's feet. He is tiring of their…insincerity."

"I understand." Geoffrey nodded as he followed the steward upstairs. Behind him, he heard Alleyne's soft footfall, the swishing of her skirts on the steps.

At the door to the hall, he paused, allowing Alleyne first entry. Like the keep itself, the hall was impressive, its solid walls only slowly showing the ravages of time. Groups of men sat chatting at trestle tables, comparing their swords and daggers. This was not a family seat – a site the size of Caen was designed to house a conquering force.

On the dais at the far end, Geoffroi, Count of Anjou, younger husband of the Empress Matilda, reclined in a large wooden chair, propped up with an array of embroidered cushions. He listened to a clerk reading a document. A nobleman, his fur cloak and jewelled fingers revealing his standing, knelt on the stone flags in front of him.

Grovelling.

Geoffrey sighed. This happened too many times both sides of the realm. Barons turning whichever way the favourable wind blew. He understood the count's bored expression, the doubt in his eyes.

Then those eyes spotted him. And settled on the woman by his side. They lit up as they raked over Alleyne's frame, and a slow smile spread across Anjou's face.

Geoffrey hid a scowl. His fears just came true.

***

Anjou's gaze met Alleyne's. Her cheeks grew hot. A piercing green. Devil's eyes. At first glance, she envied the empress her handsome husband. Judging him to be of similar age to Geoffrey, the count's tall, self-assured bearing, a shock of reddish-blond hair, bronzed skin and a set of piercing eyes the colour of the ocean, held her enthralled. On second thought she felt sorry for Matilda. She blinked. A young husband with a roving eye was no enviable fate.

She glanced at Geoffrey whose face remained impassive, almost withdrawn. He stared at the count, who dismissed the nobleman at his feet with a sharp flick of his hand, and gestured them forward. Suddenly shy, she waited for Geoffrey to make the first move. He complied by offering her his arm. As if he had guessed her frayed nerves. He knew her too well.

Pushing the thought from her mind, she placed her hand

on his arm and together they stepped forward, passing an array of nobles clearly incensed at the couple usurping their place. She took a deep breath, aware of all eyes on them.

Geoffrey stopped in front of the dais and, releasing her hand, knelt. Alleyne curtseyed before a wave of the count's hand brought them up again.

"Ahh, de Mortagne. I didn't know my wife's messengers have such delightful travel companions." He rose and stepped off the dais until he was inches away from her. "Who, pray, is this beauty and where have you found her?" A wide smile graced his features. Alleyne's gaze went to his lips. She swallowed.

Geoffrey pre-empted her reply. "My lord, this is Lady Alleyne de Bellac, recently robbed of her father, and her inheritance. She is currently under my protection."

"Is she indeed?" The smile turned into a smirk when his glance met Geoffrey's. "Well, we'll have to do something about that."

Beside her, Geoffrey stepped from one foot to the other. "We are already doing just that, my lord."

Anjou chuckled, then reached out to grasp Geoffrey's shoulder. "It has been a while since we last met. You have been staying too long in that damp, God-forsaken place that is England."

"I have indeed, my lord."

The count's eyes met Alleyne's again, and he winked. Heat rose in her cheeks. She averted her gaze to her toes peeking out from underneath the hem of her travel gown.

"We shall have a feast tonight, in celebration of our recent victories which I shall enlighten you about and, of course, our illustrious visitor, Lady Alleyne. Jacques?" Anjou turned when his steward appeared at his side. "Take Sir Geoffrey and Lady Alleyne to our guest dwellings." He took a step back and beamed. "More time for politics later, de Mortagne."

Geoffrey nodded in response, his opinion still hidden behind a mask of polite interest.

"And for feasting," the count added, his eyes not leaving

any doubt as to the meaning of his words when he met her gaze again.

They bowed and took their leave.

Only once they had crossed the hall, the continuing silence grating on her nerves, did Alleyne let out a long breath. Geoffrey had not offered her his arm this time, but had kept his distance. He followed her down the stairs. She felt his eyes bore into her as she kept her skirt lifted just enough to step around loose rubble.

Did he guess her intentions?

As they reached the bottom, Jacques the steward signalled them to follow him. "'Tis but a short walk to Caen Castle's humble guest quarters, just along here." He led them to a door on the other side, giving way to a wide corridor with doors at regular intervals. In between the oak doors, large iron sconces held burning torches illuminating the way. The corridor looked forbidding, light and shadow bouncing off the walls.

"These are the guest chambers. My lady need not fret, the kitchens and other servants' areas are on the other side of the keep. You should be perfectly safe." His smile made Alleyne wonder the veracity of his words. She prayed the door to her chamber had a lock.

At the far end, Jacques opened doors to two adjacent chambers. He gestured Geoffrey into the first, and her towards the other door.

"Thank you, Jacques," Geoffrey murmured, then nodded to her. "We shall reconvene later, my lady." He went inside, the door falling shut behind him.

Alleyne stared at the solid oak, then turned. Her chamber was the last in the corridor, behind her a dead end. Her stomach fluttered as she entered, replaced by an immediate notion of surprise. "This is lovely."

"It is all yours, my lady. I will send a maid to assist you." He bowed and withdrew, leaving her to explore the room.

The walls, solid and thick, were almost completely covered in wall hangings. She walked along the fabrics, her hands skimming the intricate patterns. Images of hunting parties with horses and hounds; a stag posing majestically before a vibrant sunrise; a lord – or king – nocking an arrow; a castle keep high up on a hill; it had to be Caen. Months of work must have gone into these precious luxuries. A scene with boys bathing.

Wait! Those were boys? Were they not? She stepped closer and immediately drew back, hand on her mouth, giggling. The scene at a lake, surrounded by lush green forests, showed women bathing. Naked!

Quickly she turned, trying to suppress her mirth as her cheeks flamed, and stared at the large bed in the centre of the opposite wall, a narrow window on each side. She rushed forward to touch the soft fur covers, the intricate stitching of the pillow covers. In another fit of giggles, she threw herself onto it, her head sinking into the thick, generously filled pillows. She closed her eyes and drew in the lingering scent of rosemary and lavender.

Oh, but for a moment's rest.

A sharp knock on the door woke her. Slowly, she raised herself onto her elbows, and stared at her surroundings. Where was she?

"Lady Alleyne." The knocking grew stronger. "My lady, are you well?"

"Yes, thank you, Sir Geoffrey. Please give me a moment." She pushed herself from the bed, reluctantly leaving the warm, soft covers.

"Mmph…" came from the other side of the door.

She smiled. Geoffrey was not a patient man. Her hand went to the lock. An icy shower prickled her back. She had forgotten to bolt the door.

"Silly," she admonished herself as she turned the handle. Geoffrey stood only inches away. He had changed clothes, wearing a clean maroon tunic and brown linen hose. His hair was wet and raked back.

"What's silly?" He studied her.

"Oh, nothing. I…I simply forgot to lock the door and must have fallen asleep." She stifled a yawn.

His brows shot together. "You should be more careful."

He glanced up the corridor, then back at her. "It's too quiet here. Not ideal for a lady on her own."

"I'll be just fine. No need to fret on my behalf. After all, I stayed at busy inns with many more folk coming and going."

"Aye." He stepped back. "And they're still safer than this viper's nest full of men at war."

"You are talking about the Count, not his men, Geoffrey. I have nothing to fear from him, I'm certain. He's bound to be honourable." She thrust her chin upward. "I have to get dressed for the meal. If you'll excuse me."

His booted foot stopped her door from slamming shut. "I'll go in search for that maid you were promised. After all, you will want to look your best if you aim to convince the count to help you. I trust you agree with the price he'll demand!" Without another glance, he withdrew his foot, and turned on his heel.

Alleyne stared after him, open-mouthed, until he slammed his door shut, then closed her own gently, sliding the bolt into place. She leaned against it, closed her eyes and took a deep breath.

Geoffrey knew.

***

Geoffrey slammed his door shut, the sound echoing his feelings. The stupid woman! Why had he not let her simmer at Will's hands? Suffer the consequences of her rash actions. She just did not learn.

Now, she was to do exactly the same thing. Rush to the first baron and plead her case. But did it have to be Anjou, of all men?

He kicked the bed frame and sat on the fur covers, elbows on knees. He had to get her away from Caen. No doubt, the count would seduce her if she stayed any longer.

They must leave on the morrow.

His mind made up, Geoffrey scanned the room, careful to keep any valuables in the leather pouch by his belt.

Satisfied he had possession of anything worth a thief's while, he searched for the steward. He found him giving orders in the kitchen.

"Jacques, a word!" He signalled from the door. The steward followed him. Uneasy in the dark corridors of the lower keep, Geoffrey walked in silence until they reached the door to the bailey. Stepping out into the sunshine, he shielded his eyes from the glare.

"My lord?" The steward stared at him, an eyebrow raised.

"I thought you would recommend a maid for the lady Alleyne. As you seem to be planning for a large gathering tonight, you can imagine she would like to look less… travel-worn." He grinned at the steward's slow smile.

"Of course. I had not forgotten." The steward bristled. "I shall call for a suitable lass to assist the Lady Alleyne forthwith. No doubt my lord will appreciate the effort."

The grin died on Geoffrey's face. "No doubt," he grunted and dismissed the steward. He walked the distance to a far wall, went up to the allure and leaned on the parapet. The town lay huddled at the foot of the castle mound. St Stephen's Church stood out in stark contrast to the cramped dwellings of the townsfolk.

A sea breeze reached his nostrils. He turned northward but the large expanse of the bailey did not allow him a clear view. The sea was still a few miles away, yet it felt closer. A clamminess not experienced since the crossing made him shudder. He had never particularly liked Caen, with its humid air and smelly lanes. He glared at St Stephen's, an inner urgency pushing him onward.

He must leave for Perche.

The hall was buzzing when Geoffrey led Alleyne into the large room. Before them, trestle tables were set up at an angle from the dais, allowing the count to watch everything that went on. His gaze met Geoffrey's, and he waved them over.

"It appears we dine at the high table tonight, my lady."

Geoffrey guided her through throngs of people – barons, knights and ladies dressed in their fineries. Geoffrey wondered briefly how the men did not sweat, clothed in furs and layers of fine silks. His eyes roamed the scene, like a play enacted for his perusal. The ladies could do with the furs, their gowns of finest gossamer and silks too flimsy for the large, dank room. Even the candles and open fires could not remove the humidity. Sweat beaded his brow. He shrugged off his musings and, smiling, bowed before the count.

Anjou, resplendent in russet shirt and blue hose, beamed at them. "My lady." He took her hand, elevating her onto the dais and kissed it a moment too long. "May I say, you look beautiful." His gaze raked over her body.

Heat shot into Geoffrey's cheeks at the *sang froid*. The count was a dangerous man at the best of times, but most vulnerable were the ladies. Although he had to agree with Anjou's observation. Alleyne was a vision in a deep green gown she had had made for her in Barfleur. Low-cut at the front, with a lace edged hem at cleavage and arms, it suited her natural curves to perfection. A circlet held a gossamer veil in place which covered her unbound hair flowing down to her hips. The flimsy material did not hide it, in fact, it emphasised the thick, wavy chestnut tresses. She was easily the most beautiful woman in the hall.

And the most vulnerable.

"My lord count." He coughed and the count turned towards him, only slowly relinquishing Alleyne's hand. Too slow for Geoffrey's liking.

"De Mortagne, come!" Anjou gestured him to a seat on his left, with Alleyne settling at the count's right hand side.

Urgency spurred Geoffrey into action as soon as a servant had filled his goblet. "My lord, as you know I carry an important message from the Earl of Gloucester. I believe it is urgent."

Anjou slapped him on his back and clinked goblets. "To your health, de Mortagne. And to my dear wife's!" He drained his wine and waved for more. "Politics come later.

For the moment, simply sit back and relax." He leaned over to Alleyne, his mouth by her ear.

Alleyne's giggles, wide eyes gazing into the count's, tore at Geoffrey's already frayed nerves. Did she know the price of her game?

"My lord, I must say…" she muttered, almost imperceptibly.

Clearly she did not have an inkling, Geoffrey mused.

He drained his wine which was instantly refilled. He watched the barons and their ladies settle into the rows of benches, and ignored the envious glances directed his way. Then the acrobats stormed in, bearing circles of fire and flying daggers. He sighed and took another draught. It was going to be a long night.

***

Alleyne's head spun. The hum in the hall, the heat from the fires and torches, not to mention the fire those incredible acrobats used, gave her a headache but any attempts at drowning such pains in wine ended in failure. The rich, heady taste did its best to muddle her senses.

The count placed another thin slice of pigeon breast on her trencher, his hand brushing hers briefly. But needs must, she had to gain his support. Once he pledged it, she would write to Matilda forthwith. Or ask him to write on her behalf. Given the attention he had lavished on her all night, she was quite certain he would agree.

His head bowed close to hers. "Are you enjoying yourself, my lady?"

Alleyne met his gaze. "Yes, my lord count. I haven't felt so elated in a long time." She bit into the delicate meat while maintaining eye contact. The game was dangerous, but it would be worth her being a little flirtatious.

After all, time was of the essence.

"I've had a thought," he whispered, then popped a grape into his wide mouth. "Why should you accompany de Mortagne all the way to his home manor, only to come back after a few weeks to return to England?"

She held her breath. "What are you suggesting, my lord?"

He leaned back, a smile playing on his lips. "I think you have more important plans to make than to traipse through Normandy countryside."

Geoffrey's head shot her way. He gave her a warning glance that should have sobered her.

Instead, she weighed up the options. She might need more time in gaining the count's support. And Geoffrey could be held up with family matters, causing unnecessary delays to her recovery of Bellac.

"I travel under my lord de Mortagne's protection. It is he who rescued me from a dreadful situation. I cannot possibly deny his hospitality when offered."

Geoffrey snorted and turned away.

The count chose to ignore him, his eyes not leaving hers. He studied her face, his own expression hidden. "Well, I can offer you my protection, as Count of Anjou and husband of the future queen of England. Would that help your cause further?"

Alleyne's head pounded. She sought Geoffrey's gaze but his attention was focused on the far end of the hall. He pointedly ignored her. It made her decision easy. She had to accept help from someone of higher rank. Her heart sank at the thought of rejecting Geoffrey again, for that was how he would regard her choice. He had risked his life for her, repeatedly. But he would be back here soon, no doubt. Then they could return to Gloucester together, in triumph.

Geoffrey would understand.

She met the count's gaze and nodded. "Yes, my lord. It would help my cause in no small measure."

Anjou raised her hand and kissed the tips of her fingers. "Then the matter is agreed. You stay at Caen and I will listen to your case."

She smiled. "Thank you. I appreciate your kind offer." She withdrew her hand and picked up the slice of meat, all appetite gone. She should feel elated, hopeful. But instead she watched Geoffrey's strong profile turned away towards a commotion near the door, his brows drawn together in displeasure. He clearly disapproved.

She startled when Anjou rose from his chair, a wide grin on his face. "What a pleasant surprise," he called across the hall. "Welcome to our court, my lord de Guines. Take a seat at my table."

Alleyne's hand froze midway to her mouth. She dropped the meat onto her trencher, her heart pounding in her ears as she glared at the man approaching the dais with a wide smile. The man she still suspected of Father's murder.

Philip de Guines.

Chapter Fifteen

Philip de Guines. Here, at the place she sought sanctuary! Alleyne swallowed hard. Her mind whirled.

At Anjou's request, de Guines inclined his head and sat next to her. "My lady."

The smile on his lips showed recognition, and she struggled to suppress her anger. Her hands shook and she folded them in her lap, clutching the folds of her gown. A black haze descended over her eyes. Now was the wrong moment to faint. She pinched herself and the nausea subsided.

"Sir Philip, are you acquainted with the lady Alleyne?" A speculative gleam hung in the count's eyes.

"I am indeed, my lord count. Our properties in Gloucestershire border on one another." His solemn, blue gaze met hers. "I was sorry to hear the sad news about Lord Raymond. Your father was a fine man. He was ambushed, they say?" He turned away briefly when a servant filled his goblet.

De Guines offering his sympathy?

How could the man do that, knowing perfectly well what had happened? The look of sincerity on his face so obviously masked his true knowledge. Alleyne fumed, the heat rising to her cheeks.

"Yes, he was killed on the road. Sir Geoffrey de Mortagne," She pointed at the under-sheriff, "came upon the attack but sadly the murderer had struck already." She glared at de Guines. Let the man know she suspected him of such treachery.

"Lord Raymond and I didn't always see eye-to-eye, I must admit, but we supported the same side. I had been called away to my Norman estate several weeks prior to the battle that ensued at Lincoln, so I could not take part." His mien serious, no trace of malice in his eyes, Alleyne's inner turmoil increased.

They had fought together? How did that fit the notion that he was Stephen's man?

Her gaze searched Geoffrey's as the count and de Guines chatted about strategies behind her back, but to her shock the under-sheriff joined in. What game was he playing? Did he really not suspect de Guines at all? Geoffrey glanced at her briefly then agreed with both men about a particular part of the count's advances into Normandy. She did not listen, her head spinning.

She must escape. Abruptly, she pushed her chair back and rose. "If you will excuse me, my lords. I feel a little tired."

After a swift curtsey to the count, his smoky eyes scrutinising her, Alleyne fled the hall and ran to her room, bolting the door behind her. Leaning against the solid oak, her breathing slowed as she forced herself to calm.

Alleyne paced her chamber. Suddenly the luxurious surroundings felt like a trap, rather than a safe haven.

Now she had no option but to leave. Under no circumstances could she stay at Caen with Father's nemesis as a guest of honour at the count's court. The men appeared to be well acquainted. Would the count believe her accusation? Or would he refuse to help if he discovered she suspected de Guines of murder? If de Guines was guilty at all. The small doubt in her head grew. Perhaps it had been Will after all…

What a mess! She shook her head.

Was it preferable to travel to Perche, with a man she trusted? But could she really trust Geoffrey? Thinking back, he had always been reluctant to believe de Guines's guilt. The ease with which he chatted to him earlier showed no sign of suspicion. But then, was that not his role, to hide his thoughts? Did she know his mind at all?

The candles cast scant light across the chamber and

tiredness won over. She took off her belt and dropped it at the bottom of the bed. Her gown followed. In her shift, she sat on the edge of the bed and combed her hair. Only when the tresses were smooth and soft, did she put the comb aside and slide under the covers. But sleep would not come, warring with her whirling thoughts.

A tap on the door made her jump. Had she dozed off after all? She stared at the candle by her bedside – it had burned down several notches. The castle must have retired by now.

A more forceful knock followed. Gingerly she tiptoed to the door, her hand halting on the bolt. "Who is this?"

A whisper reached her. "It's me."

Geoffrey? Her heart pounded in her ears. What would Geoffrey have to say to her at this ungodly hour? She drew back the bolt and opened the door by two inches.

Alleyne stepped back as the door was pushed open and in walked the count. "You?" Not Geoffrey. Aware of her state of undress, she hurried to pull a blanket off the bed and wrapped herself in it. "My lord?"

He silently pushed the door shut behind him, his eyes raking over her now covered form. "Yes, or were you expecting someone else?"

Her chin raised, despite the terror growing inside, she said, "I wasn't expecting anyone, my lord. This visit is most unseemly."

He laughed, the sound sending shivers down her spine. Suddenly she understood why they called him the Devil Count. His attractive looks, the ease with which he gained entry into a lady's chamber, his self-assured laugh and stance, his broad frame leaning against the bedpost.

She had walked right into his trap.

"I fear you misunderstand, my lord." Trying to stop her voice from trembling, she marched towards the door but he caught her wrist and pulled her against his chest. Her hands, balled into fists and holding onto the corners of the blanket, pushed against him.

"I didn't think I misunderstood, my lady. I remember

you offered." His grip tightened, his gaze lowered to her mouth.

Heat rose in her cheeks. "I did not! I merely asked for your assistance." She held her back rigid, her expression one of stern disapproval.

"And there is no way I can convince you to change your mind?" His mouth brushed hers, sending a trail of kisses along her jawline. Her skin erupted in goosebumps.

She kept her teeth clenched. Oh, he was tempting. Handsome and sensual, his hands roaming the right places, his touch gentle but firm through the blanket. A soft seduction. Unlike Will.

Not unlike Geoffrey.

Remembering the under-sheriff sobered her and she pushed back from Anjou's embrace. He released her and inclined his head. His cheeks covered in red blotches, he swallowed hard. The heat in his gaze changed to fire, barely suppressed. She had enraged him.

"My lady, I apologise. 'Tis not in my nature to force myself on unwilling ladies." He walked briskly to the door and threw it open. In the doorway he paused and turned, his expression like an angry child's. Petulant. "As to your case, de Guines has spoken to me about the disagreements over your border lands. He has but spent little time in England lately and isn't aware of any transgressions. You see, he has been in my service at various times over the past three years and if you consider him guilty, I can verify his character. At least as far as your father's murder is concerned. Philip wouldn't commit such a foul act. He'd challenge his opponent openly."

Alleyne met his gaze, shocked to hear her suspicions so easily dismissed. "But–"

"I'm afraid the culprit must be another. I hear Will d'Arques is now holding Bellac? If I were you, I would dig into his past and not spread rumours about my liege men."

"Will is an old friend of my father's. He would never–"

"Would he not?" The count's tone was frosty. "He took over your manor and held you captive. That proves a lot.

Does it not?"

"I suppose it does." Her voice shook. She sank onto the bed, dropping her hands in her lap.

Sympathy shone in his eyes. "It's time you considered the situation with open eyes, Lady Alleyne. Denial won't get you Bellac back. Action will. I wish you a good night." The door shut with a loud click.

Tremors shook Alleyne as his words sank in. Rage and disappointment stirred within her. Tears stung her eyes and she let them flow freely, her hands covering her face. Sobs racked her body.

"Oh, Father."

***

Geoffrey moved away from the door. He had heard enough. Of course he had expected the count to visit Alleyne's chamber but not on the first night, while he still resided next to her. Geoffrey only caught the end of their conversation but it was enough.

She had sold her soul, and her body, to the Devil Count for his protection. As for Lord Raymond's murder, the count's opinion matched Geoffrey's own. The evening had been insightful, with de Guines proving he was a ruthless mercenary, scouting for the count, destroying villages. But his presence in Normandy also showed he had naught to do with Lord Raymond's death. He tended to meet his victims face-to-face. De Guines focused on Normandy, on spoils of war, parcels of land. Not his manor in England.

Count Geoffroi's comments just confirmed his own suspicions. Will d'Arques was guilty. Geoffrey needed to find a way to prove it once he was back in Gloucester. The quicker he was done at home the better.

He sighed, his heart heavy with disappointment, as he crossed the room in the low candlelight. Alleyne made her bed, so now she must lie in it. The vision of her with the count sharing the same, limbs entwined, her submissive frame beneath the solid muscle of the count's, revolted him.

He swallowed back the bile that rose in his throat. Twice rejected, the pain stabbed at his heart. Never would he trust her again.

He would travel to Perche at first light, without her, then head straight back to Gloucester. Once he had brought Will to justice, he would return to take her home. 'Twas swifter this way. Simpler. His mind made up, Geoffrey dropped his hose and shirt on the floor and slid under the covers. But sleep escaped him as he stared at the shadows dancing on the ceiling.

The candle had long burnt out when light filtered in through the shutters. Dawn was breaking. Geoffrey yawned and rose, pulled his discarded travel clothes on and rolled his fine tunic and hose into a tight bundle before pushing it into his bag. He grabbed his belongings and left the room, pulling the door shut behind him. At Alleyne's door he paused for a moment, regret warring with practicality. She was better off being a count's lover, with all the luxuries that entailed, than being dragged across Normandy, uncertain of finding shelter during Anjou's warfare.

Better off than with him.

Geoffrey strode along the quiet corridor, careful not to make a noise. The count knew he was due to leave today. Fed-up with waiting to be summoned to pass on Gloucester's message, Geoffrey had arranged for the steward to hand the count his note last night. Gloucester wanted Anjou in England, to aid Matilda in her progress to London. Geoffrey had not waited long for the count's response – a messenger would take it to England. He had guessed correctly. Anjou was not leaving Normandy until the whole duchy was under his control. Matilda and England had to wait.

But that was none of his concern. He had done his duty, delivered the message, and now Perche beckoned.

Guy handed him Feu's reins as he neared the gate. "Good morrow, Geoffrey." He glanced at the sky, a deep blue only showing a pale hue in the easternmost point. "We should get far today."

"Aye, 'tis perfect for our journey. Fortune is on our side." He sat up, Feu's strong muscles beneath his thighs rearing to go. "Go, my boy!" Gladly he prodded the stallion's flanks and Feu surged forward.

"Geoffrey! Geoffrey, wait!" Alleyne's voice echoed through the deserted bailey.

He pulled the reins, his mood the same as Feu's as the stallion snorted angrily at the interruption. What did she want now? He gritted his teeth.

Guy shot him an anxious glance when, with great effort and clenched teeth, Geoffrey turned Feu and rode towards the entrance of the tower where Alleyne stood, wrapped in a fur-lined mantle against the morning chill. His eyebrows rose when he saw her toes peeking from underneath her nightdress. He sighed loudly. "Yes, my lady?"

She stared at her toes. Hesitantly she raised her head until she met his glare. She startled. What did she expect? His gratitude?

"I…I wish to accompany you."

"After all? Now why might that be, my lady?" Fury raged within him. He struggled to control his breathing as the pounding of his heart echoed through his head. Taking in the thin fabric of her nightdress where the mantle parted, and her luminous, pleading eyes, his anger subdued.

"You are safer here." Keeping his voice matter-of-fact, he forced his eyes off her shapely leg visible through the fabric. He swallowed. "The count will see to your wellbeing." His stomach contracted at the memory of the man leaving her chamber. The lass was not worth any more of his attention.

"He won't. I mean…he has offered but I have, ahem, declined." A rosy tint graced her cheeks. She averted her gaze to her toes.

"Listen. Guy and I will be much faster. Travelling in a war-torn land like this is no easy feat for a lady. You saw the damage it did in England. 'Twas wrong of me to bring you here."

"There is no need–"

"Yes, there is, Lady Alleyne. Because I must leave you now in this viper's nest while you would have been far safer at Bristol Castle, under the protection of the Earl of Gloucester. My mistake."

Shock ran through him as he watched tears roll down her face. Sweet Jesus, the woman was impossible.

"Geoffrey?" Guy's tone held an urgent note. "We must be on our way."

He nodded, his sense of chivalry not leaving him any option. "Be quick, my lady. Guy will get your mare saddled."

A sigh behind him told him Guy's opinion but all he saw was the wide smile on Alleyne's face, eyes beaming with renewed hope. "Yes, Geoffrey. Thank you. I won't be long." With that, she turned on her heel and bolted inside the building.

Geoffrey shook his head as he turned, took the reins from Guy and watched him enter the stables, shoulders slumped. It was not fair on his sergeant to travel at slow speed while they had to entertain a lady. Guy was a man of action, happiest in the thick of battle, or on a mission.

Alleyne appeared at the door, carrying her bundle. With a hint of regret, he noticed she had replaced her nightdress and slippers with a solid travel gown and boots, her cloak wound tightly around her, secured on her shoulder with a silver pin. "I'm ready." She smiled.

At this moment, Guy emerged from the stables, leading her horse. "My lady." He inclined his head and offered her his hand to help her into the saddle.

"I'm sorry, Guy. I know you would have been faster but I promise to be as swift as I can." Her smile sent colour into Guy's face and he turned away, mumbling to himself.

Geoffrey checked the sky – dawn was approaching fast – and nudged Feu towards the gatehouse. Once they passed the grunting guard, they moved through Caen at a swift trot. Early morning businesses already opened their shutters, displaying wares to people hurrying along the streets. Soon they left the city behind and the countryside opened up before them.

"*Allez*!" And this time Geoffrey let Feu have his way when he kicked the stallion's flanks.

***

The light faded when they approached the town walls of Falaise. Alleyne almost cried with relief. Geoffrey had allowed only a short pause in a small hamlet, finding shelter in a burnt-out farm cottage. In a way, the relentless pace he set had taken her mind off her surroundings, though the stench of burning crops hung deep in her nostrils. Glad he brought provisions – something she had not considered in her rush that morning – they sat for a while, eating bread and cheese washed down with draughts of ale. The countryside provided nothing for them, not even an unripe apple on a tree. The fields were a blackened mess, burnt-out stalks a sad reminder of better days. Normandy was under siege. And her gallant *saviour* – the Count of Anjou – had caused all this.

Just as he had caused her to run again.

As the breeze picked up, she wrapped her cloak tighter around her neck. The day had been hot, the sun scorching the already dry ground, but the nights were still chilly. She let her head loll back and forth to the rhythm of her mare, inured to her aching bones and muscles. After the last few weeks, her body had become used to this lifestyle. Not the most befitting for a lady but one born of necessity.

As the walls of Falaise grew closer, Alleyne made out church towers and the solid walls of the castle elevated in the centre. It must sit on a rock, another example of fine Norman defence. William the Bastard had certainly known how to defend his home.

Her gaze moved to Geoffrey's back and heat shot into her cheeks. Shame washed through her as she remembered how she had gone behind his back once more. And pleaded with him. Again. During the long day on horseback she had ample time to think. Geoffrey. Father. Bellac. Anjou. De

Guines.

Will d'Arques. The traitor.

But was he also a murderer? Everything pointed to a well-crafted plan. Only she had been so blinded by his charms she had not seen it coming, had never really suspected him of the despicable deed. Now she wondered. Will had reached Bellac quickly; his men were unmannered brutes; he taunted her about Elvire's escape. Was he responsible for the maid's disappearance, too? No word had arrived from Ancel, meaning he had not found any trace of Elvire yet. How futile was his search?

When Geoffrey spoke, Alleyne startled. "I'm sorry?"

Concern in his eyes grew into annoyance. "I said, we have arrived."

"Ah."

"Ah, yes. There is an inn near the church. I hope it still exists and hasn't suffered like the rest of this duchy." The tension in his voice finally pulled her from her own thoughts. This was his homeland. And to see it bled and tortured must hurt him. How selfish she was to focus on her own worries!

"I'm sorry, Geoffrey. Sir Geoffrey, I mean. You must be devastated."

He turned his face away but not before she had seen the grim set of his chin. He did not simply hurt; he was angry. A curt nod, all she received as a response, confirmed her suspicions.

She nudged her mare next to his stallion and glanced up. "I mean it. I am sorry about the destruction."

"You didn't cause it so you don't need to apologise."

"I know I didn't cause it. 'Tis just heartbreaking to see all the crops burnt, the farm cottages torn down, people displaced."

They reached the gate. Geoffrey hailed the guard who let them in, a suspicious frown between his eyes. "Enter at your own risk, my lord. Town's bursting with desperate folk."

His words rang true as the clamour that reached them was deafening. "Yes, people displaced," Alleyne repeated.

Geoffrey sent her a sharp glance. Had he heard her?

"This way." He pointed to the right with his hand. "Guy?"

"I'm here, Geoffrey. I'll stay behind the lady."

In a line, they rode at slow pace towards the spires of a church she had spotted from afar. Beggars lined the lanes thronging with people, pushing each other out of the way. This was where the homeless farmers had fled, seeking help from their overlords who may – or may not – listen to their woes. On a corner of Baker Street, less than thirty yards from the church, Geoffrey stopped underneath a large sign. The Duke's Head.

Alleyne briefly closed her eyes. The inn's name summed up this country. Noble against noble. Heads rolling. One man versus another. Ordinary people were the losers.

She accepted Guy's help to dismount and, her feet rooted on terra firma, she stretched her limbs. Geoffrey's eyes met hers across her mare's back, questioning. Or wondering. Her innards contracted, her heart pounded in her ears. How could she make it up to him?

"Guy, see our mounts settled," Geoffrey instructed his sergeant, as a stable lad led away the horses. Guy followed him.

With a wide sweep, Geoffrey opened the door to the tavern and let her enter first. The narrow room was crowded with bodies, unwashed, the odour hanging stale in the air. Alleyne suppressed a cough, her eyes streaming in the smoke from the central fireplace. Heat surged through her body. The air was stifling.

"Alleyne, this way." Geoffrey took her hand and led her to the back, and through a door into a small parlour, devoid of visitors. She ignored the rude calls, instead only remembering Geoffrey had called her by her given name. He had dropped the formality. Were they friends again? Hope grew in her, making her smile.

He clearly mistook it for approval of their new surroundings. "This is better, isn't it?"

She nodded as his gaze held hers for an instant almost

too long, too intense. The room, the noise outside, faded into the background. Alleyne held her breath.

Then Geoffrey broke the contact and released her hand. "You might wish to settle over there, by the table." He gestured towards a corner. "I'll go in search of Damien, the innkeeper. I shan't be long."

The noise rose when he opened the door, before muted silence fell again. Alleyne glanced around, taking in the whitewashed walls, the scrubbed tables and chairs. A small fire danced in a grate, emitting enough heat without suffocating visitors. Relieved, she shed her cloak and threw it over a bench. Then she sank into a cushioned chair near the fire and propped her feet onto a footstool. This almost resembled comfort. As tiredness took hold of her, she sank her head against the back of the chair. Grateful for the calm, she closed her eyes.

They seemed to be friends again. Hope soared in her heart. Never must she do anything to risk his... Her eyes flew open and heat rose into her cheeks.

Never must she lose him.

Chapter Sixteen

The meal consisted of mutton stew, without any trace of vegetables, and stale bread. Still, Alleyne wolfed it down as if it was to be her last. The chill that had racked her slowly dissipated as the heat from the stew warmed her insides. Content, she swallowed the last chunk of her bread and washed it down with gulps of ale. Clearly, Falaise's brewster was still in business.

Her gaze fell on Geoffrey who leaned back, swirling a half-empty cup in his hand. Only now did she realise he was watching her, an alert look in his eyes. She smiled. "This was delicious. Thank you."

"It was the only fare Damien had to offer. Little is left for folk to cook." His gaze scorched her. Her smile faltered.

"I'm aware of that. I'm simply being grateful for the meal after the hard ride today, 'tis all." It took all of her strength not to shake him. He had been in this mood since they left Caen. Of course she knew the cause.

Well, she guessed.

"Damien has a room prepared for you. The only chamber with a lock, so you should be safe. Guy will sleep on a pallet outside your door, just in case."

"There's no need–"

"Of course there is, my lady. The city is in turmoil, full of starving people looking for someone to blame. An English heiress might just fit their description of a scapegoat. Or a safe passage to riches." His tone like ice, he glared, then emptied his cup and slammed it on the table.

Deep breath!

"I'm aware of my heritage, Geoffrey. There is no need to be so…" Wringing her hands, she sought for the right words.

His brow shot up. "So?"

She gritted her teeth, forcing the word out. "Obnoxious!"

Expecting an outburst of Norman temper, she startled when he burst out laughing. Heat shot into her cheeks, embarrassment mingling with anger. Who did he think he was?

"I'm glad you see the funny side. Because I can't." She refilled her cup with a shaky hand and drained it in one go. A bad move. The strong ale made her head spin.

His face grew serious, his gaze inscrutable. "Of course you wouldn't. And you're right, there's nothing funny about our situation." He leaned back again, his eyes not leaving hers. "Fact is I'd have been far quicker without you than with you, Alleyne. To be quite honest, you have always done your utmost to rid yourself of me – first at Bellac when you called Will for help, then again in Caen when you preferred to throw yourself at the count rather than stick to our plan to come to Perche with me for your own safety. Yet…here you are after all. I wonder what prompted your change of heart this time?" His voice held a bitter tone, his back straight, showing his displeasure.

Alleyne could not blame him. He was right. Ashamed of her behaviour, she lowered her gaze and swallowed hard. He deserved honesty. No more excuses. "I…erm, the count promised help–"

"After you left him with no alternative," he cut in. His fingers drummed on the arm of his chair, the sound grating at her nerves.

Her lower lip wobbled as tears fought their way into her eyes. She forced them back, unwilling to cry in front of him. It would not gain his sympathy – on the contrary. It was clear he despised her already. Crying would make things worse.

"Yes, after I approached him for help," she admitted. "I assumed he'd write to his wife and the empress would rule in my favour. Clearly, he expected some, erm, services in return."

He snorted, his gaze raked over her body. "I'm certain he did." Geoffrey did not even attempt to hide his scrutiny.

She suddenly felt naked, exposed, wishing she had a blanket to wrap around herself. "I expected some sort of favour but not to become his whore." In stubborn defiance she thrust her chin forward. "As you see, he didn't succeed."

"My, he didn't?" His eyes darkened, reminding her of a frozen winter lake, treacherous ice underfoot.

The man was enraging. "No, Geoffrey, he did not. How dare you presume the worst!" She folded her arms in front of her chest.

Geoffrey drained his ale and refilled his cup. "Because you betrayed me once before, as I just pointed out to you. Remember Will? Remember his advances?"

Heat shot into her cheeks. He was right. She had almost submitted herself to Will, fully aware of the consequences. That was before he showed his true character. Alleyne shifted on her chair, suddenly uncomfortable in her own skin. 'Twas only because she had not believed Geoffrey's suspicions, taken them for personal dislike rather than what they were – a stark, honest warning.

The truth hurt.

"I see you know what I mean."

At this moment, drowning in that frozen lake of his eyes would be preferable. "I'm so sorry," she whispered as tears burst through. "I…I never thought Will capable of killing a friend. I thought he and Father were close." Her voice faltered.

Geoffrey pulled a linen square from his sleeve, and handed it to her. Grateful for the reprieve, she blew her nose and dabbed her eyes. She did not deserve his sympathy.

"Thank you," she sniffed, and tucked the linen into her sleeve.

"Will would remove anyone who stands in his way. If that means killing his own grandmother, he'd do it. He sold his soul to the devil a long time ago. Trust me, I know first hand of his deceptive ways."

"What has he done to you?" Alleyne had never asked him before, not without relinquishing her prejudices. Now she found herself genuinely interested. "When did your paths first cross?"

"Will and I go back to our days at the court of the Count Rotrou of Perche, my godfather. We trained together as squires, keen to impress our overlord. Keen to advance our careers." He shook his head. "But while I took my training sessions seriously, Will added to them by seducing pretty much every female at court. The count ignored it at first, even nurtured it, saying a young buck must sow his acorns widely. But later he saw through the careless attitude, the naked ambition. By then it was too late."

"What happened?" She held her breath, clinging to Geoffrey's every word. This was a side of Will's character she had never seen. Until recently. When it was too late.

"Will ensured several maids were sent away after they fell pregnant. That in itself isn't unusual – it happens in a many noble households."

Alleyne sucked in her breath. The poor girls. She had not given thought to the risk of pregnancy when she allowed Will to touch her.

Sweet Mary!

Geoffrey continued. "But it came to a head when he seduced the daughter of a lord, a close neighbour. A lass I had become fond of, and wanted to propose to." He hesitated, the ice in his gaze replaced by a faraway look. He was reliving the past.

"What happened?" she asked again. Will seduced a lady? She shuddered, realising she should not be surprised. He had almost seduced her.

"Solange was fully aware of my interest. She played me and Will off against each other. Of course, Will knew of my feelings; even more of a reason to show her what a real man he was." He laughed, the sound eerily lacking humour. "Well, he did show her in the end, in her father's stables. A visiting knight caught them in the act. Will returned home, unrepentant, even boastful. Her desperate father, aware of my intentions, offered her to me – with a tempting dowry to make up for any absence of virginity and the possibility of raising a bastard. Will's bastard. Many a knight would have jumped at the chance."

"Dear Lord." Alleyne was stunned, torn between sympathy for Geoffrey and a sudden stab of…jealousy? Where did that come from?

"Yes, indeed. I declined, sorely angered by her treachery. Although my father tried to force me into wedlock, no doubt counting the coins already in his mind, Perche agreed with me. As Will rejected Solange also, her father carted her off to a nearby nunnery. I believe the babe died at birth but she's languishing in there for the rest of her days." His eyes met hers again. "That is the kind of fate that awaits you if you put your trust in Will d'Arques." He downed the contents of his cup and set it down with a thud.

"Why didn't you tell me?"

"Because you wouldn't have listened. You were too besotted with the saintly Will to see his true ambitions. It cost you Bellac."

"No!" She rose, her chair crashing backwards, her hands balled into fists. "I haven't lost Bellac. There is still hope."

"Sit down, Alleyne!" The sharp tone made her lift the back of her chair and settle into it. "For the moment, Bellac is in Will's hands. There is neither king nor queen to listen to your case, as they are too busy waging war against each other. Will has a large contingency of his men stationed at your manor which makes an assault impossible. I'm sure that side gate we used is now fully sealed. At this point in time, you are without property, coin – apart from what you carry on you – or friends. 'Tis time to face reality."

***

Geoffrey's head pounded. He should stop drinking but the anger inside him still smouldered, so he refilled his cup. Her sympathy seemed genuine, her state of upset honest. But she had deceived him once too often, let him down too much to shrug it off easily. He must remain distant.

What was he going to do with her?

He had rushed forward to offer her a safe haven at his home, away from English warfare and politics. He had dragged her through Norman wasteland, only to leave her in Mortagne? He did not even know if his home village was indeed safe. And when he returned to England, kept fighting for Matilda and trying – with Ancel's help – to regain Bellac, had he ever thought about how he would achieve it?

This task was larger than he had anticipated. Last he heard, at Anjou's court, Matilda was finally on her way to London. Yet he could not shake off the niggling doubts in the back of his mind. How would the Londoners – Stephen's staunchest supporters – take to the empress? Diplomacy was not her forte. He only prayed her advisors were tactful enough to ensure a smooth entrance. Once she held London, the kingdom was hers.

But what if ought went wrong? Dread settled in the pit of his stomach. Alleyne's chances hung in the balance. Just as peace in England did. Both situations were too precarious.

"When we reach Mortagne, you'll be safe." His tone now soothing, he tried to ease her pain. She was only a slip of a lass, all alone. "No doubt Ancel will follow with Elvire and you'll be reunited with friends. My brother's family will welcome you, I've no doubt."

"I hope she's still alive," Alleyne whispered. "I pray for Elvire's safety every night."

Would his family welcome them? He was not certain, but it was the wrong time to divulge the old family rift. He had revealed too much already. Bertrand's wife – or widow, if he arrived too late – had no choice but to take them in. Alleyne could be a companion, sharing her grief.

His mind made up, he pushed the cup away and stood. His vision blurred. Too much ale. The pounding behind his eyes reached drumming proportions. He grabbed the back of his chair to steady himself.

"Geoffrey?" Anxiety filled Alleyne's voice. She rushed over to him, taking his arm. A stern look told him all.

"You've taken too much drink. You need to sleep it off."

He nodded. It had been a strenuous month with little sleep. He wondered for the first time how she coped. After all, he had dragged her halfway across the continent, on horseback and by rickety boat. Yet her hand on his arm was cool, firm.

She guided him towards the door and lifted the latch. "I take it your chamber is near mine?"

He nodded. "Aye, upstairs on the left." He cursed the cloud obscuring clear thought. He should be guiding her, not the other way round. He straightened but a shot of pain drove into his temple. At the foot of the steps he stopped and closed his eyes.

"Geoffrey? Come, not far to go." With a gentle nudge she pushed him onto the first step.

His eyes opened and he found his vision improved. Momentarily. A steadying hand against the wall, he heaved himself forward step by step.

Her soothing voice drifted to his numb brain. "That's right, take it slowly. Just another couple of steps and we're there."

Geoffrey dared not turn at the top of the stairs, fearful of falling. He shuffled towards the second door on the left. "This is mine, that one's yours." He pointed at the next door. "Guy should be here soon."

Their eyes met and she nodded. "Worry not, Geoffrey. You'll be fine in the morning." She lifted the latch to open his door. A smile graced her features when warm candlelight greeted them. She took his hand and, kicking the door shut behind them to escape prying eyes, led him to the bed where she pushed him into a sitting position.

Geoffrey's vision blurred as she bent close to him, an alluring scent of lavender and woman teasing his nostrils. He watched, fascinated, as she undid the laces of his boots and threw them into a corner with a thud. When she rose, he grabbed her hand and pulled her towards him. She lost her footing and tumbled onto the bed beside him, her gown thrown into disarray, displaying the rounded curves of her breasts, her auburn hair spread over the covers like spun silk.

A faerie smiling up to him, bewitching and enticing.

Ignoring the stabbing pain in his head, his arms enfolded her as he shifted on top of her. Her breathing increased, her chest rising and falling. Her gaze, curious and wondering, met his.

Sweet Mary! Send her away.

Yet the creamy skin of her half-exposed breasts proved too much of a temptation. Geoffrey slid his hand over her bodice, gently brushing the soft skin above it. She sucked in her breath, lying still. Not moving away. Not screaming.

"Oh, damn it." His voice barely a whisper, he lowered his mouth onto hers. The sweet softness, tasting of honey and barley, urged him onward. As his tongue gently probed her lips, they parted. Ditching all propriety, his mouth plundered hers in a hungry battle. She returned his exploration with eagerness. Her arms slid around his back, pulling him closer. His leg parted hers as his hand released a breast from her gown, nudging the exposed nipple until it hardened.

His breathing mingled with hers, fast, urgent. A moan escaped her, her hands grasping his tunic, kneading the sore muscles on his back. He slid his mouth down her slender neck towards her breasts. Her heart beat in tune with his, a fast rhythm neither could escape. When his mouth covered a puckered nipple, his tongue circling the sensitive flesh, her body writhed beneath him.

"Geoffrey…oh!"

His mind whirled as he sucked until her breathing grew ragged. Geoffrey heaved himself up, watching her face, as his hand roamed her neck, down her waist until it reached the folds of her skirt, her parted legs inviting him to explore. He rubbed his fingers over her softest part, the fabric of her gown only highlighting the thrill, her shaking body pliant to his touch. A moan escaped her open lips. He kissed her again.

A knock on the door pulled him from his languid stupor.

For an instant he stared at Alleyne, her eyes fluttering open, half dreamy, half surprised.

Another knock followed. "Geoffrey, are you within?" Guy's voice brought him back to reality.

He closed his eyes. What had he done?

"Wait a moment, Guy." He scrambled off the bed, offering Alleyne his hand. Hers was shaking as she pulled herself into an upright position. Her face crimson, she swiftly adjusted her gown, keeping her gaze firmly rooted to the floor.

"I'll best retire now. Good night…" Her voice trailed away but her shoulders, pushed back, showed determination. She rose from the bed and tiptoed to the door. After a nod from him, she lifted the latch and slid through a narrow gap.

"Good night, Guy. I hope you'll find the floor not too uncomfortable."

Guy stood in the doorway, a wide grin on his face, as a door slammed shut. Then the sound of a bolt being pushed into place reached Geoffrey. He released a deep breath and ruffled his hair.

"My, your arrival was timely." Geoffrey walked over to the narrow window and gazed into the dark lane below.

"It appears so. Or not, depending on point of view."

A chuckle made Geoffrey spin round. "This is no laughing matter, Guy. I seduced the lass."

His sergeant shut the door and leaned against it, arms crossed. "She didn't seem upset. I'd say, on the contrary." His mouth twitched.

"That just makes it worse." Geoffrey turned away and rested his hot temple against the cool window frame. "Unforgivable."

"No, 'tis only human. The lass has been inside your head ever since you first set eyes on her."

"She's damaged goods." Geoffrey gritted his teeth, remembering the adoring looks she had sent Will's way. "I won't have history repeat itself."

"Come now, Geoffrey. You know nothing amiss

happened."

He spun round. "Do I? Do I really?" He crossed the room in four angry strides, coming to a halt bare inches from Guy. "How do I know that? I saw her with Will, the way she gazed at him, how he seduced her with soothing words and touches. What makes you think he didn't succeed? Will always gets what he wants."

"Not this time."

"And then at Caen Castle, Anjou left her chamber in the middle of the night. What could possibly be innocent about a womaniser leaving a lady's bedroom at that time? Nothing!" He spat the last word, a bitter taste in his mouth.

Geoffrey wanted to bang his head against the wall, to rid himself of the alcohol still numbing his mind, of the images of Alleyne in Will's arms, in Anjou's bed.

Just like she had lain in his, submitted to his touch. She was no innocent.

"Damn it to hell!" He kicked the door, and tried to ignore the pain soaring through his foot. "Leave me!"

"Geof–"

"I said, leave me." He stood nose-to-nose with his sergeant, his tone cool.

Guy nodded. "As you wish." He turned, lifted the latch and slid out, pulling the door gently shut.

Geoffrey kicked it again, this time with his other foot. Dear God, he wanted to destroy something, pummel it into submission just as much as he wanted Alleyne to submit to him.

He had nearly lost himself today.

Never again.

***

The silence that had lingered over the small group became more and more awkward with each mile they covered. Again, the warm rays of the sun ensured a swift pace. Alleyne's mind worked at the same pace, never resting. Forced to look at Geoffrey's upright back for most of the journey, she had to admire the proud, alert stance, and the ease with which he talked to people from all sorts of backgrounds. Just earlier he had happily chatted to a group of English nuns undertaking a personal pilgrimage to Santiago de Compostela, now he was in deep discussion with a merchant from Rouen, on his way to Seez to collect his new bride.

Hearing only parts of the conversation, Alleyne had shuddered at the thought of the young girl, not much older than herself, who the merchant had clearly bought as companion. A glance at his exterior, the fine linen shirt and hose and embroidered gambeson, explained it all. The girl might not get to enjoy the acts of the bedchamber but she would not want for worldly luxuries.

The memory of a bedchamber brought heat to her face and she quickly averted her gaze from Geoffrey's back to the spire of Seez Cathedral looming in the distance. They would stop for the night in the small market town before they moved on to Mortagne on the morrow.

Geoffrey appeared nervous, distant whenever they spoke – which was on no more than two occasions. One such time was during a meal they took at a wayside inn. Throughout the repast, taken in the inn's main room where noise prohibited any sensible talk, he had avoided her gaze and always remained just out of reach. Only occasionally did she find his eyes on her. Fresh tears stung her eyes at the insult which hung in the air between them.

Her temper rose. She needed to speak with him about the night at Falaise, about Anjou, and about Will, but how could she begin such a conversation? He clearly deemed her a harlot. Not surprising after last night.

Guy.

She wiped away the tears and turned around to see him smile at her. He had stayed at the rear throughout their journey, not allowing her to be approached unexpectedly. The merchant's people and other travellers followed at the same pace. She returned Guy's smile and waved him forward. A swift glance at Geoffrey's back, several yards ahead of her, told her he was still chatting to the merchant, too preoccupied to look back.

When Guy reached her side she held a forefinger to her lips. "I need your help." Her voice was barely a whisper and for an instant she feared Guy had not heard her. Then he nodded.

"Of course, my lady. What would you have me do?" His expression was open, genuine.

Alleyne began to relax. "I have to speak to Geoffrey. I have to tell him all."

A shadow crossed Guy's eyes. "Whatever all may be, I would tell him before we reach the village of Mortagne. A dying or dead brother will leave him with much work, and little time."

"I know. That's why I need your help. It has to be tonight."

"I don't know his plans for Seez, but I will take you to his chamber if we must. I'm certain he will listen."

"Thank you." She stared at Geoffrey, his black hair glinting in the sunlight as he threw back his head and laughed at something the merchant said. Suddenly all became clear, as a sense of belonging settled in her heart. Her breathing grew shallow. She needed him not only to survive or to regain Bellac. She needed him in her life. She craved his attention, his touch. Last night proved it.

Oh, dear God, she was falling in love with him. She swallowed.

"Geoffrey has risked his life for you, my lady, on several occasions. He deserves your honesty."

Alleyne nodded, unable to wrest her eyes from Geoffrey's broad back. "He will have it…if it's not already too late."

"You have one chance to find out." That said, Guy slowed his pace, settling in behind her as they rode through the gates into Seez.

Ahead, the merchant took his farewell from Geoffrey, bowed to her as far as his girth allowed and rode off, down a narrow lane. His retainers overtook her and followed at brisk pace.

Geoffrey pointed ahead. "Our inn is on High Street, a few yards ahead. It will be a little noisier than in Falaise. But it will mean a speedy departure in the morning." He turned without awaiting a response and shot ahead at a trot.

She exchanged a swift glance with Guy, who nodded. Slightly encouraged, she took a deep breath and hurried to catch up with Geoffrey.

A short while later she found herself settled into a small but comfortable chamber under the eaves of a narrow town house. Evening sunshine struggled to light up the room through a small window overlooking a herb garden. Alleyne leaned against the frame and closed her eyes, letting the warm rays invigorate her face. A sharp knock on the door made her jump, and she rushed to open it.

Geoffrey stood in the narrow corridor. He had changed into his fine clothes, his hair combed back. "The landlord will serve your evening meal within the hour. In your room."

"Oh, but I don't mind eating in the guest room. It looked–"

"I have already discussed your requirements." His voice was as sharp as the knock at the door. "As I will dine with friends tonight, it's not advisable for you to venture downstairs on your own, my lady. I shall ask the landlord's wife to wake you when we depart on the morrow. I wish you good night." A perfunctory bow, then he turned on his heel.

"Geoffrey," Alleyne whispered, watching as he marched down the steep steps at the end of the corridor until she lost sight of him.

Her heart sank.

Chapter Seventeen

Geoffrey's mood was black. Having instructed Guy to keep an eye on Alleyne, he strode to the southern side of the town. The day's unexpected heat and lack of rain led to the narrow lanes being clogged up with slimy mud. He reined in his step, avoiding the worst puddles. Better not look too closely at the stinking mess. Sweat beaded his brow and he opened his cloak to cool his heated body.

Determined to escape the temptation of Alleyne's company, he had remembered an old friend. A chat with someone completely unrelated to any recent events seemed the right antidote to her wily charms. Geoffrey unclenched his fists, his breathing calmed. Tonight, he would not think about her again.

Dusk had fallen by the time he reached a large, whitewashed town house at the end of a quiet cul-de-sac which the innkeeper had directed him to. Thiebaut de Bernai did well, Geoffrey thought, as his gaze took in the lead glass windows on the upper level. The manor was surrounded by a high wall, the entrance gate solid when he knocked. The narrow window in the gate opened and a weathered face poked through.

"You are?"

Almost bursting out laughing at the level of watchfulness in the man's eyes – his heavy lids barely open, indicating he likely had been asleep – Geoffrey contained himself just in time. "Is this the residence of Thiebaut de Bernai?"

The man nodded. "This is Master Thiebaut's house. What business have you with him?"

"I'm an old friend of his. Sir Geoffrey de Mortagne."

"Are you?" The guard squinted his eyes. "He never mentioned you."

"It's a long time ago I last saw him. He is at home, is he not?"

"Yes." Cocking his head like a bird, the guard finally shuffled backward and allowed Geoffrey into a narrow yard, barely enough to let him pass. The guard gestured towards a door, which he opened for Geoffrey, allowing him in first. He shut it behind him and pointed to a chair. "Take a seat, my lord. I'll see if Master Thiebaut will receive visitors at this hour." An eyebrow raised, he turned and trundled up a narrow staircase, tutting.

Geoffrey grinned as he sat, resting his forearms on his knees. The narrow corridor opened to a large room, dark and cold. A solid oak table, easily seating a score guests, stood in the middle, devoid of any decoration. Usually, at this time of day, a family would be gathered in their main room. Where were they?

He hoped Thiebaut would see him. Truth was, he was uncertain about his reception. He had been remiss in responding to any of Thiebaut's letters detailing his happy family life. After four winters with no response, the letters had dried up.

"Now, now!" A shout from the top of the steps made him rise. "I live to see the day."

Geoffrey relaxed as Thiebaut sauntered down the stairs, a wide grin on his round face. "'Tis good to see you, Thiebaut." He returned his friend's embrace.

Thiebaut stood back, clasping Geoffrey's shoulders. "Too many years have passed without word, yet here you are, not changed at all, under-sheriff de Mortagne."

Geoffrey let his eyes roam over the other man. "Your hairline has not improved with age, old friend. But otherwise you look as sprightly as twelve winters ago."

Thiebaut laughed. "Aye, I can look after my body with good food and wine, but alas, I'm powerless against some of the more obvious signs of age. Are you going to stay with us?"

"I have a room at the Mercat Inn, together with other… travellers in my company."

"What a pity! But you'll share my dinner, won't you?"

"Have I ever refused your generous hospitality, Thiebaut?" Geoffrey smiled. "I thank you for the offer. I must admit I'm famished from my travels."

"Follow me to the solar, then we'll talk." He barked an order at an invisible servant for another trencher and cup as he climbed the stairs.

Geoffrey followed him slowly, his bones aching with each step. The last few weeks had been gruelling and, for the first time in his life, he craved rest.

Thiebaut ushered him into a cosy room. Windows on either side let in the early evening light. A small fire in a grate kept away the chills. His host slumped into a seat at the head of a narrow table in the centre of the room, and gestured to a comfortable chair to his right.

"Be seated, Geoffrey. You look in need of a good night's sleep, if I may say so." He signalled to a young lad to fill the cups before he raised his. "To old friends, Geoffrey."

"To old friends." Geoffrey tasted the ruby liquid, allowing its warmth to spread through his limbs. "This is a fine drop."

His host chuckled. "An excellent grape from Burgundy."

Geoffrey nodded, relishing the strong taste. He looked around the room. Elaborately embroidered tapestries covered the walls, the furniture – cabinets bearing fine dishes and two large chairs buried under a sea of cushions by the grate behind Thiebaut – showing wealth and comfort. Soft rugs covered the stone floor. He nodded in appreciation.

"You have done well for yourself. Is business still going well despite Anjou laying waste to all of Normandy?"

His host leaned back, stretching his legs dressed in russet hose. "Ahh, this wretched war has an impact, of course. My couriers have been robbed of their wares, both by mercenaries and by Anjou's men, so many times I have lost count. Almost." A sly smile graced his mouth. "But I keep finding new ways of sending my goods to their destination. A small civil war doesn't stop me."

Geoffrey chuckled. "You're as clever as I expected. But tell me, where is your family?"

Thiebaut grew sombre. He sipped at his wine before meeting Geoffrey's gaze. "I sent them to Poitiers. This country isn't safe for a wife and three daughters."

"You have three daughters?"

"Yes, and no son." He shook his head. "Amelie wished to stay, but the safety of our children is our priority. They have been in Poitiers at her sister's manor for the past year."

"That's a long time to be without your family. Have you visited?"

"Only once, at Christmas." His eyes clouded over.

"You miss them."

Thiebaut nodded. "Aye. But at least I know the girls can go to the markets and buy trinkets without worrying about attacks. 'Tis but a small price to pay." He swallowed as he stared into his cup.

A servant pushed open a door, a tray of bowls with steaming meat and vegetables in his hand.

Thiebaut straightened, shrugging as if shaking off gloomy thoughts. "Let's eat. And then you tell me all about your life."

Geoffrey grinned. "All of it?"

Thiebaut laughed. "Of course. You owe me for all those unwritten letters."

***

Geoffrey leaned into the cushioned chair and stretched his legs towards the fire, a brimming cup of wine in hand. He stared into the dancing flames as childhood memories flooded his mind. Memories he had successfully blocked for the past ten years. Memories his conversation with Thiebaut had re-awoken.

His father had always detested him, though Geoffrey never discovered the reason. If the man even needed one…

Geoffrey stopped long ago counting the times he had tried to impress his stern father, unable to break through the hard shell Father had built around him, unable to make sense of it. Bertrand, the first born, the favourite son, always received praise. True, they did not share a mother, Bertrand's having died in childbirth, as had his own mother, God rest her soul.

Bertrand always escaped with any misdeeds. He could do no wrong, even when he drowned Geoffrey's favourite puppy in the pond or accused Geoffrey's favourite childhood friend – the daughter of their steward – of stealing. Without much ado, she had a hand cut off and her family was banished from Father's lands. She had been innocent. A shiver ran down Geoffrey's spine.

On Geoffrey's thirteenth birthday, Father had arranged for him to join the Benedictine Abbey in Caen. Refusing to accept his fate, a desperate Geoffrey bolted to the court of the Count of Perche. Admiring Geoffrey's daring spirit, his godfather accepted him as a squire. Grateful for the chance, a young Geoffrey had done his utmost to earn Perche's respect, accompanying him on his journeys to Spain to fight the Moors. As expected, it had been easy for him to settle into the life of a fighting man.

On return to Mortagne, Perche knighted him, an act approved by King Henry. Then Bertrand's jealousy could no longer touch him. The count had turned him into the man he was now, a well-trained spy, a knight walking among the great of the realm. He chuckled.

"What are you thinking of?" Thiebaut cut into his thoughts, his voice low.

Geoffrey looked up. Thiebaut settled back into his cushioned chair, feet propped on a foot stool. A smirk graced his friend's face as he swirled his cup in his hand.

"I just remembered Count Rotrou's court." He grinned. "My training was impeccable. I guess he knew long before I did where my path would lead me."

Thiebaut nodded. "Aye, I agree. Perche is a wily fox. He knows a good man when he meets him. That's why he trained you so mercilessly before you left for England." He took a sip, his gaze on Geoffrey over the rim of his cup. "And that's why he kicked out Will d'Arques."

Geoffrey's brows shot up. "He did what?" His mind whirled.

"Oh, you don't know? My, you have been too far away from home. I thought your brother would write and tell you all."

"I hadn't heard from Bertrand until I received word of his illness." A bitter taste lay on his tongue.

"Well, you'll be pleased to hear that young Will d'Arques was sent away in disgrace. He was found guilty of seducing the count's ward, a young lady who had come to live with him after she had lost her parents, a year or so after you left. While men tend to overlook the same charge in a servant, leaving a girl in the care of one's liege lord pregnant is not acceptable. Perche forced Will to wed the girl. When Will beat her on their wedding night, leaving her covered in bruises, he was duly dismissed from service and his wife retired to a nunnery. It seemed Perche had been waiting for an excuse. His fury was staggering."

"Will is married?" That new piece of information stunned Geoffrey. When Thiebaut nodded, he murmured, "The man was about to wed the lady in my company, for her inheritance." Suddenly it all became clear; Will's attempted seduction of Alleyne, his reluctance to wed her swiftly and make the affair official. Would he have wed her anyway, knowing his wife was safely tucked away in faraway Perche? Committed bigamy? He shook his head in disbelief. Another lady's life Will had destroyed.

"Ahh." Thiebaut gave him a grave look. "That explains his prolonged absence from Normandy. His goal has always been to find a rich heiress."

Geoffrey's teeth gnashed as fury rose in him. Will had built up a reputation in England, grown rich on doing dirty jobs other men would decline to even consider, garnered favours from the rich and powerful.

He must tell Alleyne. It would crush her, but also served

as a final warning if she needed one. She had a narrow escape.

"The worst is, though, that Will now holds Lady Alleyne's manor lands. I'll have to find a way to regain them for her, but with the empress not interested in petty squabbles, and King Stephen captured, we can't expect any support at this point." He took a large draught of wine and refilled his cup from a clay pitcher on the small, round table between them.

"Yes, I've heard of the king's capture. The situation in England is tenuous." Thiebaut shook his head. "I don't think it possible to fight Will until one or the other is securely on the throne and you can openly petition for a return. If Stephen regains his freedom, you would have to prove your allegiance, as your lord, Sheriff Miles, is openly supporting Matilda. No doubt, Stephen will know your allegiance. He wouldn't trust you."

Geoffrey agreed. "Whichever way I'd try, my hands are tied. But I have no choice. I must find a way to win back Bellac."

Thiebaut leaned forward and patted his arm. "I have no doubt you will. It might just take longer than expected. But then, you'll likely be held up at Mortagne for a while anyway."

Geoffrey's head shot up. "Why? Once Bertrand has recovered, I can return to England."

"And what if he dies? What of your inheritance?" The quizzical look in Thiebaut's eyes made Geoffrey's skin crawl.

"What inheritance?"

"You should ask your brother before he dies. About your mother. About her property, her title."

Geoffrey snorted. "My mother had no title, as you well know. And no lands. She was a minor knight's daughter."

Thiebaut laughed. "You definitely have been away for too long. Rumours are rife with who your mother really was, ever since Bertrand tried to have her grave dissolved some years ago. An order from Perche stopped it. Her remains were then taken to the chapel of the counts of Perche and Mortagne, to be interred near the late Count Geoffrey."

"What? Why did I never hear of this?" Geoffrey's vision swam.

"Ask your brother."

***

Alleyne sat near the open window, the evening breeze tickling her skin. She had briefly contemplated to refuse the food brought up by the innkeeper's wife, but the pleasant aroma of herbs proved too much of a temptation. With unusual appetite, she had devoured the stew down to the last morsel. Wheat was scarce, as was meat, but as long as rabbits roamed the countryside, crafty innkeepers knew how to feed their clients.

Now, her hands folded loosely over her belly, she leaned back, watching townspeople hurry home before darkness descended fully. Days were long this time of year. Though tired from her journey, the balmy air pulled at her, keen to lead her out into the encroaching night. A church bell rang out, echoing through the narrow lanes. She leaned forward and craned her neck but could not see any spires. Was the cathedral open this late? Guy had mentioned building works when she told him of her wish to pray for her father. Apparently the Lady Chapel was intact, he confirmed, but he suggested she go in the morning. Taking a deep breath, she made up her mind. She would not wait.

She needed to pray for Father and seek guidance from God about her future. About Geoffrey.

Taking her cloak from the hook behind the door, Alleyne secured it with a pin. The chapel was likely to be cold, as all places of worship were. Softly, she raised the latch and pulled the door open. Expecting Guy outside, she stared at the empty corridor. Perhaps he was still in the main guest room, partaking of a cup of ale, or two.

She smiled and pulled the door shut behind her. The

dimly-lit corridor led to the narrow staircase, she remembered from her arrival. With one hand, she hitched up her gown enough for her feet to find secure foothold on the steps, while seeking to steady herself on the wall with the other. At the bottom, another short corridor led to an outside door at the far end. She hurried past the open entrance to the inn's main room, the noise of dozens of patrons muffling her steps.

Outside, she glanced up and down the lane. Dark shadows loomed underneath the overhanging buildings on either side, with dusk settling across town. They had crossed a square not far from the cathedral. She darted towards it, staying firmly in the middle of the lanes to avoid the mud. Between houses, a spire of the new cathedral loomed large. Her blood surged through her body as she rushed towards the high peak. Only a few men paid her attention, her step too fast to invite any comments.

Finally, she emerged from a darkening lane into a wide, open square. A half-built tower stood tall, the foundations of another only yards on the other side. She gazed up in awe. Once the spires were completed, this would form an impressive entrance to the new cathedral. But at this moment, the gaping hole between them made her skin crawl. Building sites were unsafe, and Alleyne kept at a distance.

She circled the front until she came to the Lady Chapel. Its narrow door opened into a small space, illuminated by dozens of candles. She crossed the threshold and held her breath. A wave of warmth enveloped her. Tallow candles lit the small space. Not the large, cold space other chapels were. A statue of the Virgin and Child, united in their close embrace, stood by a small, rectangular altar several steps up from the ground. Not taking her eyes off the statue, she knelt on the lowest step. Only then did she close her eyes and lower her head in prayer.

As the heat from the candles spread through her limbs, she repeated words she had not spoken since Father's burial. Tears streamed down her face, part in mourning, part in relief of finally finding peace. "*Ave Maria*," she whispered, crossing herself. "*Gratia plena…*"

An ache seeped into her bones. With a start, Alleyne came to from her prayers, blinking at the bright flicker of the candles. How long had she knelt here? She stared at the Virgin, whispered words of thanks, and crossed herself. She pushed herself upright, her aching shins protesting, and she furtively stretched them. Physical pain became bearable when someone listened. Smiling at the statue, she nodded. She had an ally. Now she knew what to do.

Feeling her resolve strengthened, Alleyne walked back to the door and cast a final glance at the altar before leaving the chapel. Gone was the warmth, replaced by cool night air. She must have spent hours in prayer, or so it seemed, as the square was deserted. The shutters of the houses facing the cathedral were closed, families gathered inside, no doubt. She must hurry before it became unsafe for her to be wandering about.

Clutching her cloak tighter around her, the hood pulled over her head, she darted across the square. Then she stopped. Which lane had she come from?

Panic rose in her chest as she stared around. Several narrow, darkened lanes led away from the square. Oh, why had she not made sure she remembered a marker? The houses, with their overhanging upper storeys, all resembled each other. A shout rose from one lane, with laughter following ribald suggestions.

She ventured towards the entrance of that lane. In the dim distance, a sign creaked at an angle. An inn! Was it on the correct side of the lane? What was her inn called again? She cursed herself for not paying more attention, but as she had stayed in many inns on the way, they all blurred into one.

There was only one way to find out. She balled her trembling hands into fists, keeping tight grip on her cloak, and strode forward. As she neared the inn, high noise levels rose from its interior. The building was whitewashed, true, but so were nearly all houses in Seez. As the door was thrown open, she merged into the overhanging shadow of the house opposite. Two men staggered out, clasping each other for support. They appeared deep in their cups, their steps unsteady. As the men hobbled past her, she held her breath. But her new ally must have kept an eye on her, as they soon disappeared around a corner. She released her breath and, thanking the Virgin, hurried to the still open door of the inn. A quick glance inside told her it was the wrong place. She must return to the square and take another lane.

As her gaze drifted away from the crowds gathered within, it fell onto two men sitting at a narrow table in a corner. One, an older man with receding hair, was dressed in expensive materials. Another, his back to her, resembled…

"Geoffrey?" A whisper escaped her as she watched, mesmerised.

A blonde woman, her unbound hair falling forward, bent over him, revealing ample cleavage, her hand firmly clasping his shoulders. He turned his face towards the harlot, showing a wide smile.

"Sweet Mother!" Aware she should leave, Alleyne stood rooted to the spot, her eyes not leaving the man she had come to love. She shook her head. No, the man she thought she loved. A man who now pushed a handful of coins into the woman's hand. Alleyne felt her mouth go dry as the blonde pressed a kiss on Geoffrey's mouth, her hand weaving around his neck.

Her vision blurred. She must go. Stumbling away from the inn, she pushed her way through a group of men.

"Hey, sweeting. I've only just arrived." A hand grabbed her arm. "Why the hurry?" Laughter followed his words.

Alleyne pulled herself free from his grasp and shot forward into the darkness. Only when the noise had receded, did she stop. She swallowed hard, looking around. This was not the square by the cathedral. As voices reached her from different directions, she spun around but the lanes lay in darkness.

"Sweet Mary, help me!" she whispered and crossed

herself. The sound of footsteps made her step into the shadows of a house. If the town guard spotted her, they might think her a whore. She would end up in gaol.

She watched the guard pass and delve into the lane she had come from. Good, they would be busy with the inn's patrons.

As she gazed across the small square, she recognised the fountain. They had turned left after they passed it earlier that day. Her eyes firm on a wider lane ahead of her, she shot from the shadow and hurried along. Another sign loomed large outside a tall house. She approached, but her relief was short-lived. As she stared through the narrow gap serving as a window, her fear grew. Inside, women clad in nothing but the faintest shifts draped themselves over the laps of several townsmen, ranging from skinny to portly. Alleyne's skin crawled. A whorehouse.

A hand touched her shoulder and she shrieked. Swiftly she turned, ready to ram her knee into the attacker who jumped back.

Chapter Eighteen

At dawn, the innkeeper's wife woke her. Alleyne had no recollection of how she returned to the inn the previous night, nor how she ended up in her bed. She sat up. "How–?"

The rotund woman, old enough to be her mother, turned from the opened door and tucked a strand of brown hair into her wimple. "The sergeant brought you in. He carried you halfway across the town. When I saw the state of you, I couldn't sit back, could I?"

"You took me here, to bed?" Alleyne felt heat rise in her cheeks.

A loud laugh cracked through the silence. "Aye, and don't worry – I've seen plenty of young lasses to their beds safely after they've been out. Too much wine's not good for the head." She tutted and pulled the door shut behind her.

"But I'm not drunk!" Alleyne stared at the door, her protestations loud in the quiet room.

Her temples pounded but it was not drink that caused it. Memories flooded back and she choked back tears. Geoffrey with a harlot. And she had thought she loved him. How could she? A shudder wracked her body.

She slid her toes from underneath the covers. Best she rose soon, so Geoffrey did not have to wait. A knock on the door made her cover up again.

"Who is it?"

The door opened and a young girl poked her head through the gap. The resemblance with the innkeeper's wife was startling. It must be the daughter. "I'm here to help you dress, my lady."

"Come in." Alleyne threw the covers back. "We must

hurry."

Once dressed and packed, she joined Geoffrey and Guy in the small yard behind the inn as they readied their mounts. She ignored Geoffrey's scrutiny of her attire and beamed at Guy. A warning glance told her he had kept her outing from Geoffrey. She busied herself with her cloak, then approached her mare, stroking the soft mane. "I'm ready."

A grunt from Geoffrey made her look at him more closely. His skin pale, bags showed beneath his eyes. He appeared to have enjoyed a long night. No doubt with that harlot from the inn. Men! Revulsion tore through her. She swallowed back the bile that rose in her throat. Men were all the same.

"Are you chilled, my lady?" Geoffrey's voice cut through the silence. The storm in his gaze made her squirm.

"No, my lord. I'll just be glad to arrive at your manor."

"It's not my manor but my brother's," he said brusquely, and mounted. "You would do well to remember that."

Grateful for Guy's assistance, she eased into her saddle. "Thank you, Guy."

He nodded and went to his own horse, still not uttering a word. Something was amiss between the men but she could not think of a cause. Had Guy dared reprimand Geoffrey for his late night? Or had Geoffrey told him off for leaving her alone, unattended? She glanced from one to the other but as neither met her gaze, she shrugged it off.

Geoffrey led the way through the lanes bustling with tradesmen. Outside the town gate he came to a halt. "We will cross into Perche lands soon and should be in Mortagne by midday. Then we can rest and plan."

Alleyne thought she heard him say, "I hope", but was not certain. Checking her cloak was tightly fastened against the morning breeze, she urged her mare into a canter.

The sun had risen over the crests of distant hills by the time Geoffrey slowed. She reined in her mare when Guy appeared by her side.

"My lady." His voice was barely above a whisper.

"Geoffrey isn't aware of your, erm, escape last night. I'd rather we keep it that way."

She nodded. "I understand. Of course, we shall keep this between us. But tell me," she added, "why is he in such a strange mood?"

Guy's jaw set in a grim smile. "I think the visit to his friend's house stirred too many memories. He returned, deep in his cups, and stayed up most of the night. I'd wager he took more drink, from the empty jug I found on the floor this morning."

She sent him a sharp glance.

"I know, my lady. I should have taken the ale from him."

He had misread her. "He was at our inn all night?"

Guy's glance was open, curious. "Aye, why?"

"Because I–"

"Over there's a good place to break our fast, don't you agree?" Geoffrey shouted from ahead, pointing at a clearing on a nearby hillside. "We need to talk before we reach Mortagne."

Alleyne exchanged a glance with Guy as they nudged their horses to follow Geoffrey's direction. "That sounds ominous."

The sergeant nodded.

***

Geoffrey tied Feu to a low branch, took the bag containing their provisions and dropped into the grass. The scent of wildflowers hung in the air, their colourful display dotted the meadow. The lush grass swayed in the soft, warm breeze. Chestnut trees loomed large behind him, reminding him how close home was.

Home? No, Mortagne was not his home. Gloucester was. He shook his head to rid himself of such treacherous thoughts.

Guy threw a blanket across the grass and gestured to Alleyne to settle onto it. She untied her cloak and crouched, tucking her heels beside her thigh. Geoffrey caught a glimpse of an ankle and averted his gaze to a distant valley. He must forget that damned attraction. Alleyne was never going to be his.

He must tell her about Will.

Guy handed Alleyne the water flask. Unholy thoughts flashed through Geoffrey's mind as he watched her swallow sip by sip. His mouth went dry. He turned away and unwrapped the bread and cheese the innkeeper had given them. Laying the bundle in the centre between them, he broke off a corner. He took a bite and regretted it instantly. The bread tasted stale. 'Twas yesterday's, if not older. He forced it down and took a deep draught of water. His temples had not stopped pounding since he rose. Too much wine the night before.

Thiebaut had taken him to his favourite inn, where the owner's daughter had taken him under her wing. He had given her several coins to ensure he was served the best wine. In hindsight, his head aching, that had turned out to be a bad decision.

He leaned back on his elbows, watching Alleyne as she washed down a morsel of cheese. He waited until she lowered the flask. "Will d'Arques is married." There, the secret was out.

The colour drained from her face and the hand holding the water flask shook violently.

He flinched at his own carelessness and shot up to kneel by her side. She stared straight ahead, into the distance, unseeing. It must have shaken her to the core. "I'm sorry, Alleyne. I shouldn't have blurted it out like I did."

"You clearly shouldn't, my lord." Guy's cynical tone hit him.

"Leave us, Guy! Go water the horses." He glared at the sergeant. Guy rose without another word, untied the horses and marched off towards the tree line whence the trickling of water reached them.

"Damn." Geoffrey swore, and pulled Alleyne's hands into his. Hers were like ice. "Alleyne?"

She raised her gaze, meeting his. "Will is married? Since

when?"

"For many years, before he came to England. I'm sorry."

She withdrew her hands and rubbed them, as if ridding herself of his touch. "No, you're not. It suits you very well."

He sat back, crouching on his knees, and frowned. "What do you mean?"

She stood, her hands firmly on her hips. "You know what I mean, Geoffrey. You have always suspected Will ever since he arrived at Bellac. I know what Anjou said – Will is likely behind Father's murder. But so far that has not been proven, so you've had to hold your judgment. But now this story emerges and again Will is under suspicion. Yes, perhaps he is guilty. But why can't you admit you have no idea who did it? Is it not enough that I'm stuck here, in this war-torn wilderness, with you?"

Tears ran down her face. Geoffrey leapt to his feet. She spun on her heels and ran down the meadow towards the stream, her ragged sobs echoing behind her.

Did she still love Will? He thought she had gotten over him. Clearly, that was not the case.

Geoffrey rubbed his hands over his face. Whatever he did, he could not do right by her. He bent to pull the rug from the floor and picked up the water flask.

"Guy!" he shouted, his voice hoarse. "Let's move!"

After Alleyne joined them again, Geoffrey kept a fast pace. She ignored him. His mind whirled while the throbbing at his temple intensified. His hopes had died the moment she had run from him. Perhaps he always imagined the spark he thought burned between them. After all, how could he compete with Will? Bile rose in his throat and he swallowed hard. Always Will! He even won when he was hundreds of miles away.

Concentrate on Mortagne. He must focus on Bertrand. Thinking of his brother made his head feel like splitting. They had parted on bad terms, and now he returned to his brother's sickbed. Like a vulture.

"Geoffrey, look. Up ahead. Is that Mortagne?" Guy's voice cut through his musing.

He raised his gaze. The town perched on a hill above him remained unchanged. Like a tapestry, consigned to memory. The town walls stood solid, rooftops and church spires hovered above the parapet.

"Welcome to Mortagne, the seat of the counts of Perche. My home town." He could not hold back a bitter note creeping into his voice.

As he turned, Alleyne's eyes were on him, full of… sympathy? Pity? He quickly turned back and spurred Feu on. The final part of this misbegotten play awaited.

A guard at the town gate held out his pike. Geoffrey halted Feu; Guy and Alleyne stopped behind him.

"What do you want?" The guard, his uniform stretched over a large stomach, shuffled his feet, a distinct look of suspicion on his face. "We don't have need to folk fleeing Normandy. We're a small town."

The guard considered them refugees. Geoffrey shook his head, chuckling softly. "We're not fleeing Normandy, man. I'm Sir Geoffrey de Mortagne, brother of Master Bertrand, godson of the late Count Geoffrey. Are you still trying to stop me?"

The guard flushed, leaned his pike against the parapet and hurried to open the gate. "Apologies, my lord. I've never met you."

Geoffrey grew serious. It had been too long. "No, you haven't. Thank you."

Once inside, he paused.

"Geoffrey?" Guy's voice held concern.

He smiled at his sergeant. "I'm fine. Just nervous, 'tis all."

"You'll do the right thing by your brother. I know it."

Geoffrey chuckled. "I wish I had your confidence." He glanced at Alleyne, but her gaze roamed the buildings around them.

"Mortagne is an old town, my lady. Folk are gruff but only on the surface. You'll come to like the place."

The chill in the gaze that met his was unmistakable. "I don't intend to stay long enough to find out."

She might as well have slapped him. Geoffrey glared at her, then nudged Feu at a slow walk down a lane following the town wall. She was not his biggest problem at this moment. He finally came to a halt outside a three-storey town house. The stone wall surrounding it was easily eight foot, but crumbled in places.

Bertrand should pay more attention. But then, he had been unwell.

Geoffrey heaved from the saddle and led Feu to a double gate. It was locked. Using his fist, he banged three times against the solid wood. Behind him, Alleyne and Guy hovered, uncertainty writ large on their faces. None knew what lay ahead.

After what seemed like an eternity, the gate opened to reveal a young lad of no more than ten years. "Yes?"

"I wish to speak to Master Bertrand. I—"

"Master Bertrand is indisposed. You have to come back another time." He swung the door to close it but Geoffrey edged his foot into the gap.

"Not so fast, my lad." He pushed the door open, pent-up anger close to eruption. "I'm his brother."

The boy's eyes widened and he released the door, turned on his heel and raced across the yard. "He's here! He's here!"

Geoffrey shook his head, pushed the gate fully open and led Feu into a yard. Alleyne came to his side, reins in hand. "This is your home?"

He nodded, unable to deny the truth. "It's one of two manors in family hands. The other is outside the village, another five miles through the forest to the east. I thought Bertrand was here, given his illness. Quicker for the apothecary to see to him. And the priest, if necessary."

She nodded and gave him a thin smile. It was enough to make his hopes soar. Perhaps she could settle here after all? For a while at least.

"I'll close the gate." Guy's voice reached him. "Give me Feu."

"Thank you. Go along the side of the house and you'll

find small stables." He gestured to a narrow path between the house and the fence.

Guy took his reins. "All will be well, Geoffrey. Don't fret." He took Alleyne's reins and led the horses away.

Before Geoffrey opened his mouth, a cry went up from the front door. "Sir Geoffrey! Finally!"

Geoffrey swallowed hard when he came face-to-face with the steward, an old man of three score years, his white hair wispy and sunburnt face wrinkled. "Aubrey. What a pleasure to see you so well. I thought you'd retired a long time ago?"

The steward bowed before engulfing him in bony arms. Geoffrey steadied him when he stumbled. "It has been too long, my lord. Your presence has been sorely missed in this house. Come within."

Only then did Aubrey appear to notice Alleyne. His shrewd eyes went from her to Geoffrey. "Your lady wife, my lord?"

"I'm Lady Alleyne de Bellac, no lord's wife, and a guest of Sir Geoffrey." Alleyne's voice was quiet, yet determined.

The steward shuffled his feet. "My apologies, my lady. I deemed a beautiful lady as yourself a most suitable spouse for this young lord."

Geoffrey laughed. "Don't worry, Aubrey. The lady Alleyne is to enjoy our hospitality for as long as she wishes to stay." His gaze met hers and she returned his smile.

"Very generous, my lord," she breathed.

He grew serious, turning back to Aubrey. "But tell me, how fares my brother?"

Aubrey's face fell, worry etched in his features. "Master Bertrand has been poorly since the winter but has deteriorated over the last few weeks. I fear, my lord, you have arrived just in time."

Aubrey led them into the hall, where Geoffrey imagined Bertrand sitting at the head of the large oak table in the centre of the room following Father's death. Even before, Bertrand had enjoyed playing lord of the manor, with Geoffrey the unwanted sibling. Geoffrey knew in later years his brother was consumed by envy. Bertrand owned manors, and miles of pastures and farm land, but a noble title had eluded him. Now the hall was deserted, the tops of the table and cupboards bare.

Aubrey gestured to a chair by a narrow grate. "My lady, if you wish to rest while I have your room made up? I'll get the boy to light the fire against the evening chills."

Alleyne took his arm. "Thank you, Aubrey. You've been most welcoming. 'Tis too mild for a fire so please don't fuss on my behalf." She cast Geoffrey a glance he could not decipher, and settled into the chair, untying her cloak, and propped her feet up on a footstool.

"My lord, I'm certain Master Bertrand awaits your company."

Geoffrey followed Aubrey up the stairs. At the top of the landing, the steward took his cloak. "He's right through there, in your father's old chamber. In the meantime, I'll ensure your rooms are readied."

Geoffrey stood in the open doorway and stared at the large four-poster bed. The figure lying beneath mountains of cushions and throws did not resemble his brother at all. At their last encounter, many years ago, Bertrand had been a large man, known for his love of food, the finer things in life. The body in the bed before him was a skeleton, the skin on his face so stretched, the bones of his arms stood out. Geoffrey went to the foot of the bed.

"Hello, Bertrand."

The skeleton opened his eyes. Geoffrey remembered well the look. Proud, jealous, full of envy. Of hate. His past merged into the present.

Definitely Bertrand. He had not changed.

***

Alleyne stared into the cold ash in the grate by her feet. What was she to do now?

The enormity of her journey hit her when the steward took her to be Geoffrey's wife. Of course, everyone here would.

Heat rose in her cheeks at the mere thought of the meaning of those words. Geoffrey's wife? Certainly not after her discovery in Seez. He clearly liked cavorting with harlots, something no husband of her's was ever going to be permitted. But how could she stop such transgressions in any husband?

Men were all the same. Even Will. Will had a wife!

Alleyne swallowed hard. He had pursued her throughout his so-called friendship with Father, all the while having a wife somewhere in Normandy. How could she have been so wrong? Strangely, though, she now felt nothing but pity. None of the excitement he caused in her every time he had visited over the years.

Instead, her heart mourned at the thought of Geoffrey sharing his bed with a harlot. Tears stung behind her eyes and she closed them quickly. She would not cry. But she had to speak with him. About what she saw.

About her future.

Footsteps on the stairs brought her out of her reverie, and she opened her eyes. The steward approached her. She returned his open smile.

"My lady, a chamber has been prepared for you. If you'd like to follow me?"

"Of course, Aubrey. I thank you for arranging this with no notice given. I'm sure life in your household must be difficult enough, even without unexpected guests." She followed him upstairs. They passed a door where she heard lowered voices. One was Geoffrey's.

"Is this..?" She pointed at the closed door.

Aubrey nodded. "Yes, it's Master Bertrand's chamber. Sir Geoffrey is with him. I assume you know their history, their, erm, enmity."

"Yes, Geoff–, Sir Geoffrey mentioned a rift. I hope they can mend it before Master Bertrand passes."

Aubrey's face was serious. "I've prayed for a reunion for many years. But both lords are stubborn. And there's also the question of Sir Geoffrey's–" He stopped short, obviously aware he was gossiping, opened a door and gestured her inside.

"The question of Sir Geoffrey's what?" She entered a small but comfortable chamber; a lady's chamber. Sumptuous wall hangings covered the stone walls, a fire danced in a grate, the large, delicately-framed bed inviting with covers of embroidered cushions and covers.

He stared at his toes. "I hope the chamber is to your liking, my lady. It belonged to Lady de Mortagne, Master Bertrand's late wife, Marguerite." Ignoring her question, he turned away. "I'll have your belongings brought up."

"Thank you, Aubrey." Alleyne spoke to an empty room. What had he meant, the question of Sir Geoffrey's…what? Aubrey's comment had her intrigued.

She hung her cloak on a hook by the door, then walked to the narrow window on the opposite wall. Leaning out, she drew in her breath. A neatly kept garden opened below her. Climbing roses bloomed against the whitewashed wall of the manor, their scent rising to her window. Rows of herbs occupied either side of a square lawn. A small paradise.

Beyond the garden stood other houses, clean and well kept. Mortagne must be a wealthy village. A sleepy place, given the lack of sounds reaching her. Apart from voices. Male voices from the room next to hers. She froze.

"I will not have it, Geoffrey. Not in my house." The voice croaked the more it rose in volume.

"She's not—"

"I don't care where you got her from, but she's not staying under my roof, living in sin."

"Bertrand, for God's sake! Alleyne is not my mistress. How often do I have to say it?"

Heat shot into Alleyne's cheeks, as aware of his words as of her eavesdropping. Still, she needed to know.

"Not…in…my…house! Wed her, then! You said she owns a manor?"

"Yes, but—"

A coughing fit interrupted him. "See, what you've

done?" The coughing subsided. "Either you wed her or she leaves. Don't care where she goes."

"You haven't changed, Bertrand. Still the pompous, stubborn fool! I really don't know why I came back."

A door slammed and silence descended. Alleyne leaned back and briefly closed her eyes. Suddenly all was clear.

Geoffrey did not want her. 'Twould seem he did not even know what to do with her now they were here. She threw her hands to cover her mouth. What was she to do?

***

"That went well." Geoffrey swore as he went downstairs in slow steps. On the table in the hall, he spotted a clay jug and four cups. At least he could rely on Aubrey.

Filling a cup to the brim, he drained it in one large gulp before replenishing it. He slumped into the seat Alleyne had taken earlier, his mind whirling. Why had he not thought of that? Now he was due to stay for several weeks – Bertrand did not have much longer in this world, he was certain – what to do with Alleyne? Bertrand was still head of the household.

Reluctantly, his anger subsiding, he had to admit Bertrand was right. Both men could not live under the same roof as a young, beautiful heiress. An unwed heiress with no lands, and no chaperone.

He had taken her from England to keep her safe from men like Will d'Arques, like Philip de Guines. Only she ended up with him instead. A second son, without property other than a cottage in Gloucester, without wealth, leading a life full of dangers. Perhaps he should have left her in Gloucester, asked Sheriff Miles to take her under his wing, petitioned the empress to find her a husband.

Those were futile thoughts as neither Matilda nor Miles had the time, nor intention, to protect a young lady with a stolen inheritance. Alleyne would have been pushed from one protector to another, and eventually married off to someone who took her for her beauty only, out of sympathy.

Not the greatest prospect either way.

At this moment, he also had no idea how to fight Will and regain Bellac. Perhaps once Matilda was crowned and settled as queen of England, she would listen and rule in his favour. A favour she owed him for years of risking his life.

He took a sip. He knew what to do. "Aubrey!"

The steward arrived from the corridor linking the room to the back of the house. "My lord?"

"Fetch me–"

The sound of hoofbeats outside diverted his attention. He strode to the door, a step ahead of Aubrey, to find Guy, grinning widely, holding the gate open to a rabble of riders.

"What the–? Ancel?" Geoffrey stepped forward and took the reins of the nearest horse. The captain of Bellac Manor's guard pulled down his hood. He laughed as he heaved himself from the saddle.

"Sir Geoffrey, I'm so glad to see you safe." He patted his horse's neck when Geoffrey handed the reins to the boy who had let him in earlier.

"I'm mightily relieved to see you, too, Ancel." He looked up to find the second rider – a woman – throw back her cape. "Elvire? You're alive!"

Guy helped her from the saddle. Elvire beamed.

"Yes, my lord. Thanks to this man." She pointed at Ancel. "His men kept me safe when d'Arques sent his bloodhounds on me." She stumbled forward and Geoffrey was quick to catch her by the arms.

"Aubrey, tell the lady Alleyne we have visitors."

"Yes, my lord. Please all, come within." Aubrey scurried up the stairs

Geoffrey led Elvire to the cushioned chair he had recently occupied. "Guy, would you pass the wine, please." He gestured to the table with his head.

Ancel dropped into a vacant seat and accepted a cup of wine from Guy. Geoffrey took another cup from him and handed it to Elvire. "Drink. You're safe now."

A small shadow fell over the doorway. Geoffrey turned. A gangly lad stood there, studying the tips of his boots.

"Alfred?"

The boy grinned. "Aye, Sir Geoffrey. 'Tis me. I couldn't just let Ancel go off by himself, could I?"

Geoffrey laughed and exchanged a glance with the captain. "No, you couldn't. You've grown since we last met…"

Ancel chuckled. "You tell him, Sir Geoffrey. He'll want some wine next."

"And why not?" Guy handed the boy a cup. Alfred cradled it gingerly with long fingers. "He deserves it."

Light footsteps sounded on the stairs, then Alleyne whirled into the room. "Ancel?" When he nodded, she beamed. "I'm so glad you're here. Oh, Elvire!" She turned to her maid, nearly knocking the cup from Elvire's hand as she embraced her in a firm hug. Tears stood in her eyes. "You're alive."

"Aye, my sweeting. I'm alive." The maid stepped back and squeezed Alleyne's hands. "And I'll never leave your side again."

Geoffrey's heart wrenched. What had they endured? He must question Ancel later, once the women retired. The captain returned his gaze and nodded in silent agreement.

Aubrey appeared by his side, a brimming pitcher in hand. "My lord, Master Bertrand wondered about the commotion. I informed him we have more visitors. He has ordered a pig to be slaughtered for our guests. I've just told Cook."

Ancel stood. "I'm aware your lord is unwell. I can find an inn for myself and Alfred to be out of the way."

"My lord is dying," Aubrey said bluntly. "But he wishes to extend his hospitality to all Sir Geoffrey's guests, including the ladies. I trust you stay in your lady's room?" He glanced at Elvire.

The maid nodded, squeezing Alleyne's hand. "Of course I will."

Aubrey looked at Geoffrey. "We have several pallets we could lay out here in the hall. Would that suit?"

"Aye, I'm sure it'll be the best solution. What say you,

Ancel?"

"Thank you, Sir Geoffrey." Ancel turned to Aubrey. "Please pass our thanks to your lord."

Geoffrey took the pitcher from Aubrey's hand, settled into a chair and raised his refilled cup. "To returned friends!"

"To friends."

Alleyne finally relinquished Elvire's hand and sat beside him, facing Ancel. "So what's the word from England? Has the empress finally been crowned?"

Ancel stared at his cup, clearly reluctant to answer.

Dread settled in the pit of Geoffrey's stomach. So much for leaving politics until later. Trust Alleyne, wishing to keep abreast with developments. Perhaps they were not so different after all. Or mayhap she simply wanted to know who to appeal to.

After a long silence, Ancel raised his head, a grim look on his features. "The news is grave, my lady. Last we heard before we boarded for Normandy, the Empress Matilda and her court were chased from London after she showed an apparent lack of tact. It appears her cause has lost its momentum." He took a deep draught, then pulled a folded parchment from his gambeson and held it out to Geoffrey.

Instinct told him to not touch it. He had had enough of politics. Reluctantly, he stretched out a hand. "What is it?"

"A message from Reginald."

"He is still with Queen Maude's followers?"

Ancel nodded. "Yes, he thought it prudent to stay where he was. He accompanied her march on London, where much land was burned. I briefly met with him there before we hurried to Dover. It appears the queen is set for revenge."

Next to him, Alleyne straightened. He met her gaze as he unfolded the paper. She was as tense as he felt.

He read his sergeant's scribbles once. Twice. Then he dropped the note on the table and closed his eyes.

How would he explain this to Alleyne?

Chapter Nineteen

Alleyne stared at the message she had just painstakingly deciphered, then dropped it to the floor. The colour drained from her skin. Her hands shook. A sense of foreboding engulfed her, and she closed her eyes.

'Twas all over.

"Alleyne?" Geoffrey took her hand.

She blinked, unable to meet his gaze, snatched her hand away and crossed her arms under her chest. "He has won." A sob escaped her.

Beside her, a chair scraped on the floor, then Elvire's warm hands were on her shoulder. "I'm sorry, child."

She leaned back into Elvire's embrace. Tears threatened and she let them fall. Everyone's eyes were on her. Ancel. Alfred. Everyone knew. She was the last to find out. The last to discover that Queen Maude had praised Will d'Arques for his tireless actions in their pursuit of the empress. The wretched queen granted him lands in return for his services. A large manor in Kent. A town house in Winchester. The manor of Bellac.

"He's taken my home." Her voice was barely a whisper.

"We're going to win it back, my lady." Ancel's soothing tone did nothing to ease the pain. He cared, but against the decision of a queen he was helpless.

"No, we're not."

Geoffrey leaned over. "We will. I gave my oath to Lord Raymond, and I'll give it to you now, as his daughter and heir, here before all these witnesses. We will retake Bellac, your rightful inheritance."

Unable to avoid his eyes so close to her face, she blinked back the tears. "But how?" Her voice quivered.

He straightened, his expression strained. "I don't know yet but I'll find a way. We may have to wait until Matilda regains the upper hand."

Fear gripped her heart, the beats pounding in her ears. "That could take years."

His gaze bore into hers, unrelenting. "Yes." The single word said it all.

"What…what am I to do in the meantime? I can't depend on your hospitality. You'll soon return to England. The empress needs you there."

"As much as my brother and I dislike each other, I won't leave until he has recovered, or…" He crossed himself. "I suggest we take it one step at a time. You're safe here, as are your people."

She looked past him, to Ancel's tired face, to Alfred hovering by his side. She clasped Elvire's hand and her gaze met Geoffrey's again. "But we're intruders. Surely, our presence must upset your brother. He shouldn't have to fret about strangers in his house when he lies abed, sick."

Geoffrey crossed his arms. "This is also my home and therefore you are welcome for as long as you need. Here in Perche, you are now under the protection of the Count of Mortagne, wherever he may be, and the Count of Anjou. We can bide our time."

"How will I ever repay you? After everything you've done for me?"

A glint of determination shone in his eyes. "I shall think of something."

***

After a restless night spent pondering his future, Geoffrey rose at first light and went to the window to push open the shutters. His chamber faced the side of the house. A mild early summer breeze fanned his face and bare chest. He leaned over the narrow ledge and gazed across the narrow lane at the town wall looming on the other side. Sentries walked the length, stopping at intervals to exchange words. 'Twas peaceful here, so unlike Gloucester, his chosen home. The calm surroundings soothed his frayed nerves.

He chuckled. He must be getting old!

Hearing sounds from within the house, Geoffrey turned, pulled on a linen shirt, fastened his hose and went downstairs. Guy and Ancel sat at the table, ale in hand. "Good morrow."

Geoffrey poured himself a cupful and settled into a chair. "You're awake already, given the strenuous journey you've had?" His eyes met Ancel's.

"I couldn't sleep." Ancel's words echoed his own thoughts.

"He was thinking about finding employment here," Guy said. "Possibly with Anjou's army."

Geoffrey nodded. It made sense for Ancel to seek employment. Not one to take alms, the former captain clearly needed to be occupied. "We'll go to Anjou together, Ancel. But first I have to write to Sheriff Miles. And, of course, see how my brother fares over the next sennight." He held up a hand when Ancel opened his mouth. "No objections, Ancel. You stay here as long as your lady needs you."

"I've no manor to defend, so how can I serve her?" Bitterness clouded his words.

"But you are still her captain, responsible for her safety. As long as she remains unwed, you have a responsibility."

Ancel's dark eyebrows shot together but Guy nodded. "Geoffrey's right. You're needed here for the moment. Later, you can join Anjou's army. Or return to England to fight for the empress." He stared at Geoffrey. "First of all, we need to find the Lady Alleyne a protector."

Ancel's eyes lit, a sly smile on his face. "Why don't you wed her, Sir Geoffrey? She'd be safe with you."

Geoffrey fidgeted with the hem of his linen shirt. Not keen on wedding talk, he must find another solution. Though the notion of Alleyne in his bed brought heat to his face. "Nonsense! We shall find her a husband who has enough power to take up her cause."

"Someone like you." Guy cocked his head.

"No!" His hand hit the surface of the table. "Enough of this talk of marriage. We'll take her to the count's court once my brother has, erm, recovered. I don't doubt she'll be able to choose a suitable man." He ignored the stab at his innards.

"May I be blunt, my lord?"

The sharp tone in Ancel's voice made Geoffrey glower. Why were the two men so determined to annoy him? "Go on, then. As you obviously wish to ruin my day."

"My lady has been watching you right from the moment you arrived at Bellac. I know, don't say it," Ancel held up a hand, "she had a liking for d'Arques, but I believe she now has truly been healed of her affliction. That brought her back to you. Lady Alleyne has always been a wilful, determined lass. That's why it's so clear to me. She would never have agreed to come with you to Normandy, here to Perche, unless she wanted to. She could have insisted on staying in Gloucester, or appealing to the empress. But no, she came with you. She depends on you to deal with d'Arques." He paused, taking a deep breath. "She depends on you with her life."

Geoffrey rose, his mind in turmoil, and went to stand by the window, his gaze sweeping the yard. He ruffled his hair. Was Ancel right? Was marrying Alleyne the solution? He despised the thought of losing his freedom, his independence. But the lass needed someone reliable to take care of her. Other suitors might not bother with her small inheritance, considering her beauty enough for producing the required offspring. Her wish to regain her home might be ignored. He swallowed hard.

It was still to be a marriage of convenience. After Solange, he had sworn never to lose his heart again and he had no intention of changing his credo now. Alleyne did not love him anyway, her attitude very obvious. Their only shared goal lay in fighting Will and regaining Bellac.

Hearing Aubrey's voice above, he made up his mind. "I

need to speak with my brother."

He ignored the grinning miens of his companions. But as he climbed the stairs, he remembered how thin the bond was between him and Bertrand. Yet he must reach out to him; his brother was dying. 'Twould be their last chance.

Aubrey came towards him, balancing a bowl of murky water in his hands. "Sir Geoffrey, your brother wishes to see you. He's very poorly this morning."

Geoffrey nodded. "Thank you, Aubrey. I'm on my way to him anyway."

Aubrey stopped when they reached the same step. "This time it's serious, my lord. As if Master Bertrand has been waiting for this day." A sombre look on his face, the steward continued down the stairs

Geoffrey swore under his breath as he reached the door to his brother's bedchamber. Bertrand lay propped up against thick cushions, his skin sallow, stretched tightly over prominent cheekbones.

"Bertrand." He entered and closed the door. Slowly, he walked to a chair by his brother"s bedside. "I'm here."

Bertrand blinked, the veins in his eyes a deep red. "Geoffrey." His shallow breathing rattled. "I've not much time left on this earth."

Geoffrey shook his head and opened his mouth but Bertrand's hand shot up and grabbed his wrist.

"You know the truth – look at me! The fever's had me in its grip for nigh on a whole season. 'Tis time for me to let it run its course."

"Has the apothecary been called?"

Bertrand shook his head, then winced in pain. "He's done everything he could already. But let's not waste our breath on useless words."

Geoffrey lowered his gaze to his wrist, where Bertrand's bony hand loosened its grip. He took it in a firm grasp. "I know we haven't always seen eye-to-eye."

Bertrand managed a wry smile. "Never, really. And do you want to know why?"

Geoffrey stared at him. "Because you were the elder, and

Father…he preferred you."

"Ahh, but that's not the whole truth, Geoffrey."

A shiver ran down his spine. The hairs on his neck rose. "Not the whole truth?"

"No. I was always jealous of you."

"I know. But why?"

Bertrand sighed, withdrew his hand, and clasped both hands together as if in prayer. "Because of your… background."

"You hated my mother whilst she was alive. I never knew why, though I guess her lowly status didn't fit your ideal."

"Yes, I despised her. So much so I rejoiced when she died giving birth to you." He shook his head and briefly closed his eyes.

Geoffrey's blood froze. "Continue."

Bertrand stared at the ceiling, his gaze far removed from the chamber. "Your mother was not a minor knight's foster child, Geoffrey. That's what Father thought when he seduced her, deeming her nobody of importance, but he was wrong. And he regretted his action to his death."

Geoffrey sat still, his mind numb. Why had his father never told him the truth?

As if reading his thoughts, Bertrand said, "Father never liked being caught in a trap – but caught he was when he discovered your mother's true identity after she fell pregnant with you." Sadness clouded his gaze when he met Geoffrey's. "Your mother was a natural daughter of the late Count Geoffrey's younger brother, Fulk, God rest their souls."

The revelation hit Geoffrey like a fist. He staggered back. His godfather was in fact his uncle? He shook his head. "This can't be true."

"Oh, but it is." Bertrand coughed and Geoffrey hurried to hand him a linen square from a side table. Blood stained the thin fabric when Bertrand dabbed his mouth.

"You must rest, Bertrand. We can speak later." A dreadful suspicion settled in his stomach. First Will, now his father. Did men never learn? Questions whirled in his mind, but his brother's health was more important.

"No, Geoffrey. There won't be another chance. I…I can feel the life drain from me."

"You're just tired–"

"Shut up and listen! When I'm gone, this manor and all its lands will be yours. But you are also due your mother's inheritance."

"My mother's? She had an inheritance?" Geoffrey's head pounded. 'Twas too much.

Bertrand's eyes shone, tears trickled down his gaunt face. "You never knew about this because Father swore me to secrecy. In Perche's absence, he ensured that she was buried without fuss."

"And she was later moved to the Perche family chapel?"

Bertrand's mouth twitched. "Indeed. When Father failed to mould you according to his will, he despised your courage, your success as a fighting man, a knight. And he fouled me with his evil thoughts, ordering me to keep your inheritance. I should have told you a long time ago instead of hiding behind this." He gestured at the room. "My wife died two summers ago. I destroyed her with my constant envy. I have no children. My life is worthless."

Geoffrey leaned forward and clasped his brother's thin arm. "Nonsense! You have been a successful merchant, expanding Father's property. You are an important member of the guilds. Your life hasn't been worthless."

Bertrand wiped away his tears with the bloodstained cloth. Geoffrey took it from his hand and gently dabbed his brother's face, his emotions warring inside his head. His father's behaviour had sown too much hatred. It had destroyed their family.

"Not completely, I agree. At last, you know the truth. I just don't know why Perche never told you."

Geoffrey mused. "I assume I was still young when I left his service. Still, it is surprising. Perhaps a family link as ours embarrassed him. Or he didn't want to be seen to favour me through a thin blood line rather than my hard work."

"Possibly. You can always ask him when he returns." Bertrand nodded, a move that induced another coughing fit. He wiped his mouth with the back of his hand. "You are a rich man, Geoffrey. You own your mother's manor and large swathes of fertile Perche lands. All the documents are in that chest by the desk." He pointed at a large table by the window, beneath which a solid oak chest stood with its lid shut. "You're now rich enough to consider the pretty lady I spoke to last night your match."

"What?" Geoffrey stared at his brother. "You spoke to Alleyne?"

Bertrand's lips parted in a pained smile. "Yes," he whispered. "She's a beauty, that one. And she has courage and brains. A deadly mix in a woman, if you ask me, but perfect for you."

Geoffrey shook his head. "She doesn't want me. Although–"

"Oh, but she does. I saw it in her eyes whenever your name cropped up. With your mother's inheritance, and mine, you'll be able to fight for her home. But first, I guess, you must fight for her hand." He coughed again. "Please remove a cushion. I wish to rest now."

Geoffrey slowly lifted Bertrand forward and pulled a cushion from behind him. Gently, he lowered him again.

He turned at a knock on the door. A priest entered, with Aubrey hovering behind. "May I come in, Master Bertrand?"

Geoffrey glanced at his brother, his face even more pallid than earlier. It had cost Bertrand dearly to talk for so long. "Yes," he said. "My brother has need of you." He squeezed Bertrand's hand and met his eyes, knowing it would be the final time.

After he pulled the door shut behind him, he let out a long breath.

Aubrey's expression was grave. "I'll have the servants say prayers for Master Bertrand." The steward descended the stairs with a heavy step.

Geoffrey swallowed hard. Soon this would be his household. Plus whatever manor his mother had bequeathed him. With property came responsibility. Was he ready for it?

Alleyne's door opened and Elvire emerged. When she spotted him, she hurried to his side and lay a hand on his arm. "How fares Master Bertrand?"

"He lies dying." The words held a bitter aftertaste. His whole life he had spent fighting his father, and Bertrand. Relieved he and his brother had made peace in the end, he was saddened by the cold light of reality. Bertrand would not survive the day.

"Is your lady within?" He gestured to Alleyne's chamber.

Elvire straightened and removed her hand, a suspicious glance in her eyes. "Yes, she is. Why?"

"Because I have something to discuss with her." He walked past her. When she turned, he added, "Alone."

Outside the solid door he paused, listening for any signs of Alleyne but the room was quiet. Mustering his courage, he knocked.

***

Alleyne rose from her seat by the window and answered the door. Elvire had just left. She would not knock.

She opened and took a step back. Geoffrey.

With shaking hands, she adjusted her gown, uncertain of what to do.

"May I enter?" His voice was calm, gentle, yet it held a tone of something different.

Determination.

"Of course." She glanced past him. "Where is Elvire?"

He stepped over the threshold and kicked the door shut. The latch clicked into place. "She went to join the servants in praying for my brother."

The blood drained from her face. "Is it that serious?"

He nodded. "Yes, I believe his time has come. That's why I'm here."

"Ahh, to tell me about your brother? 'Tis very thoughtful

of you." She sighed in relief. Surely, he would leave now.

"No, actually not just that. I..." He folded and unfolded his hands, his gaze never leaving hers.

Was Geoffrey nervous?

He cleared his throat. "I've come to offer you a pact."

"A pact?" Intrigued, she gestured for him to sit before she lowered herself into the other window seat. "Pray tell me."

He sat, only to rise again immediately. "Erm, not quite a pact. A proposal."

"What?"

He pulled her from her seat, cradling her hands in his. The grip was tender, yet firm. "Yes, a damned proposal. We spoke about it last night, remember?"

A sense of recognition hit her, sending a shiver down her spine. "We spoke about what?" Her voice barely rose above a whisper.

His strong jaw was set in that determined way she had noticed whenever he took action. "About your future."

The combination of his touch, their hands entwined, and the seductive tone of his voice made her head spin. "I have to sit."

"Not so fast." His arms circled her waist, holding her firmly against him. "Truth is, I wish for your hand in marriage, Alleyne. With my inheritance, I shall have the means to support your cause to retake Bellac. You won't want for anything."

Tears stung her eyes and she wriggled from his embrace. His arms fell to his side as she pushed past him and leaned against the window ledge for support. The warm breeze caressed her heated skin. She wanted him, so what was the problem?

Thoughts warred in her head. He was only bound by duty. His inheritance? Oh, she would have taken him anyway, if only he cared for her instead of cavorting with harlots. But marrying out of duty, no doubt finding a suitable lover once she fell pregnant?

"What happens when we regain Bellac?" Her voice

wavered. She must know.

Footsteps sounded behind her. His breath tickled her neck. "If you wish to live there instead of Mortagne, we can come to an arrangement. But we're going to fight d'Arques for it."

Tears rolled down her face and she quickly wiped them away with her sleeve. He did not care for her.

"You'd dump me there while you go fighting, or spying, or whatever it is you're doing?" Sobs racked her body.

His hands reached out and gently turned her to face him. He lifted her face to meet his gaze. His thumb brushed away traces of her tears. "Why are you crying?"

"Bec…because I don't wish to marry out of duty. I…I always wanted to marry for love. And I find it hard to love a man who takes whores to his bed."

"What?" He stood back, his eyes the colour of a frozen lake. "Who takes whores to bed?"

"You!" She thrust her lower lip forward, not trusting herself. The truth was out, now he could do whatever he wished. She watched in stunned disbelief when he began to laugh. "This is no laughing matter, Geoffrey."

His face grew sombre, yet his gaze shone with something she did not recognise. "Does that mean you care?" Geoffrey pulled her against him.

"No!" She wriggled but this time he held her tight. Unable to resist any further, she nodded, her gaze firmly fixed on his collarbone. "Yes."

"My sweeting, I take it as your agreement, then?" His thumb caressed her cheek, down the contour of her neck. The sensation sent shivers across her skin.

"Like I said, my lord," she emphasised his title, "I can't possibly wed a man who takes–"

His mouth covered hers in an instant. The warm taste of his lips made her head spin. His teeth nibbled her lower lip and she opened them, allowing his tongue access. Her body pressed against his, her arms weaving their way around his neck. A wave of excitement engulfed her.

When he finally broke the kiss, her eyes fluttered open.

A smile graced his lips. "I've never lain with whores apart from once, when I was fourteen, and I never shall again. As you know well, I take my vows seriously."

The memory of his promise to Father struck her, yet it was a feeling of peace. Father believed Geoffrey would come to her aid. Father would have approved of him as a husband.

"But the woman in Seez? In the tavern?"

"Ahh, yes. Guy mentioned you were jealous." He chuckled.

"I was not jealous, just…disgusted."

He laughed, pulling her closer, her chest meeting firm muscle. "Clearly not observant enough, as you would have spotted me talking to an old friend all night. A male friend who is very much a family man. The lass you consider a harlot is the innkeeper's daughter who made sure we had the best wine."

"Oh," she whispered, heat shooting into her cheeks. "I thought…"

"Well, you thought wrong, Alleyne." He lowered his lips to meet hers again.

***

They emerged from the forest several miles east of Mortagne and slowed their mounts to a walk. With the day of their wedding only a fortnight away, Geoffrey eventually agreed to seek out his mother's manor where they were to make their home. Alleyne raised her gaze, her eyes widening with delight.

Before them, at the top of a large hill covered in meadows bursting with wild irises, daisies and violets, a large whitewashed manor house stood proudly, encircled by a sturdy wall. Whilst the walls and narrow windows provided ample protection, towers three storeys high on every corner gave the impression of castle. The view from the top must be breathtaking. A narrow wooden bridge across a ditch led to a sturdy double gate.

"It's beautiful," Alleyne whispered.

Geoffrey brought Feu to a halt beside her and sat motionless in the saddle. He stared at the hill, deep in thought. Finally, he broke the silence. "The manor of Nonant, my mother's legacy."

"It looks well kept." Alleyne's assessed the fortifications.

"Aye. Bertrand, God rest his soul, looked after it well." He crossed himself. "This is our home now. Until we recover Bellac. Do you approve?"

"Oh, yes." She smiled and squeezed his hand. "Shall we?"

Epilogue

August 1141

Will d'Arques dropped the parchment on the table and grabbed his tankard, a smirk playing on his lips. Now he knew for certain what he had long suspected. He leaned back and gazed around the bustling hall of Bellac Manor. The wall hangings, Lord Raymond's pride, hung singed in places where men had been careless with the torches. The stink of tallow candles strong in the air, the floor rushes sticking in a muddy mess to the ground.

Will did not care. His men, mercenaries and disillusioned soldiers alike, crowded the tables, playing dice. Several whores leaned over shoulders, or straddled laps, their low-cut gowns and hitched skirts displaying their goods. Dice, women and plenty of ale, replenished as soon as they were emptied, kept the men content. For the moment. They were restless, itching for a fight. A skirmish would improve their mood.

He took a draught, his eyes scanning the message in front of him. Alleyne had fled to Perche with de Mortagne, apparently settling in his family manor. They were wed. Will raised an eyebrow. Oh, they deserved each other; the coward and the scheming witch.

He chuckled, a weight falling off his shoulders. The threat of their potential return anytime soon diminished, Will was finally free to join Queen Maude and her army again. They had been on Matilda's tracks ever since the Londoners chased the arrogant hag from their city, uncrowned. Will nodded. Maude needed men like him, fearless, without conscience. His mercenaries could work off their aggressions. He would emerge on the winning side, rewarded for his support. Once Stephen was restored to the throne, Will was certain the king would grant him more honours. Who knows, he might even make him an earl.

A young whore, no older than fourteen, came towards the dais, her round hips swaying, blue eyes promising satisfaction. It still irked him that he could not subdue Alleyne. Rage grew within him at the memory, replacing embarrassment.

Well, he would show this harlot! His gaze roamed over her body, the painted mouth, her long blonde hair, half obscuring her full breasts squeezed into a tight gown, her slender waist. Perfect. Will set aside his tankard and waved her over.

"Why, my lord! What can I do for you?" Giggling, the girl hopped on the table and settled her long legs either side of his chair.

Will grabbed her hair and pulled her towards him. A flash of pain shone in her eyes. His heart pounded in his ears as his body responded. Grinning, he ripped open her gown to expose her fully. "Yield," he demanded as his hands kneaded the girl's soft flesh, "and I might let you live."

Let Alleyne rot in God-forsaken Perche. He would deal with her later.

After he had killed Geoffrey.

Thank you for reading this Ocelot Press book. If you enjoyed it, we would greatly appreciate it if you could take a moment to write a short review.

You might also like to try books by other Ocelot Press authors. We cover a small range of genres, with a focus on historical fiction (including mystery and paranormal), romance and fantasy.

Find Ocelot Press at:

Website: **www.ocelot-press.com**
Facebook: **www.facebook.com/OcelotPress**
Twitter: **www.twitter.com/OcelotPress**